TOM CLANCY'S
NET FORCE®

CLOAK AND DAGGER

CREATED BY

Tom Clancy and **Steve Pieczenik**

Written by

John Helfers and Russell Davis

BERKLEY JAM BOOKS, NEW YORK

This is a work of fiction. Names, characters, places, and incidents are either the product of the author's imagination or are used fictitiously, and any resemblance to actual persons, living or dead, business establishments, events, or locales is entirely coincidental.

TOM CLANCY'S NET FORCE: CLOAK AND DAGGER

A Berkley Jam Book / published by arrangement with
Netco Partners

PRINTING HISTORY
Berkley Jam edition / March 2003

For information address: The Berkley Publishing Group,
a division of Penguin Putnam Inc.,
375 Hudson Street, New York, New York 10014.

ISBN: 0-425-18303-3

BERKLEY JAM BOOKS®
Berkley Jam Books are published by The Berkley Publishing Group,
a division of Penguin Putnam Inc.,
375 Hudson Street, New York, New York 10014.
BERKLEY JAM and its logo
are trademarks belonging to Penguin Putnam Inc.

PRINTED IN THE UNITED STATES OF AMERICA

10 9 8 7 6 5 4 3 2 1

SHADOW OF HONOR

Was Net Force Explorer Andy Moore's deceased father a South African war hero or the perpetrator of a massacre? Andy's search for the truth puts every one of his fellow students at risk . . .

PRIVATE LIVES

The Net Force Explorers must delve into the secrets of their commander's life—to prove him innocent of murder . . .

SAFE HOUSE

To save a prominent scientist and his son, the Net Force Explorers embark on a terrifying virtual hunt for their enemies—before it's too late . . .

GAMEPREY

A gamer's convention turns deadly when virtual reality monsters escape their confines—and start tracking down the Net Force Explorers!

DUEL IDENTITY

A member of a fencing group lures the Net Force Explorers to his historical simulation site—where his dream of ruling a virtual nation is about to come true, but only at the cost of their lives . . .

DEATHWORLD

When suicides are blamed on a punk/rock/morbo web site, Net Force Explorer Charlie Davis goes onto the site undercover—and unaware of its real danger . . .

HIGH WIRE

The only ring Net Force Explorer Andy Moore finds in a virtual circus is a black market ring—in high-tech weapons software and hardware . . .

COLD CASE

Playing detective in a mystery simulation, Net Force Explorer Matt Hunter becomes the target of a flesh-and-blood killer . . .

RUNAWAYS

Tracking down a runaway friend, Net Force Explorer Megan O'Malley discovers that the web is just as fraught with danger as the streets . . .

ACKNOWLEDGMENTS

We would like to acknowledge the assistance of Martin H. Greenberg, Larry Segriff, Denise Little, Brittiany Koren, Lowell Bowen, Esq., Robert Youdelman, Esq., Danielle Forte, Esq., Dianne Jude and Tom Colgan, our editor. But most important, it is for you, our readers, to determine how successful our collective endeavor has been.

—TOM CLANCY AND STEVE PIECZENIK

1

Mark Gridley stared at the decrepit, run-down house looming before him. A flash of lightning highlighted its broken windows, peeling paint, and rickety, weed-choked porch. The front door slowly swung back and forth in the breeze, its screeching hinges adding a macabre touch to the setting. Even standing several yards away, Mark smelled the mustiness of the place, overlaid with sharp ozone from the approaching storm and the dry, grassy scent of the blighted brown lawn. Thunder rumbled in the distance, and he felt the vibrations deep in the pit of his stomach. Running a hand through his damp, windblown hair, he shook his head.

"Well, this is definitely the last time I open my big mouth," Mark said as he walked through the light rain toward the ramshackle building, brittle dead grass crunching under his shoes. "I can't believe I agreed to this."

He stopped just in front of the porch. From here, the house looked like a malevolent face, with windows for eyes and the front door a leering, crooked mouth. The door swung faster on its squealing hinges, beckoning him in. *Okay, there are three of them, and they're somewhere in there, waiting for me,* Mark thought, trying to shake the creepy feeling the scene gave him. "Chameleon finder on," he commanded, activating his scanning program. "Let's play."

With his program engaged, the house glowed in unearthly colors ranging from deep indigo to bright crimson. Studying it closely, Mark saw the computer commands that made up the veeyar site. The basic foundation of the house, the walls and the roof, was composed of fairly simple "cool" code, shades of black and blue, with extra details, such as movable parts like doors and windows, emphasized in hotter colors. The program, which Mark had written himself, would give him the edge he needed to hunt his quarry. *At least, I hope so*, he thought as he walked up the creaking stairs onto the porch and entered the house.

Mark walked through the doorway and found himself in a narrow hall with a steep staircase leading to the second floor next to it, both decorated in ancient, peeling wallpaper and large patches of greenish-gray mildew. The powerful smell of decay was everywhere, making him wrinkle his nose in disgust. Mark scanned the dusty floor in front of him, looking for any sign that someone might have passed this way.

A loud *bang* behind him made Mark jump. He whirled around to see what was sneaking up on him. It was nothing. The rising wind had slammed the front door shut. Feeling an uncomfortable trickle of sweat on his forehead, he swiped it away with his hand. Mark shook his head. *Get a grip,* he thought. *You used to love this stuff as a kid—Halloween haunted house sites, the whole works. But those were just spook programs. It's a lot different when it's real.*

Mark looked around again. "Come on," he whispered, "Where are you?" The old house shifted and groaned around him as he crept through the hallway, alert to the slightest movement or variation. Dust trickled down from the ceiling and tickled his nose.

A floorboard creaked above his head. Mark froze, trying to decide whether it was just the house settling or someone creeping around upstairs.

It sounded like someone was up there. Mark was listening so intently that he almost didn't register the vague human form outlined on the peeling wall to his left, barely visible against the blue code of the hallway. Distracted as he was, he nearly took another step forward—which would have placed him directly in front of the camouflaged person hiding right next to him.

He paused, looking down at his feet as though searching for traps, and examined the blue silhouette out of the corner of his eye. Now that he was aware of it, the figure was plain as day, and Mark fought to keep a triumphant smile off his face. His program worked as well as he'd hoped, but there was no sense in warning his target that she'd been spotted. Not when he could have a little fun instead.

"Computer," he said, using the programmer command mode so the scenario froze and no one in it could hear him. "Run Markclone2."

He paused a moment, then took a cautious step to the side. An exact duplicate of Mark remained standing where he had been. Mark looked at the blue form, which was still poised on the wall. He nodded. *Usually I just use this program to escape boring Netizens I stumble on in chat rooms,* he thought. "Computer, run Unseen program on me, then continue walking Markclone to the end of the hall. Execute."

Now Mark could smile. The Unseen program made him invisible—unless someone had a spotter program as good as his own, and Mark knew no one here did.

He watched as his double drew closer to the blue figure. As it approached, the outline of a hand detached from the wall and reached out to tag Mark's clone—and passed right through the computer simulation. The blue figure, caught off balance, took a step forward and cried out in surprise.

Before it could right itself, Mark stepped forward and slapped his hand on the blue form. At his touch a flash of white energy surged through the figure, freezing it in place.

"Gotcha," he said. "That's funny, Megan, I never figured you for a wallflower."

The blue silhouette morphed into a lithe brown-haired girl who kept staring at the floor without saying a word.

"Oops," Mark said. "Computer, thaw head."

"Thanks," Megan O'Malley said as she turned her head to look at him directly. "You spotted me from the beginning, right?"

"Just about. You were hidden pretty well from any casual

observer, though. One down and two to go." Mark eyed his fellow Net Force Explorer speculatively. "I don't suppose you'd give me any hints as to where they went?"

Megan shook her head. "Nice try, Squirt, but I'm not going to make this any easier for you."

"You know, I could just leave you like that," he said with a mischievous smile. "I'm sure it could get very uncomfortable just standing there for a while. Come on, just one small clue, and you'll be free."

But Megan shook her head. "Even if I did know, I'd think you'd rather have the pleasure of finding them yourself. But I don't have any idea where Daniel and Maj are. We all split up and took a different part of this place."

Mark nodded. "Swell. I'll just have to find them the hard way. See you outside."

"Actually, do you mind if I come along and watch?" Megan asked. "I won't give you away."

"All right, as long as I have your word on that," Mark said. "Computer, thaw body." He waited until Megan melted back into the wall. There was a strange new odor in the hallway, and it took Mark a moment to place it. *Wallpaper,* he thought to himself, *rotting wallpaper.* He shuddered as he thought of pressing his body into the grimy peeling wall, virtual or not. *Yuck.* "How can you stand the smell?"

"It was worth the chance of catching you," Megan said.

The rules of this contest were simple: the three other Net Force Explorers, Megan O'Malley, Madeline Green, and Daniel Sanchez, had ten minutes to hide themselves in the house in any manner they chose. Mark then had ten minutes to go in and find them using his program. If any of his friends escaped detection and were able to tag Mark first, they won. If Mark found them all without being tagged, he won.

Mark tried to hide his smile as he watched Megan move along the wall beside him. He had a feeling the reason Megan was hanging around now had more to do with Daniel Sanchez than with any desire to see his program work. No problem. In fact, Mark was looking forward to taking Daniel down a peg or two when he caught him. The more people who witnessed that, the better.

It had been Daniel who'd suggested this whole business

in the first place. Twenty minutes ago Mark had been safe and sound at home, visiting some of his friends in veeyar at the Net Force Explorers' online headquarters. They'd been discussing the latest project he had been working on, a program designed to scan for abnormal variations on the Web, theoretically making it possible to spot lurkers, people who surfed the Net without visible personas.

Usually, lurkers were just harmless people who didn't want their presence known for personal reasons, but Mark knew his father, Net Force commander Jay Gridley, was concerned that lurkers were using the anonymity of the Web to spy on others. With so many business dealings and so much information accessible on the Web, online security was always a high-level concern. That was where Net Force came in. A branch of the Federal Bureau of Investigation, Net Force was created specifically to combat crime online. The agents who worked there dealt with state-of-the-art equipment, as well as state-of-the-art criminals. Mark's program, if it worked, would go a long way toward helping Net Force catch lurkers who were up to no good.

When Mark had described what he'd been working on, Megan and Maj had listened to him without saying much. But the fourth member of their group, Daniel Sanchez, had just laughed when he'd heard what Mark was doing.

"There's nothing on the Web that can't be tampered with," Daniel had said. "But I'll tell you what—since you're so confident about this, how'd you like to play a little game of hide-and-seek? Meg, Maj, you interested?"

The two girls had exchanged glances. "We're listening," Megan had replied.

And that was how Mark found himself here. He cautiously searched the other rooms, all too conscious of how little time he had left. The rest of the first floor was empty, just dusty floors, cold damp air, and wind and rain whistling through broken windows. Mark scanned the deserted rooms one last time, in case Daniel or Maj was playing a waiting game, hoping to sneak up on him on the stairs. He found nothing. If his program was doing what it was supposed to, this level of the house was now empty, save for the disguised Megan.

Standing at the foot of the stairs, Mark looked into the

shadowed hallway. Was it his imagination, or did a dark shape flit across the top of the stairs? Mark trotted halfway up the staircase, then stopped. Were Daniel and Madeline working together, one distracting him while the other sprang an ambush? Despite the relative harmlessness of the situation, Mark felt sweat again on the back of his neck. He knew Daniel was very competitive and would do whatever it took to win this little contest. *I can't leave anything to chance,* Mark thought.

Moving more slowly, Mark reached the second floor. The stairway ended in a landing here, with three doors in a row in front of him. Mark looked down and saw footprints in the dust leading to the nearest room on the right. *Why didn't I see those downstairs?* he wondered. Tiptoeing over to the closed door, Mark looked at it closely, making sure it wasn't Daniel or Maj in disguise, then pushed it open.

The room it swung into was filled with furniture and boxes, all stacked haphazardly. *The perfect place to hide,* Mark thought, *at least until now.* Although the profusion of junk would keep anybody from being spotted in a normal scan of the room, Mark's program cut right through the mess, looking for the colored data that would indicate one of the hidden Net Force Explorers.

Mark looked around through his program. His sweep of the room came up empty. There was no one here. Mark frowned as he stood in the doorway. *Maybe they thought this would be too obvious.* After a last look around, he backed out, closed the door, and kept moving.

The next door on this side of the hallway opened up into what appeared to be a bedroom of some sort. A broken-down mattress occupied the middle of the room, with a dusty desk and an overturned chair next to it. Ragged floor-length curtains fluttered at the window, startling Mark for a second until he realized that it was just the program-generated wind that was moving the drapes, not someone standing behind them.

No need to get jumpy now, he told himself. Mark was about to enter the room when he saw the small glowing line that trailed off the chair and across the floor. With a start, he realized just who the chair actually was. Looking closer, he saw the underlying blue form of another one of his targets.

Just waiting for me to stroll right in, eh? Not this time, he thought. "Computer," he commanded again, "center gravity on me."

Mark waited a second, then took one step onto the wall, then another. No matter what surface of the house he stood on, gravity would always be right under his feet. Mark walked up the wall and stopped near the ceiling. He reached into his pocket and took out what looked like a small circle of inky black cloth. He slapped it on the wall next to him and waited as the program ran, enlarging the spot into a hole big enough for him to enter.

"Computer, run Unseen," Mark said, then climbed into the hole.

He came out on the other side of the wall, inside the room with the suspect chair. Mark folded the black circle and put it back in his pocket. He moved quietly up the wall to the ceiling and went to the far side of the room, coming down behind the chair/person. Not even bothering with an illusionary Mark this time, he walked up to the chair and grabbed it, the white light freezing the pretty girl it caught into a remarkably chairlike posture. Mark set the chair down and considered taking a seat in it. *Nah, that would be cruel.* "Computer, thaw head. Nice try, Maj, but you'll have to do better than that," Mark said.

He could see the girl's annoyance at being caught. "That easy, huh?"

Mark thought about it before answering her. "Not really. That last room lulled me into a false sense of security, so I almost wasn't ready for you. You'd also disguised yourself really well with that chair overlay. If I hadn't been able to spot the data trail from your computer to this site with my program, you'd've had me for sure. Megan's keeping me company, so if you want to stick around and watch me find Daniel, you're more than welcome to join us."

Maj smiled. "I think catching Megan and me has made you overconfident. I'd watch yourself if I were in your shoes," she said. "Don't forget about his father. I think Daniel just might surprise you."

"What about his father?" From what Mark could remember, Daniel didn't talk about his family very much, if at all.

"He's a Secret Service agent. Daniel's probably picked up a few things from him through the years," Maj said.

"Uh-huh. We'll just see about that." Mark grinned. "Just stand back and watch me in action."

Maj shook her head as she faded into the wall. *What? Doesn't she think I have what it takes to do this? I'll show her! So far, so good,* Mark thought as he crept out into the hall.

At the other end of the landing, standing out in the open not more than ten feet away, was Daniel Sanchez. Mark nearly jumped out of his skin in surprise.

"Come get me, Squirt," Daniel challenged, tossing him a wave as he turned and ran through the far door. Mark followed more slowly, stopping when he was beside the door. Taking a deep breath, he stepped into the room, ready for anything.

Daniel stood on the other side of the room, apparently waiting for him. Mark looked around and cautiously advanced toward the center of the room. "You know, I think you've taken the cliché 'hide in plain sight' a bit too literally," Mark said. Daniel said nothing. Mark started to feel uneasy. He scanned Daniel's persona, finding nothing out of the ordinary about it. Right down to the data string, the person standing in front of him was Daniel Sanchez.

So why do I feel like I just walked into a trap? Mark wondered. The answer to his thought came all too quickly.

"Perhaps," Daniel said. "But which one of us is the Daniel Sanchez you want, and which one of us is a veeyar-generated ghost?" This time the voice came from behind Mark.

Mark whirled to find another Daniel Sanchez standing in the doorway. He was surrounded. The hunter had become the hunted.

He didn't want to be chased through the house by two Daniels, so Mark moved to the middle of the room. The two Daniels slowly approached him, making sure that the doorway was blocked at all times. Mark looked at the second Sanchez, trying to find some discrepancy or error that would tell him if this was the real one or not. The persona looked like the first one, right down to the logon tag.

"I think this is too easy for you, Squirt," the Daniel by the door said. As it spoke, it split in half, each part becoming a fully formed Daniel Sanchez.

"I want to stack the odds in my favor a bit more," the Daniel on the far side of the room said as it copied itself. Now there were four Daniels homing in on Mark.

"Assuming your program doesn't find a mistake in one of us—" the Daniel by the window said.

"—which we're pretty sure it won't, you'll just have to guess which one of us is real," the Daniel blocking the door finished.

"It's a one-in-four shot, so what do you have to lose?" the third Daniel asked.

"Except the game," the fourth Daniel added.

Mark took a few steps backward, only to feel the wall behind him. Frantically he looked from one Daniel to the other. Finding camouflaged Explorers was one thing, but trying to tell a clone from a real person was something else.

Something Mark had said in his earlier conversation with Daniel came back to him. ". . . the basic components of a lurker's identity . . ." *One thing every real user has is the logon trail of data that leads back to his computer,* Mark thought. Quickly scanning the four Daniels, he discovered that they all had the red lines of logon tags. He traced the cords back to their source, in this case Daniel's computer.

The four Daniels were slowly closing in on him, identical lazy grins on their faces. *The way he's stretching this out, he's certainly enjoying this,* Mark thought, still trying to figure out how to tell one Daniel from another. *There has to be a difference somewhere,* he thought. *Only a few seconds left . . .*

That's it! Mark scanned the data strings again, this time looking for whichever one had been created most recently. He discovered that while one of the Daniels had been online for almost three hours, one of them had only been here for one minute, and two others had been created within seconds of each other. That meant—

Mark jumped forward and grabbed the Daniel who was blocking the door. "You're the real Sanchez," he said.

The other three personas shimmered and exploded in a

flash of multicolored light. Daniel's shocked expression changed to a frown for an instant, then finally a smile. "Not bad, Squirt, and that wasn't a guess. How'd you know?"

Mark told him about the logon tags and how he had discovered which constructs had only existed for a few minutes. As he spoke, Megan and Madeline solidified into the room as well.

Daniel listened to the explanation, then asked, "So what happens when I come on the Net next time and create a construct right away, or have one waiting online twenty-four/ seven, to use whenever I see fit?"

"I don't know. You're right on that account. If you had made a copy of yourself that predated your current logon, I would have grabbed the wrong one. I'll have to come up with something better to cover that possibility," Mark said.

"Your program is a nice idea, Squirt, but you'll always be playing catch-up," Daniel replied. "Just when you think you've got it beat, some hackmaster tooling away in his basement will come up with the next rung on the ladder, leaving you to climb after him."

"They'll be findable if I set the scan program to look for the fundamental items of a Netizen's computer link into the Web. There will always be basic elements of the Web that can't be tampered with," Mark said, bristling slightly. Barely thirteen, Mark was years behind the rest of the Explorers in age. The fact that his parents also worked at Net Force hadn't helped his popularity, either, and for the first few weeks after joining the Explorers he'd heard more than his share of comments about being in the program only because his parents had let him in. But his unquestionable computer skills had proved he belonged here and brought the rest of the Net Force Explorers around in the end. However, he still hated being talked down to, and usually ended up making the person messing with him eat his words—online, of course.

"My program suite needs work, but as I said before, there will always be a way to detect lurkers on the Web," Mark said. "As the invisibility programs get better, so will the countermeasures. I recorded this little game, so I can take a look at the different masking procedures later. Thanks for the help, guys," Mark said.

"As much as I hate to break this up, if we don't get to the Net Force Explorers meeting, we're going to wish *we* were constructs," Madeline said.

"You're right," Mark said. "Hey, Daniel, where did you find this setup? This would make a great haunted house for Halloween."

Daniel looked around the dilapidated mansion one last time as the kids started to leave the house. "There's a place out in California that re-creates sets from old movies. This one was from an ancient 2-D called *Psycho*."

"Which is probably just how Captain Winters is going to react when we get to the meeting late," Megan said with a grimace as the house faded out around them. "Let's go!"

2

A second later Mark, Daniel, Megan, and Maj appeared in the Net Force Explorers' virtual meeting room, a nondescript auditorium containing kids of all ages and descriptions. Dozens of teens from Net Force chapters around the tristate area had logged on for their weekly meeting, and the four were acutely aware of everyone watching them as they appeared in the crowd during the meeting.

"Wow, it's pretty bad when the people who actually live *in* D.C. can't make the meeting on time," Andy Moore, another member of the Net Force Explorers, said. Andy, like several of the kids, lived just outside of Washington, D.C. Right now he was grinning like a contented cat. But even he turned serious when the man at the podium in the center of the room cleared his throat. The veeyar room was set up so everybody, no matter where they were standing, had a direct view of the man.

"And the reason you're late is . . . ?" Captain James Winters let his sentence trail off. He didn't look happy.

The four exchanged glances, then Mark spoke up. "Sorry, sir. The experiment I was running took longer than I thought it would."

Surprisingly, Captain Winters accepted that. "It's easy to

lose track of time on the Net, but next time don't forget about your responsibilities." The four nodded, and the meeting started.

"We have a special guest speaker for tonight's meeting," Captain Winters began. "Special Agent Ryan Valas is a liaison from the Central Intelligence Agency, who is working with Net Force to develop electronic protection and countermeasures for international data transmission. He's going to give a brief overview of the history of electronic crime worldwide, and then he'll talk a bit about what's being done to keep it under control these days. Agent Valas?"

The tanned, handsome man who had been sitting to one side while Captain Winters was speaking stood up and took the podium amid polite applause from the audience. Mark scanned the other members of Net Force. Most were watching with interest, although Andy Moore was already discreetly stifling a yawn. Valas was getting much more attention from Megan, Maj, and the rest of the girls than he was from the boys. *Is there any guy they don't think is cute?* Shaking his head, Mark turned his attention to the lecture.

"Thank you, Captain Winters, and thank you all for the gracious invitation to be here tonight. As I'm sure every person here knows, with the vast amount of information that travels around the Net worldwide, Net crime is rising at a staggering rate. Sophisticated code breakers and eavesdropping programs are available to just about anyone, and any Netizen who wants to can access an incredible amount of information that should remain private. And, in case some of you think that the job of catching Net criminals consists of just tracking people down in veeyar, let me remind you that virtual crime spills out into the real world more often than anybody would like—and often violently."

Valas waved his hand, and a scale hologram projection sprang up in the middle of the room. The scene depicted was a burning apartment complex surrounded by police cars and SWAT vans. Police officers in body armor and helmets were pointing automatic rifles at several men and women being led out of the building; most of the prisoners were injured in some way.

"Most of you probably caught this on HoloNews when it

happened. Seven months ago the headquarters of an international industrial espionage ring was raided by Net Force in San Francisco. The suspects were well armed and had a few seconds' advance notice because they intercepted police communications. A six-hour standoff ended in a firefight in which one officer was killed and three were wounded. The police had to use tear gas and flash-bang grenades to subdue the suspects." Valas nodded at Captain Winters. "Net Force was instrumental in assisting with much of the intelligence-gathering for that operation. So, before we get to the exciting world of Web security, who here can tell me what electronic crime first gained national prominence and really made on-line security a worldwide concern?"

Several of the Net Force Explorers exchanged glances, then Charlie Davis spoke up. "Wouldn't that be the 1994 Citibank case, where a Russian hacker named Vladimir Levin tried to electronically embezzle almost ten million dollars by transferring the money into dummy accounts?" Charlie was studying criminology, hoping to use it with Net Force in the future.

"Correct," Valas said. "A cooperative effort by the law-enforcement agencies of several nations caught him and his accomplices in England, Israel, and the United States."

Andy Moore nudged Charlie. "Way to pross that ancient data!"

Charlie smiled and gave him a high five, his dark brown skin looking even darker contrasted against Andy's sun-burned pink hand.

Valas watched the byplay with a smile, then said, "That case, and the capture of hacker Kevin Mitnick, who disrupted computer systems, stole credit card numbers, and even bugged investigating FBI agents' phones, made the federal government realize that online crime was going to be a big problem as our planet moved into the virtual world.

"After several fierce battles on Capitol Hill over such issues as free speech and privacy, limited regulation of the Net began in earnest in the first years of the twenty-first century. Along with that regulation came Net Force, created specifically to monitor, track, and apprehend online criminals."

As Valas spoke, Mark looked around and saw that everyone in the room was keyed in to the presentation. Even Andy, who had a three-second attention span on a good day, was listening intently. *Our meetings haven't been this quiet since Captain Winter announced the Shadow Program*, Mark thought. His gaze suddenly met the intent look of Captain Winters, who was looking at him and frowning slightly. *How does he do that? It's like he reads my mind sometimes.* Mark quickly turned his attention back to the lecture.

A half hour later Valas wound his lecture down and opened the floor to questions. The first one came from Charlie Davis.

"How does a person get your job?"

Valas had to wait until the Net Force Explorers stopped chuckling before he could answer. "Hard work and perseverance," he said. "College is essential, too. I've got a degree in criminology. That or a business or computer-science degree is practically required to get anywhere in this field. Experience is a plus—which you're getting here in the Net Force Explorers. Once you've gotten your degree, apply to the CIA, and if you're good enough, the rest is a piece of cake. That is, if you like long hours, dead-end leads, and cases that take months and sometimes years to resolve. If you're thinking the CIA is a glamour job, it's time to rethink that idea. The work's no picnic, but if you're looking for a challenge, you'd be coming to the right place."

"Do you see the Net changing much in the future?" Mark asked.

"The Net is always changing. In that respect, it's exactly like the real world. With the growth of Web-based political movements and continuing experiments into online consciousness, the first totally online community is not far away, we think. And as that evolves, so will the criminals on the Net. I hope some of you will be around to catch them." Valas smiled. "I see that our time is up. I thank you for your attention, and I'm sure we'll be seeing each other around. Thanks again." He left the podium to enthusiastic applause.

Captain Winters shook hands with Valas. With a final wave, Valas popped out of veeyar.

"If I could have everyone's attention before we break for the evening," Winters said, "I'd like you to be sure to look at the posted schedule for our next meeting. Our new shadow program is also getting under way, for those of you who would like to learn more about the different departments of Net Force. Sign up for the position you would like to learn more about, and someone from Net Force will contact you to schedule a shift accompanying an agent doing that job. That's all we have for tonight. I'll see you next week."

There was a buzz of conversation as the meeting closed down. Several of the Net Force Explorers said their goodbyes and disappeared, logging off to their homes. Mark, Daniel, Megan, and Maj all stayed behind for a minute.

"Yeah, I could see myself doing that in ten years. Daniel Sanchez, cyber-cop, busting the bad guys on the Net," Daniel said.

"Sounds like a bad holoprog," Mark teased.

"Yeah, well, laugh all you want, but when I'm famous, you all can say you knew me when. Heck, even you, Squirt," Daniel said.

Mark rolled his eyes, but before he could reply, Megan broke in. "All right, you two. Does anyone want to get together real-time tonight? Maj is spending the night, so she'll be at my place."

Mark shook his head. "Thanks anyway, but I'm booked."

Daniel also had plans. "Nope, I'm connecting downtown with some friends of mine. We're going to see what kind of trouble we can get into at the Monuments game."

"Well, don't get into anything you can't handle, Daniel," Maj said. "In that case, we'll see you on Monday."

"Trouble I can't handle? Hey, this is me, remember?" Daniel grinned, waved, and vanished.

"That's what I'm afraid of," Maj said to no one in particular, shaking her head.

3

Actually, Daniel hadn't told the other Net Force Explorers the whole truth. He wasn't sure he was going out. He was only sure he was going to try to. He had logged into the Net Force Explorers meeting from school. Unfortunately, he had forgotten his tickets for that night's game. Now, to get them, he had to get in and out of his home without being spotted. The only problem with that was he might see his father. Right now that would be most uncool.

So I'll just slip in the house real quiet-like, Daniel thought as he trotted up the autumn leaf–covered walk to his parents' house. Located in Georgetown, the colonial home blended in perfectly with the rest of the upscale neighborhood. But as Daniel looked up and down the street, he couldn't help but feel like he always did—out of place. He knew his parents had worked hard to get where they were today, but they were still the only Hispanic family on the block. Even the fact that they had lived there for more than five years did little to alter Daniel's view. His family was well liked and respected in the neighborhood, but he still felt like an outsider. And he knew that nothing he or his family did could change that.

Shaking his head, Daniel keyed in his combination to un-lock the front door. The smell of baked ziti filled the front hallway and foyer. That was a bad sign, because it probably meant that his father was either home or due in shortly. Ramos Sanchez loved Italian food, and Daniel's mother, Carol, usually made it on the nights when his father could be home for dinner. Her career as a fourth-grade teacher kept her busy, but she still tried to make time for at least one home-cooked meal a day for Daniel and, when his job allowed him to join them, Ramos.

But not tonight, Daniel thought. *It's hot dogs at the ballpark if I can pull this off.* Slipping his backpack off, he crept upstairs to his room. He dropped his backpack in the corner and picked up his baseball glove, putting the plastic baseball park pass into his pocket. Tonight's game featured rising pitching star Steve Lafflin of the Seattle Mariners against one of Daniel's personal heroes, Jose Rodrigo, currently the player with the highest batting average in the entire league. It was going to be a power-hitting showdown, and Daniel's friends had gotten them prime seats. Maybe he could even come home tonight with a ball that had been crushed into the stands by Rodrigo himself.

Yeah, but only if I make it to the game, he thought. After checking to make sure he had everything, Daniel walked to the stairs and peeked down into the hallway. He could hear his mother preparing the dining room for dinner. His father was nowhere in sight, and Daniel couldn't hear him, either. Taking a deep breath, he started down the stairway.

He had just reached the foyer when he heard a sound behind him. Daniel sighed as he turned around to see his father standing in the dark archway that led to the garage. Although several inches shorter than his son, Ramos seemed to fill the hallway with a quiet, unshakable confidence.

With a sinking heart, Daniel realized that his father must have been watching him the entire time. *Man, sometimes having a Secret Service agent for a father just sucks,* he thought. Still, he had once chance left, and he grabbed for it like an out-of-control skydiver grabs his reserve parachute cord.

"Hey, Dad, I didn't see you there." Daniel smiled. *That was telling the absolute truth,* he thought. "I'd love to stop and talk, but I'm running late for the game, so I'll catch you later, okay?"

"Not so fast, son. I'd like to talk to you for a minute." Ramos's voice halted Daniel just as he was about to turn the doorknob. "I was hoping you would come see me before you left, but apparently you decided this was the easier way out."

Daniel started to speak, but his father held up his hand. "You are aware of how I feel about your schoolwork, yes?"

Numbly Daniel nodded.

"Your grades for the quarter were posted today, as I'm sure you know."

Actually, I was hoping they wouldn't have gotten here yet, Daniel thought, but didn't dare say. *It's just not my day.*

"I told you that you could go to the game if your grades were acceptable. I think you know what your scores were."

Of course Daniel knew. He had always been an excellent student, able to nail the highest scores in his classes with little effort. Because of that, he had recently been moved into Bradford Academy's toughest Advanced Placement classes, where he'd actually had to think for a change. The difference had caught him unprepared, and his grades reflected that.

"I know, Dad, you're right. Some of the finals for last semester caught me a little off guard, that's all. So I got a couple of B's. My scores are still in the top ten percent of my class. Let me catch the game, and I'll hit the books for the rest of the weekend, I promise."

"I'm afraid that's not possible, son. The top ten percent may be good enough for school, but that doesn't cut it in the real world. To be the best, you have to rise above everybody else, work harder than everybody else," Ramos said.

While listening to his father, Daniel felt a familiar hot tingling begin in the pit of his stomach and start spreading throughout his body. *Here we go again*, he thought. He knew his father was usually intractable on these kinds of things, but he had to try one more time.

Taking a deep breath, he smiled and said, "Dad, I already do all that. You know I work hard, it's why I'm in these classes in the first place. Hey, I'm actually being challenged for once. Okay, so I admit I didn't ace every test. As I recall, even Einstein failed more than one math class. Just let me have tonight, and you'll barely see me until next quarter's results are posted, and you won't be disappointed, you have my word."

Ramos shook his head. "I told you at the beginning of the quarter what I expected of you, yet you didn't make the grades I asked for. As long as you get straight A's, you can go out with your friends. Until then you stay home and study."

The tingling was much stronger now, and Daniel felt like his head was on fire. He swallowed hard, trying to clear his dry throat. "So, just because I didn't get a perfect report card, you're grounding me?" he asked.

Ramos nodded. "I demand better from you than you've given me this semester. We both know your capabilities. You didn't hold up your end."

"Well, maybe I'm just plain tired of holding up my end!" Daniel shot back. "I go to school, I come home, and I study. I'm not playing in any sports programs, and I don't spend a lot of time hanging out with my friends. I work my butt off at school and at home, even in the Net Force Explorers. I'm sick of you constantly hanging over my shoulder, making sure I'm always working. Nothing is ever good enough for you. Well, I'm tired of working! When is it my turn to enjoy myself for a change?" Daniel said.

"Lower your voice," Ramos snapped.

"No!" Daniel noticed his mother standing in the hallway. He hated it when she got caught up in these arguments, which had been occurring more frequently than ever lately. He locked eyes with his father again. "I'm tired of discussions and compromises! I'm not you, and I never will be, so quit trying to run my life to fit your plans!" Daniel clenched his hands into tight fists, his whole body shaking with long-suppressed anger.

"Whether you are tired of it or not, you are my son, and you will respect me in this house," Ramos said, his voice even.

"That's funny—you sure don't respect me, so why should I extend you that courtesy?" Daniel said.

"Daniel!" his mother exclaimed. Father and son stared at

each other, neither one willing to be the first to back down. Finally Ramos sighed.

"I was hoping we could discuss this rationally, but I see that's impossible. Go to your room. We'll talk about this in the morning. I'll let your friends know you won't be joining them this evening," Ramos said.

"Maybe if I stay up all night, I can come up with enough reasons for you to get off my back," Daniel said over his shoulder as he started up the stairs. *No problem,* he thought. *In five minutes I'm out my window and off to the stadium.*

His father's voice cut through his thoughts like a virus through an unprotected program. "And please don't try sneaking out your window. I've set the home security system. I don't want to have to explain to the police why my son was breaking *out* of my house."

Daniel froze for a moment, then, without looking back, continued up the stairs, a prisoner in his own home. At the top of the stairs he paused, listening to his mother and father conversing in low voices.

"Ramos, don't you think you were a little hard on him?" his mother said.

"No, I don't. I told Daniel to keep his grades up if he wanted to go out on school nights. He didn't, and until he does, I want him right here where I can keep an eye on him. He needs to learn responsibility. In the real world he'll only get one chance, if that, to earn other people's respect. Whatever career he chooses, he'll be required to do his best no matter what. I expect him to have that lesson well learned before then."

I sure can't learn anything when my "teacher" keeps repeating the same old lessons like a stupid parrot, Daniel thought.

"Are you sure that's why you read him the riot act over his report card?" his mom said.

"What do you mean?" his father asked.

"I know what you went through during your early career in the Service. Are you sure you're not pushing Daniel hard so that he doesn't have to go through the same thing? After all, times are different now."

Yeah, so different they're leaving my dad behind, Daniel thought. He heard his father sigh.

"There will always be someone who will hold his heritage against him. Times will never change enough to prevent that. I'm challenging Daniel to be the best, because someone will always assume he isn't, and then he'll have to work that much harder to overcome that prejudice."

"Ramos, I'm not so sure you're right about that. The kids in my classes get along fine. Their fights and squabbles aren't race-based. They're just children being children."

"Perhaps, but odds are Daniel will encounter prejudice at some point in his career, and I want him to be ready for it," Ramos said.

Daniel shook his head. *Why does he still think I can't take care of myself? Any problems I run into, I'll handle on my own. I'm not a kid who has to be looked after anymore. What does it take to make him realize that?*

"Dinner's getting cold," his mom said. "Shall I call him down?"

"No, not yet. Let him sit up there and think about what I said for a while. I'll take a tray up and try to talk to him later. Besides, I doubt he'll have much appetite right now," Ramos said.

Amazing, that's the one thing he's gotten right about me so far this evening, Daniel thought.

"It might help if you explained where you're coming from," Carol said.

"I've tried, but it just doesn't seem to sink in. Honestly, I'm not sure how to get through to him anymore," Ramos said.

"Well, give him time to cool off and try again later. Come to dinner."

The conversation continued as Daniel's parents walked out of earshot. Daniel remained where he was for several seconds, trying to control the anger surging through him.

How can he possibly know what I'm going through? This is my life, not his, Daniel thought as he turned and headed down the hall. *I'm responsible for my decisions, no one else. Why can't he just see that and give me the freedom I deserve?*

Once he reached his room, he resisted the urge to slam his door shut behind him with a loud slam. Daniel waded through the crumpled piles of clothes on his floor. *Someday*, he thought, *I'll prove my father wrong, and I can't wait to see the look on his face.* He briefly toyed with the idea of logging on and catching the game in veeyar, but what was the point? Even though veeyar would be indistinguishable from the real game, in this case being there was the whole idea, getting out of the house, getting away from his family and being free to do what he wanted. *Besides,* Daniel thought as he logged on to his system, *I'm sure Dad's already locked me out of the game.* Which, he soon found out, was exactly the case.

Resigned to his fate at least for the night, Daniel downloaded several virtual texts for a project he was working on for the Net Force Explorers. *If I can't lose myself at the game, I might as well get something accomplished. It's clear I won't be going anywhere for a while. And at least this will be interesting.* With a sigh, Daniel plunged into his research.

4

Mark lashed out with his bullwhip, the end curling around the tree branch above him. With a gulp and a quick look down, he jumped off the ledge he was on and swung across the yawning chasm. He landed on the other side with an audible thump, and suddenly realized his heels were still sticking out over the edge. *Oops, that's a long drop to a bad logoff.* Stepping carefully forward, he breathed a sigh of relief once he was well away from the canyon wall. Turning, he flicked his wrist, freeing the whip, then coiled it and hung it at his side.

"Eat your heart out, Lara Croft," he said, pushing his fedora back on his head. The entrance to the lost Aztec temple was just ahead. This time he'd recover the treasure for sure.

Abruptly the scene before him froze in place. *What's this?* Mark wondered just before an all-too-familiar face appeared before him.

"Sorry about the wait, son. Ready to go?"

"Dad!" Mark said. "I just made it to the temple on level twelve of Cities of Gold! We can't go now! Just five more minutes, please?"

"Mark, it's already eight o'clock. We're lucky your mom's also running late, or we'd be in for it. We'll grab something on the way home for dinner. How does that sound?" Jay Gridley asked.

"Japanese tempura shrimp?" Mark asked.

"Depends on what your mother says. Save that program and meet us at the entrance, all right?"

"All right, all right." His dad blinked out of existence in the veeyar scenario. *Frack! I've been working to get to this level for two months, I'm just at the door and the 'rents show up. If I'd crashed and burned and had to start all over again, he wouldn't have come in for hours.* Mark saved his game, disengaged his neural connection, and shut down the computer system.

He was sitting in a veeyar console chair in the middle of a featureless room at Net Force HQ. His parents both worked there, so he often came to meet them at the office after school. He got up, stretched the kinks out of his muscles, and was soon navigating the maze of corridors that comprised Net Force HQ. In a few minutes he saw his folks. They were waiting by the front reception and weapons-detection area talking about work. They broke off when they saw him coming.

"Hey, Mom, Dad!" Mark said as he trotted over to them.

"Ah, here at last. Everything taken care of?" Mark's mom asked.

"Yeah, let's go. I'm starving," Mark replied. As he passed the reception desk, he held his ID badge up for the electronic scanner. It beeped, clearing him from the building. His parents followed suit.

"So how was the Net Force Explorers meeting?" Jay asked as they walked to the parking lot.

"Great. That guy from the CIA, Ryan Valas, spoke to us about online crime and all that stuff. You should have seen Charlie prick up his ears. Sounds like Valas'll be a good addition," Mark said.

"Ryan joined about six months ago, and came very highly recommended. I'm enjoying working with him. Speaking of work, how's that detection program of yours coming along?" Jay asked.

Mark tried not to brag as he replied, "I just ran a beta test today in an open system. I found everybody—Daniel, Megan, and Maj—in less than ten minutes. You should've seen the looks on their faces." *Especially Daniel's,* he thought.

"Sounds promising. Did you ever find a way to isolate the logon tags?" Jay asked.

"It's funny you should mention that, Dad," Mark said, then launched into the story of how he caught Daniel. "Of course, this was an isolated test with unsecured links, and they knew I was looking for them. Still, I'm going to have to work out a better way to find hidden and encrypted links."

"All right, you two, enough shop talk for one evening. Sometimes I think you'd both live online if I gave you the chance," his mom said. Mark and his father exchanged glances. "And, no, that chance will never come, so forget about it. Instead, why don't you two geniuses think about where we're going to eat this late."

"How about Sakimura's?" Mark asked.

"Honey, that would be great, except we'd still have to wait forty-five minutes for a table."

"Actually, if we step on it, we can just make the nine o'clock reservations I made online," Mark said.

Both of his parents looked at him, then at each other. "I took a guess as to when you'd both be done," Mark said. "What can I say? I got lucky."

Jay smiled at his wife. "Lucky as well as intelligent. And he even has your good looks."

His wife shook her head. "Flattery will get you everywhere, but right now, I'd settle for just going to the restaurant."

"Agreed," Mark's father said, glancing down at Mark, who also nodded. They passed through the secured lobby and checkpoint and went out to the parking lot, where a Dodge minivan waited.

The October air made all three of them shiver in their jackets. *Too bad it's not one of the limousines,* Mark thought as he and his family trotted across the wet asphalt. *Dad could have had the driver meet us at the door.* He had gotten to ride in one of the armored limos when his father had assumed command of Net Force. *There are definitely advantages to being the Net Force commander's son,* Mark thought. *Of course, there are risks as well.* When Mark's dad had accepted the position, he'd had a long talk with Mark, explaining the dangers of his job. The position of Net Force commander wasn't all glory and veeyar surfing. A previous commander, Steve Day, had been assassinated back in 2010. Day's successor, Alexander Michaels, had also been a hitman's target. *"With great power comes great responsibilities,"* his father had told him, *"and also deadly enemies."*

Mark knew that all too well, having gotten into his own share of scrapes both on and off the Net, often when he was trying to help out his fellow Net Force Explorers. But he wouldn't have traded those adventures, or his friends, for anything in the world.

At least it's been quiet lately, Mark thought. *Almost boring. But nobody's shooting at my dad, so boring's okay by me.* Even if it meant that he would have to settle for the Plain-Jane ride tonight. He'd sit in a cloth-covered seat instead of a leather one, look out the minivan's windows instead of the tinted, bulletproof windows of a sleek limo. The side door slid closed, and a minute later Mark and his parents were headed for the heart of Washington, D.C.

Three hours later Mark munched on a peanut butter cookie as he headed to his room. He still had a ton of work to do on his program. Dinner had been great, but Asian food was the same the world over—even if you stuffed yourself, two hours later you were hungry again.

Mark logged on to his veeyar site, which at the moment resembled the world of his favorite e-comic, *Past Perfect*, which was about a group of time-traveling scientists who kept trying to fix the world's mistakes, often with ridiculous results. The wallpaper of Mark's site looked like the inside of the machine they used to travel through time. A bright ball of light resembling a white dwarf star was directly in the center, with millions and millions of separate time strands radiating out from it. As Mark drew closer to the center, he could see the individual time lines passing him, thousands upon thousands of branching alternate universes. In some, dinosaurs still ruled the Earth, and glaciers covered New York. In others, Rome had never fallen, and the streets were filled with kids in togas driving chariots. The millions of time strands contained every strange permutation of reality possible.

Mark froze the site so he wouldn't be distracted and scanned his virtmail. A message from Joanna Winthrop, the head of Net Force Internal Operations, was waiting for him. Mark had virtmailed her earlier that morning to set up a meeting to discuss his progress on the lurker program. Selecting the message with her icon on it, Mark saw Joanna's face appear.

"Hi, Mark. I got your message and would love to discuss how things are going. I'm working the nightshift at HQ, so if you're still up for it, stop by in veeyar later tonight, and I'll take a look."

Mark brought up the log file that had recorded the hide-and-seek game he had played earlier that day, viewed it, and realized he still felt pretty good about it. Sometimes, when he reviewed his programs later, he wasn't as happy as he could be, but this time he was satisfied. *Just a few things to check out before I head over*, he thought.

Mark looked at several security programs that would scan for the hidden logon tags his father had mentioned earlier. Absorbed in his task, he didn't notice how late it was getting until he found himself nodding off.

"Time," he said. A glowing readout appeared before him: 12:47 A.M. "I'm beat. I'd better get going." Mark saved his work and iconized it. He activated the Net launch program and took off for Net Force's Web site.

When Mark took off, he did so literally, soaring out into the electronic world that was the Web. He could have just materialized at his final destination, but what was the fun in that? *Flying World War II airplanes is fun, but nothing beats this*, Mark thought as he left his site behind at Mach speed. Below, he could see tens of thousands of various sites represented by buildings and other icons as he flashed by. The pathways that connected them all were represented by highways on which millions of people traveled at the speed of light, getting to where they had to go in the blink of an eye. Of course, like Mark, many people preferred the illusionary freedom of flying through Net space to instantaneous arrival.

Flight contraptions of all kinds filled the air, from hot air balloons to hang gliders to personal rocket packs. Mark liked the simplicity of superhuman flight. *After all, the Net is the one place that makes the impossible possible.* If Mark had seen a purple dragon with pink polka dots fly by, he wouldn't have given it a second glance. The Net freed people from what many considered the confines of ordinary life and allowed them to pursue whatever interests or hobbies they had, from mountain climbing to Formula One auto racing. In here the universe was like putty in the palm of a person's hand, ready to be molded into whatever form and function the user could think of. What they did with it was limited only by their imagination.

A few more minutes' travel brought Mark closer to the icon that represented Net Force online. *Traffic is still heavy, even this early in the morning,* Mark thought. Once he started following the pathway that led to the Net Force site, the traffic flow lessened considerably. By the time he reached the site, the area was deserted, or very nearly so. Mark saw a single proxy leaving the Net Force area. *I wonder who else is working in the wee hours?* Mark thought. He swooped down to take a closer look.

The flyer that left the building was a sleek European model Mark couldn't place. It moved like lightning, taking him by surprise as it accelerated past him. He saw that the flyer was supposed to be invisible, but with his scanning program activated, Mark could see the logon tag that the aircar was following.

Techtronix? Hmm, I wonder what they're doing here so late? And why all the secrecy? Techtronix was an international multicorporation with branches on every continent, involved in just about every aspect of Net business, from electronics to manufacturing to communications. It was almost impossible to walk into any store or shop online without seeing the Techtronix logo on something.

Maybe they're meeting with Net Force about industrial espionage. I'm sure a company like that has plenty to worry about in that area. But you'd think their main office people, the kind who'd meet with Net Force, would be nine-to-fivers.

Mark soared lower toward the Net Force site, aiming himself for the main entrance.

He had just passed the first door when the portal slid shut behind him. Instead of the destination menu that usually appeared for Net Force Explorers, a flashing red light went off.

"Unauthorized entry detected. All system ports have been shut down. Please stand by for identity confirmation scan," a modulated computer voice commanded.

What the heck is going on? Mark thought.

"Confirming, please wait," the voice said.

As if I had another choice, Mark thought, tapping his foot. *Something must be going on.* After an interminably long few seconds, the voice spoke again. "Identity and retina scan confirmed. Access permitted." With that, the Net Force Explorers menu appeared. Mark immediately noticed that the Command Center icon was inaccessible. *The Command Center isn't usually off limits unless there's been a major intrusion,* Mark thought. *It's not off limits to me, however, and I am supposed to be meeting Joanna. . . .*

Mark selected a small icon from his fanny pack and activated it. After a few seconds the Command Center icon flashed twice, and a door appeared in the far wall. Mark jumped through the door as fast as he could—the program he'd inserted would only work for a few seconds before deleting itself.

Whether in real time or veeyar, walking into the Net Force Command Center always gave Mark a rush that nothing else could match. He paused for a moment and looked out over the virtual site, which was constructed to look exactly like its real-world equivalent. Veeyar consoles, each manned by a Net Force operative, were arrayed in a semicircle three rows deep, all facing a central area where several massive viewscreens were constantly updating the condition of the Net, from monitoring possible intrusions to verifying security for thousands of banks, military bases, and government departments, both online and in real space. Mark could hear snatches of various people's conversations, from the undercover agents who set up sting operations against online arms dealers and software pirates to security consultants who tested high-level protection programs for Fortune 500 companies. He drank it all in. Mark loved programming; in fact, he loved anything that involved computers in general. He figured he'd be working on veeyar programs until the day he died. With his skills he could get an excellent job at any number of companies that would test his limits every day. But actually being a part of Net Force, however small that role might be right now, gave him a deep sense of pride. *Besides,* he thought, *it is more fun busting the bad guys.*

Mark scanned the rows of consoles, looking for one particular person. He found her at the far end of the room, a tall woman with her hair tied back in a simple ponytail.

Mark activated a ghost program, which allowed him to be invisible, and drifted over. Net Force headquarters suffered dozens of intrusion attempts on a daily basis. A lot of basement hackers thought it would be fun to try and put something over on the best of the best. Unfortunately for them, practically all of them were caught and arrested for criminal Net trespassing. Despite Net Force's high success rate at catching these hackers, and the stiff prison sentences the hackers often got for their trouble, too many Nerds and Nerdettas kept trying to beat the police. *I hope that's just what happened tonight,* Mark thought. *Although if it is, these guys were good, good enough to get past the perimeter. Most hackers don't even get past the front door. It's a good thing we've got great internal security.*

The woman he was standing behind was Joanna Winthrop, the head of Net Force Internal Operations. She was studying a three-dimensional replay of the intrusion, watching as the hacker accessed various files. Finally the hacker realized he'd poked where he apparently shouldn't have, because he disappeared just before the alarm sounded.

Joanna turned to the tech seated next to her. "I wish this was just a simple outside intrusion, but that isn't the case. According to all of our data, the hacker was internal. More specifically, it was one of the Net Force Explorers."

For a second Mark thought Joanna was playing some kind of sick joke, although if she was, he didn't see the humor. *All of us have struggled and sacrificed to get here.* Mark couldn't believe that any Explorer he knew would throw all of that away to play a prank.

"What was the hacker accessing? Is the breach still open?" the tech asked.

"No," Joanna replied. "We've got the whole site locked down, but that didn't stop him from grabbing some of the data he was after."

"What did he get?"

"He was in the Southeast Asian Operations File. We're still assessing exactly what he managed to download before we clamped down on him," Joanna said.

"Who was it?" the tech asked.

"Just a second, I'm pulling his file now. Here he is."

The picture came up, and Mark got a horrible feeling in the pit of his stomach. There, staring back at him from an official Net Force ID displayed on the screen, was the face of Daniel Sanchez.

Suddenly Mark heard a stern voice behind him. "What are you doing here?" He realized that the security crackdown had stripped off the ghost program—he was visible!

Joanna looked up and Mark smiled weakly at her. "Hey, Jo, what's going down? Another hack attempt?" he asked.

"Besides yours, you mean?" she asked, frowning.

Busted, Mark thought. *And I know I'm gonna get it this time.*

5

"What?!" Daniel cried. He had gotten a call from Captain Winters to come down to Net Force headquarters with his parents first thing Sunday morning. Since his mom and dad were both already out of the house, he paged them, letting them know where he would be, and took the autobus over to the Net Force HQ. Now he found himself listening to the most unimaginable news possible.

"I'm sorry, Daniel, but your veeyar persona was recorded trying to access unauthorized files. The security system even matched your DNA scan." Captain Winters paused. "Personally, I don't believe it was you, but I saw the evidence myself. Until we get to the bottom of this, I'm afraid I have to suspend you from the Net Force Explorers pending a full investigation. I'm sure this is a mistake of some kind, but our policy is absolute in a situation like this. Effective immediately, your membership in the Net Force Explorers is suspended until the matter has been resolved to Net Force's satisfaction."

Daniel sat frozen, stunned by what Captain Winters was saying. "Net Force's satisfaction? What about my satisfaction? I didn't do anything! I wasn't even online that much this weekend, and I never came near the Net Force site!

Besides, what possible reason would I have to break into Net Force files? This is unbelievable! I didn't do it!" Daniel protested, tightly gripping the arms of the chair he sat in to keep himself from leaping to his feet and doing something he'd regret.

"Hey, relax, I'm on your side," said Captain Winters. "I know how upsetting this is for you. Why don't you tell me what you did this weekend, and I'll see if I can pick up something that would explain this."

Daniel gave Winters a quick rundown of the last few days, which mostly involved staying home and doing schoolwork.

"When were you online yesterday, Daniel?" Captain Winters asked.

Daniel thought for a moment. "Off and on throughout the day, I guess. My virtual hang-gliding club met yesterday, so I logged a few hours sailing over the Rockies."

"Sounds like fun," Captain Winters said. "So you didn't access Net Force about an hour after midnight last night?"

"Of course not. I was online, but I was nowhere near the Net Force HQ. Can't you check the usage log from my computer, get the list of sites I visited, and match them up with the time the hack happened?" Daniel asked. "That would clear me right away!"

Captain Winters nodded. "Good thinking. But I've already had Joanna do that. And the logs show that during the time the hack occurred, you were online and in HQ. I believe what you're telling me, Daniel, but the evidence is against you. I'm sorry, but we have to follow the rules. I'm sure this must be a mistake, and I'll work night and day to correct it."

Daniel shot out of his chair and paced around the room. "Yeah, there's been a mistake made, all right, and when I find out who screwed me over, I'm gonna show him what a mistake it was!"

"Daniel! Sit down!" Captain Winters snapped. He waited until the boy slumped back in the chair again. "I've called and asked your parents to come down so we can discuss this. Right now—"

"Great, that's just what I need, my dad, Mr. Authority, coming down on me again. No, thanks, count me out," Daniel said. *Perfect, that's just perfect. Now he can come down here and chew me out in front of the captain,* he thought.

"Daniel, I'm trying to help you out here. If you didn't do anything, then why are you resisting? Help me, and help yourself," Winters said. "I realize you're angry, but try to look at this from my side."

"May I go now?" Daniel asked through clenched teeth.

Winters shook his head. "You're dismissed, but I want you to stay around here until your parents arrive. And, Daniel?" Captain Winters said as Daniel stalked toward the door.

"What?" Daniel said, without turning around.

"Like I said before, I believe you. Let's try to figure out what's going on together. Don't try to do anything yourself. That could only get you in more trouble."

"Look, I know you're trying to help me out, Captain, but I'm not gonna lie down and let whoever did this walk all over me. Besides, it sounds like Net Force has already made up its mind, no matter what you think. And I don't even want to guess what my dad's going to say when he hears this." *I don't have to guess,* Daniel thought as he stepped out the door. *He's going to kill me.*

Winters watched the doorway for a few seconds, listening to Daniel's angry footsteps fade away. When he was sure Daniel had gone, he logged on and called a meeting with a select few Net Force Explorers.

"What?!" Megan cried, her voice sounding surprisingly like Daniel Sanchez's earlier that morning. She looked around at Maj and Mark, the other members at the meeting, then back at Captain Winters. "That's impossible!"

Captain Winters nodded. "Every instinct in me wants to agree with you, Megan, but Joanna is fairly certain that Daniel was behind the intrusion."

"If all you have is a Web signature, that can't possibly be enough to suspend Daniel. Why don't you ask him about that night?"

"Don't forget we also have the DNA identification tag, which is extremely difficult to reproduce," Captain Winters said. "Anyway, I did ask him, and he denies it, says he wasn't anywhere near HQ when it happened, but his alibi doesn't hold up. With his own computer log telling us that

he was online and at Net Force at the time, we really have
no choice but to suspend him pending further investigation.
Besides, against my instructions, he seems to have left Net
Force headquarters."

"He got mad and took off?" Mark rolled his eyes. "That
certainly sounds like Daniel." The stern looks he got from
the other three caused him to look around. "What? He's a
hothead, that's all. I didn't say he was hacking and stealing
files."

"Is there any chance he'll really run?" Megan asked. "I
mean, for good?"

"I would find that hard to believe," Winters said. "I think
he was just upset over the accusation and needed some space
to think about it. That's part of the reason I called the three
of you here. Normally, this would be an internal investigation. But, since Mark is already aware of what has happened," Winters said, turning a stern gaze on Mark, who was
suddenly looking everywhere but at Captain Winters's face,
"I decided to bring all of you here to try and help. Of all the
Net Force Explorers, you three seem to have the best rela-
tionship with Daniel."

Could have fooled me, Mark thought, but kept his mouth
shut.

"I'd like you to stick with Daniel during the next few days
and see if there's maybe something he wouldn't tell me that
might help clear him. And above all, I want you to make
sure he doesn't do anything rash. He's already in enough
trouble, and I don't want him getting in any more. So keep
an eye on him, all right?" Winters said.

Maj, Mark, and Megan nodded, exchanging glances
among themselves.

Mark spoke up. "Any intel on the *real* intruder yet?"

Captain Winters shook his head. "Not yet, but Joanna is
chasing down a couple of leads. Now, we all know about the
various disguise programs that are floating around on the
Web these days, many of them very sophisticated. If Daniel
is innocent, then someone either actually used Daniel's
veeyar system to gain access or managed to copy his persona
and signal perfectly, linked it back to make it look like Daniel's system was the source, and used that to try and access

our files. That's my current theory, anyway. But until I can prove it and Daniel is cleared, he's on suspension. So, like I said, you guys keep an eye on him for the next few days, and let us handle this."

"Right, Captain," Megan said. Mark and Maj nodded.

"Okay, this meeting is adjourned. I'd like to emphasize one thing," Captain Winters said, looking at each of them. "Clearing Daniel's name is the first priority on my hot list right now. I'm in his corner as much as you guys are. If anything should come to light that you think might help me, let me know right away, all right?"

The three Net Force Explorers nodded.

"Then you girls can go," Captain Winters said. "Mark, I'd like to speak with you alone for a moment."

Uh-oh, Mark thought, *here we go again*. He turned to Megan and Maj. "Why don't you go on ahead, and I'll meet up with you later?"

After the girls were gone, Mark leaned back in his chair, grinning weakly at Captain Winters. "Look, I know what you're going to say—" Mark began, when Winters cut him off.

"I'm sure you do, Mark, because this isn't the first time we've had a conversation like this. How can I get through to you that hacking into headquarters will not be tolerated?"

"But I wasn't hacking! I was supposed to meet Joanna!" Mark protested. "You can ask her!"

"I have asked her," Captain Winters said. "She agrees— up to a point. That point is where she caught you intentionally eavesdropping during an obvious security alert. You weren't supposed to be in the Command Center right then and you knew it. Under the circumstances, you should have either logged off or made your presence known immediately. If you'll recall, she was the one who turned you in."

"Yes, well," Mark said, "it was worth a shot, wasn't it?"

"Not really. Mark, I've tried to be patient, but this is serious. Because you're the son of the commander of Net Force, I've cut you a little slack when your hard work in other areas warranted it. But the fact is that you're a Net Force Explorer, and therefore subject to the same rules that everyone else has to follow. Do not break into areas you're not supposed to be in again. If you do, commander's son or not, I'll have no choice but to bring you up on the same charges Daniel is facing. Do I make myself clear?"

"As crystal, sir," Mark said past the dry lump in his throat. *He means it this time*, Mark thought. *I'd better cool it for a while.* "You're right, Captain. I'm sorry, and thank you for the second chance."

Captain Winters nodded. "Good," he said. "You'll let me know when you find Daniel, right?"

"Yes, sir," Mark said.

"Then get out there and start looking. I'll talk to you soon. You're dismissed," Winters said.

Mark got up to leave, and he could feel Captain Winters's eyes on him as he walked to the door. Once outside, he breathed a sigh of relief. *I guess what Dad says is true—if you stick your neck out long enough, sooner or later someone's going to take a chop at it. That was a little too close for comfort.* Shaking his head, Mark logged out of the Net Force site and went in search of Megan and Maj.

"I just can't believe that Daniel would do something like this," Megan said. "I mean, why work so hard to get into the Net Force program to throw it all away?" Mark had tracked the girls down in a Parisian café site, where they now sat drinking virtual cappuccino and discussing their meeting with Captain Winters.

"I hope you're saying that as a reason to believe him?" Maj said, frowning.

"Of course I am. It just doesn't pross," Megan replied. "By the way, Mark, what did Captain Winters want with you after we left?" she asked with a knowing grin.

"Okay, yeah, I got caught somewhere I shouldn't have been again," Mark said, "but if I hadn't been there, we wouldn't know anything about this, and wouldn't be able to try to help Daniel."

"Weren't you just telling Winters what a hothead Daniel is?" Megan asked. "Are you sure you want to help him?"

"Look, maybe Daniel and I don't always get along so well—" Mark began.

"That's the understatement of the year," Maj said under her breath.

"But," Mark continued as if she hadn't spoken, "this could've happened to any one of us. And any one of us could be the next persona this chameleon uses to try to get into Net Force. I may not like Daniel all the time, but we all know he's innocent. If we work together, maybe we can help him—and ourselves—out."

"You're right, Mark. It *could* have been any one of us. What did you have in mind?" Megan asked.

"I've got something I need to take care of at headquarters that won't take long, then I think all three of us should find Daniel and talk to him," Mark said.

"Do you have an idea about what's really going on?" Maj asked.

"Maybe. I was going to see if my lurker program could discover who's behind this," Mark said.

Maj nodded. "I'm not slamming you, Mark, but Joanna's the best there is. I'm pretty sure she'll find the real person behind this."

Mark grinned. "I know, and I'm hoping she does, too, but she doesn't know everything. Just trust me."

Maj exchanged glances with Megan, who pointed at her watch. "Whatever. We've got a ton of research to do for our history sim on the Battle of the Bulge, so we'll get started on it while we wait for you. Let us know when you're through here, and we'll all go visit Daniel."

Mark nodded, and the three split up, heading for their respective destinations in cyberspace.

Daniel had struck out blindly from Net Force Headquarters after his dismissal, not caring where he went. Eventually he ended up on the elevated hover-trains of the local mass-transit system in Washington and the surrounding suburbs. He rode the rails using his E-pass, jumping on and off when it suited him, traveling through several neighborhoods, all the while feeling the burning of the familiar cold ball of anger in the pit of his stomach.

During all his traveling, however, one thought kept flaming in his mind. *Whoever did this to me is going to pay. I*

guarantee it. I don't care how long it takes me to find them.
For a second he thought about going home, but immediately dismissed the idea. *No doubt Dad knows about this, and he's waiting for me. I'm not dealing with him until I have to. The way things have been going lately, he wouldn't even listen to my side of the story. I'm sure he's just aching to ground me for the next twenty years or so, and then I'd never find out what's going on. Anyway,* he thought ruefully, *we'd just get into another argument if I went home now.*

As Daniel stared out the window at the cityscape below him, he was reminded of the early twentieth century hobos who used to ride the trains cross-country, traveling from job to job, going wherever chance took them. *I'll bet that was some kind of life, going where you wanted, when you wanted, with no one to answer to.* For a wild second he thought of ditching it all and taking off, heading out of Washington to see the rest of America, maybe even the world. *Find out what it's like to be my own boss for a change,* he thought.

But the fantasy passed as quickly as it had come. *I couldn't put Mom through that. She'd lose it if she didn't know what had happened to me,* he thought. *Besides,* he realized, *I need to find the chameleon who skinned me and teach him a lesson. And to do that, I'll need some help. Someone still connected to Net Force. Someone like . . . the Squirt. Yeah, he can go a lot of places I can't, and keep me informed as to what's going on with the investigation. Jeez. That irritating little . . . But he's about the only one who can save my rear. I'm gonna hate asking him, but I don't have a choice.*

For now I'd better get home and face the music. The longer I wait, the worse it will be. Daniel turned to the view screen set in the back of the chair in front of him and asked for the most direct route to Georgetown. In a few minutes, he was heading toward home . . . and the growing storm on the horizon.

Mark looked at the locked red door to Net Force file storage. Based on security clearance, virtual doors within Net Force appeared either red or green, indicating access or a lack thereof. *The security protocols aren't a problem, but Captain Winters will be a big problem if I get caught,* he thought.

Daniel had better be worth the risk I'm taking. This isn't the Command Center, so I should be all right. But I'd better pull this off without anybody knowing. Mark slipped a shiny silver icon from his bag of tricks and applied it to the door. He watched as it seemingly sank into the metal, and the door slowly changed to green. Mark slipped through the door as fast as he could and retrieved the icon from where it had appeared on the other side.

He headed straight for the Net Force storage files. In a few minutes he had located what he was looking for—not the internal security records, but the logs of visitors accessing the Net Force site. He called up the file for early Saturday morning, looking for anyone leaving during the time that Daniel was supposedly accessing the files. Isolating the logs during that time, he scanned it, searching for anything out of the ordinary.

"Here's the Techtronix car taking off," Mark muttered. "Right after the internal alarm was tripped. Wait a minute. . . ." Now that he was able to watch the car at his leisure, he noticed that it was only a shell, basically an electronic signal programmed from another source. There was no high-flowing data stream that would indicate someone had logged on and was actually using it as their vehicle. Which meant . . .

It was a decoy, in case someone was watching. That means that there was still someone else here that night, Mark thought, someone with something to hide. *Now all I've got to do is find him.* He looked for a logon tag, but found nothing. *It's a slave program, probably meant to head back to its source, in this case, Techtronix. Spam mail, perhaps?*

He slowed the time frame down to increments of one-one hundredth of a second, then ran the log through his lurker program. Seven hundredths of a second before the alarm was sounded, what appeared to be a pinpoint of light appeared for a millisecond, then vanished. Mark backed the clock up and stopped the log, bringing the flash up and examining it closely.

Gotcha! What he'd found was an encoded burst transmission, compressed to travel on extremely high-bandwidth frequencies. *Now to trace you back to your source.* Mark backtracked the signal to where it originated, which led him back into Net Force headquarters, to one of the terminals used to monitor Net traffic.

Finally getting somewhere, he thought. Calling up that system's internal logs, he found, as he had thought he would, that the signal was coming from an outside source. Tracing that, he stared at the logon address that popped up. . . .

Sighing, Mark shook his head. The address he was looking at was Daniel Sanchez's. *Whoever set this up, they're really, really good. I think I've found out all I can here. I wonder if Joanna's come up with anything else yet?* Mark left the file storage area and reactivated the security program on his way out. Turning down a hallway, he flew toward the command center.

Once he reached the center door, Mark sent a message to Joanna, asking to see her.

A minute or two later Joanna appeared at the door. "Hey, Mark, what's up?

"Hi, Jo," Mark said. "Uh, I'm really sorry about the sneak-in last night."

The tall woman smiled. "That's all right. I hope you understand why I did what I did."

"Yeah, all too well. Anyway, the reason I'm here is that I was wondering if you'd come up with anything more about that hack last night?"

"Nothing yet," Joanna said. "Why?"

"Well, I was thinking about something I saw on my way into headquarters last night. There was a Techtronix car leaving really late, which seemed odd enough that I looked a little closer at it. It was right at the time of the hack, and the car seemed fishy somehow." Mark carefully omitted mentioning the transmission burst he'd found in the visitor logs. *The last thing I need to do is get in trouble with Joanna a second time*, he thought.

Joanna nodded. "I caught that. We saw it and traced it. The Techtronix shell was just a front to cover up the hack, though it was a nice piece of programming in its way. We traced it back to your friend. Funny, I didn't think Daniel had it in him. I mean, he's a competent programmer, but I didn't expect anything this complex from him."

"You don't think he actually did it?" Mark asked with a sinking feeling. If Joanna thought Daniel was responsible for the break-in, it would be hard to prove his innocence.

"I believe in all you kids, but the evidence speaks for itself. Right now it's all against Daniel. Has he given his statement yet? I'd like to hear what he has to say," Joanna said.

"Captain Winters talked to him about it, but nobody's taken an official statement, as far as I know. I guess Daniel bailed when he got the news," Mark said, aware of how bad that sounded. "Megan, Maj, and I are going over to talk to him, see what we can find out."

"Well, if some evidence contrary to what we've got so far doesn't come up soon, I don't see any recourse but to bring him up on charges. Look, if—and I'm only saying if—he did do it, try to get him to come clean. A plea bargain would be a lot quieter than a court case, and the punishment less severe. He'd probably just receive a probationary sentence," Joanna said.

"But he'd be out of the Net Force Explorers," Mark guessed.

"I'm afraid so. We can't have any security risks here, Mark, you know that," Joanna said.

"Yeah, well, we're going to prove it wasn't him and clear this whole mess up once and for all," Mark said.

Joanna nodded. "I'd love to see that, Mark, but don't go off half-cocked. Right now all we've got to go on is Daniel's word, but if he really didn't do it, then this whole thing smacks of more than just a kid poking his nose where it doesn't belong. If you do turn something up, come see me or Captain Winters, all right?"

"Don't worry, if I find anything unusual, I'll let Net Force know."

"I'll hold you to that. And Mark?" Joanna said. "Good luck. Just remember . . ."

"I know, I know. Don't get in over my head. Thanks, Joanna," Mark said. "Oh, there is one more thing. If you can tell me, that is. What was the hacker going for?"

"He broke into some security programs and some corporate, military, and private files," Jo said. "We were on to him before he got any further into the system."

"What would Daniel want with that kind of stuff?" Mark asked.

"That's a pretty good question, Mark," Joanna said. "If Daniel comes in, maybe he'll tell us. I'm wondering if someone's forcing him to use his access to Net Force to retrieve information. That seems more likely to me than Daniel doing this as a prank. Sooner or later we're going to find out whatever's going on. If Daniel came in now, it would go a lot easier for him, and for us."

"I'll try and find him for you, Jo, and thanks again," Mark said. *I know we can find him. I just hope we can do something for him when we do*, he thought.

It was dusk when Daniel trotted up the walk to his home. The front of the house was dark, and for a brief instant he thought his parents might not be home. *Wishful thinking, I'm sure.*

He hit the combination and opened the front door. At the end of the main hall a soft light flickered in his father's study. *I'm not running this time. I didn't do anything wrong.* Daniel kept telling himself that as he slowly walked down the hallway.

At the doorway he looked in and saw his father sitting in a leather wingback chair, staring at the fireplace. Taking a deep breath, Daniel rapped lightly on the door.

"Come in," Ramos said. Daniel walked over to him. Ramos motioned to another chair opposite him. "Sit."

Daniel did so, keeping his eyes on his father all the while. Besides the three words he had spoken, Ramos had not looked up at him or acknowledged his presence in any other way. *Fine, he wants to give me the silent treatment, two can play that game*, Daniel thought. The silence stretched out between father and son, punctuated only by the crackling of the logs in the fire.

"I was almost ready to call the police. I've been driving around town for the past six hours looking for you," Ramos said after several minutes.

"To find me or arrest me?" Daniel said without thinking. His father looked up then, the hurt in his eyes plain to see.

Daniel's insides twisted at that gaze, but he didn't say anything. *The truth hurts, doesn't it?* he thought.

"What am I supposed to think? I get a call from Net Force Headquarters to come down for a meeting, where I learn my son is suspected of stealing classified documents. Then, when we're supposed to meet and try to work this out, you're nowhere to be found, disobeying a direct order from Captain Winters, I might add. So I scour the city but find no trace of you. I don't know if you've run away, been abducted, or what. Now you casually stroll in like nothing even happened. So, tell me, Daniel, what am I supposed to think? If you were in my place, what would you do?"

"I'd believe in my son, that's the first thing I would do," Daniel replied.

"Can I?" his father asked.

Daniel snorted. "If you have to ask that, then I don't even know why we're having this conversation."

"Dammit, this is not a game!" Ramos shouted, leaping to his feet. "We're not talking about school grades or a baseball game. We're talking about a crime that could ruin the rest of your life!"

"No, what we're talking about here is trust, the trust a father should have in his son. And, apparently, it's a trust you don't have in me!" Daniel also stood, face-to-face with his father. His voice escalated in volume as the pain in his gut grew with every bitter word. "When it's really counted, I've never given you a reason to doubt me. Now, when it appears—*appears*, mind you—that I've done something wrong, you're so eager to take everyone else's word for it, to believe what you've been shown, that you won't even stop to consider that I'm innocent!"

Daniel felt the hard-won control over his emotions that he'd fought for all day slipping away. He took a deep breath. "You're right, this isn't a game. It's deadly serious, and it could ruin the rest of my life. Why would I throw the rest of my life away for a stupid prank?"

"Have you already forgotten what happened here Friday? I placed my trust in you, and you let me down. You know how I feel about your schoolwork. I expect you to be the best. That was a trust between us. Trust is important, and once that trust is broken, it takes more than words to get it back. So tell me, why should I trust you now?" Ramos asked.

"Because I came back." For a moment father and son stared at each other, breathing hard, and Daniel saw the pain welling up in the older man. *Why does he always doubt me? Is this how it's going to be, us always at each other's throats?* Daniel made a conscious effort to relax, and sat down in a chair. He unclenched his fists, seeing the red crescents on his palms from his nails pressing into the flesh. "I came back here to ask for your help because I *am* in trouble. And I came back to tell you that I didn't do anything wrong." *You should know, you're the one who kept me grounded all weekend,* he thought. *And restricted my Net access like I was three years old.*

Ramos still hadn't sat down. "Don't you know how leaving made you look? Why didn't you stay at Net Force and wait for me?"

Because I didn't want our dirty laundry aired in public, Daniel thought. "I was so angry at the thought of being set up that I couldn't sit still. I knew I couldn't accomplish anything waiting around there. I wanted to start doing *something* to clear myself. And, let's face it, Dad, I didn't want to have the kind of fight we're having now at Net Force Headquarters. I knew you'd be upset when you found out what was supposedly going on," he said.

Ramos stared at his son for a moment, then nodded and slowly sat down. "Son, I know there's been a lot of tension between us, but this has got to stop." Daniel started to speak, but Ramos held up his hand. "All I want right now is for you to tell me what's going on, whatever it is, and we'll take care of it. It doesn't matter what you're involved in—what's important is that we end it now, before it goes any further. You're in serious trouble here. I don't think you're aware of just how serious it is. Talk to me, tell me what you're mixed up in. We can make it right, but you have to tell me what is going on."

As Ramos spoke, Daniel's sense of hope was slowly replaced by a feeling of incredulity. When his father had finished speaking, Daniel just stared at him, hardly able to comprehend what he had just heard.

"I can't fracking believe you!" Daniel said. "I *came* here asking for your help. I said I didn't do anything, and you don't believe me. You never believe me, or believe in me. Nothing ever changes, does it? I'll never be good enough for you!" Daniel got up and stomped toward the door. "That's fine. If you won't help me, I'll get the bastard who did this on my own. Then we'll see who's right!"

"Daniel, wait!" Ramos cried.

Daniel ignored him and pounded up the stairs toward his room. At the top of the stairs he paused, expecting his father to come after him. From his vantage point Daniel could see the hallway below, and he watched his father's shadow cross to the bottom of the stairs. Finally Daniel heard a deep sigh, and the shadow retreated.

Will things ever be right between us? With a sigh of his own, Daniel entered his room and logged into veeyar, shutting out any possibility of conversation. Some things just hurt too much.

6

Mark took a quick break from his online activity to grab some dinner. His parents were still at work, probably trying to figure out what was going on with the Net Force break-in. *It's just as well,* he thought. *I've gotten in trouble before for sticking my nose in where it doesn't belong. Mom and Dad would probably take a dim view of what I'm about to do.*

As he nuked some leftovers, Mark thought about why he was investing so much time on this problem. *Maybe because it could have just as easily been me facing a charge like this. Annoying or not, Daniel is a Net Force Explorer, and he deserves a fair hearing. No one should be punished for something they didn't do.* And, deep down, Mark knew that Daniel was innocent.

After gulping down his hurried meal, Mark headed back to his computer. Jacking back in, he found a message waiting from Maj and Megan. Since Daniel had taken off, they had been watching the Net all day, hoping he'd show up. It looked as if they finally had something.

"Hey, Meg, Maj, I'm here, what's happening?" Mark asked as he appeared before the two girls.

"Daniel's finally online. He's running some kind of sport

simulation. Hang gliding, it looks like," Maj said.

"Wow, nothing like living on the edge. Well, what are we waiting for?" Mark asked. "Let's go talk to him."

The Arizona desert was hot and dry, with wind-worn rock formations studding the landscape like giant fingers poking out of the earth. Daniel stood in his hang-gliding harness on the edge of a sheer 500-foot cliff face, feeling the scorching wind blast his face. The sun was bright and merciless, even through the expensive sunglasses perched on his nose. He looked down across the barren plains, seeing nothing but scrub brush and the occasional yucca plant. He was utterly alone.

Right now that's just the way I like it, he thought. Daniel had discovered virtual hang gliding two years ago, after getting real world lessons for a birthday present, and had been in love with it ever since. The sensation of silently gliding above the earth, with no noisy engine propelling you and no cramped cockpit to stuff yourself into, was like nothing else. It was just him, the fresh air, and the open sky.

He stepped into the body glove of the hang glider and fastened it around himself, leaving the lower half undone so he could get a running start off the cliff. He did a final safety check, and was just about to take off when a voice caused him to start and look around.

"Daniel?" Standing a few feet away were Megan, Maj, and the Squirt. Daniel sighed and picked up his hang glider again.

"Not now, guys, I'm really not in the mood." Daniel stepped closer to the edge of the cliff and gauged the wind, preparing for his launch.

Mark stepped forward and grabbed the edge of the blue glider's wing. "Yes, now, Daniel. You can't keep running from this, you know. You have to face it sometime."

Daniel glared at him, his aerodynamic sunglasses making him look like a huge humanoid-insect hybrid, and shook off the younger boy's hand. "Look, I'll come back to HQ and give whatever statement they want when I'm good and ready, not before. I just have to think about a few things first."

"What's to think about? Come back now and work with Net Force, not against them. Work with us, too," Megan said.

"I'm sure you guys know all about it. Everyone at Net Force is already convinced I'm guilty," Daniel said.

"Daniel, you know that's not true. We know you're innocent. Captain Winters is on your side. But we need your help to get to the bottom of what happened. Why don't we go talk to Captain Winters now?" Maj said.

"Nothing doing," Daniel said. "I'll talk to you later." And with that, he stepped off the cliff and soared into the air.

"Just a second, I'll be back," Mark said, then followed Daniel right off the cliff face, leaving the two girls standing there.

"Boys! I've got a sim that will let us catch up with them," Megan said. "Assuming we want to go after the jerks who just left us here."

"We're supposed to be watching Daniel, remember?" Maj said. "So boot up your sim and let's go."

By the time Mark had caught up with Daniel, he was soaring in an updraft, climbing higher into the azure sky. Mark stayed on him, pulling alongside as the older boy leveled off his hang glider.

"Ya know, Squirt, you're kind of spoiling the scenery right now," Daniel said without looking at him.

"What? Oh, yeah, the flying thing," Mark replied. "Well, since you didn't want to talk down there, I figured maybe you'd be more comfortable up here."

Daniel suddenly pulled the control bar of the hang glider toward him, causing the craft to swoop toward the ground.

Why is he making this so hard? Mark wondered as he followed. When Daniel's glider leveled off, Mark was still beside him, saying nothing. They continued this way for several seconds, with Daniel casting sidelong glances at Mark, and Mark ignoring them. Finally Daniel said, "Freeze sim," causing his hang glider to stop in midair, and catching Mark by surprise, but just for a second. He stopped immediately and whirled on Daniel.

"Listen, Dexter, if you don't want any help, then fine, just stay in here and hide from everything. That's not going to do you any good, but then, I won't have to worry about you anymore, will I? It won't be my problem." Mark could see

Megan and Maj approaching in some sort of fifteenth-century Renaissance hot-air balloon. He waited for Daniel to respond. When he did reply, the words were so low that Mark almost missed them.

"You're right," Daniel said, then repeated himself more loudly. "You're right, Squi— I mean, Mark. This whole deal has just got me so angry I can't see straight, even to accept a helping hand."

"Um, yeah, okay," Mark said, caught off guard. "So why don't we head back down and talk about this."

"Race you," said Daniel. "Resume sim." And with that, he plunged the glider down in a steep dive, heading back toward the launch spire.

"You're on," said Mark, diving alongside him and signaling Maj and Megan to head back.

By the time Daniel and Mark had returned to the mesa, the two girls were waiting for them, neither looking particularly happy.

"Are you two through?" Megan asked with her arms crossed.

Daniel looked at Mark and nodded. "Yeah, and thanks for coming by. I'm sorry I haven't been more sociable. Like I just told Mark, this whole thing has gotten me so ticked off I can't see straight. I apologize for giving you the runaround. If you guys can help me, I'd appreciate it."

Mark saw Maj and Megan thaw noticeably. *Smooth*, he thought. *If I had done something like that, they'd probably be a bit more ticked off. I'm undoubtedly the better programmer, but most of the Net Force Explorers treat me like a younger brother. Daniel, however, got an entirely different reaction from those two.*

"All right," Megan said, wiping her brow. "But can we talk someplace where it isn't so hot?"

Daniel chuckled. "You mean you don't like the 110-degree heat? I prefer to hang glide in the summer desert when the thermal updrafts are at their peak. Just a sec, I think I've got something here you'll all like. Watch this." He turned to the vast barren expanse and said, "Alter simulation, dusk, late April. Set temperature at seventy degrees. Go."

The environment shifted around them, the sky changing

from a clear light blue to a rich tapestry of orange, purple, and red, all blended together as far as the eye could see, as if someone had taken a giant pastel set and colored the sky. Instead of beating down on them with intolerable heat, the sun had turned into a fiery red sphere that was dipping below the horizon. The temperature dropped to a much more comfortable level, and Megan, Mark, and Maj could hear the sounds of the desert nightlife making its presence known. They could hear the hoots of owls hunting for food, the chirps of crickets, and the occasional coyote howl. All around them the desert floor was coming alive in a way it never did during the day.

The four kids just stood there for a moment, taking it all in. Daniel spoke first. "I love the desert. It's so peaceful, so . . . empty. Here, it's like you're the only one in the whole world."

"It's beautiful. Did you do this?" Maj asked.

Daniel smiled and shook his head. "Not all of it. It's a section of Chupadera Mesa, out in New Mexico. I downloaded the basic topography, then fiddled with it until it looked the way I wanted. It really speaks to me—I keep coming back here."

Watching the way Megan and Maj were both looking at Daniel, Mark rolled his eyes. "So," he said, ready to get back to the reason why they were here. "How do we figure out who's really doing this? And, once we do that, how do we catch him? Whoever's doing this is good, I mean really good, 'cause Joanna and the internal security team haven't found him yet. Course, that could be because they're too busy looking at Daniel to find the real culprit." Mark succeeded in snapping the other three back to the problem at hand.

"I don't even know where to start," Daniel said. "I mean, *I* know I wasn't near the Net Force site at all this weekend, but someone sure went to a lot of trouble to make it seem like I was. That sounds like a serious hacker to me. One who had a plan, and a goal."

"You got that right," Mark said. "Before we go any further, give me a minute." Mark reached into his fanny pack, pulled out an icon that looked like an empty cartoon speech balloon, and threw it into the air. The icon flew up about ten feet and expanded into a dome that settled over the group. "That should give us some privacy, just in case anybody's listening. Here's what I found out at HQ earlier today," Mark said, summarizing his search of the security logs and the Techtronix decoy he found, as well as the logon address that led back to Daniel's computer.

"Jeez, somebody *really* has it in for me," Daniel said.

Mark shook his head. "I'm not so sure. I think you were just the unlucky test subject. I mean, I think you were picked at random. It might have just as easily been Megan, Maj, or myself." The other three looked at him. "Well, I think skinning me would be pretty hard, but that's not to say it couldn't happen."

"You said test subject," Megan said. "So you think this will happen again?"

"Undoubtedly," Mark said. "Daniel's right. This guy has a plan. First, the chameleon program worked perfectly, as far as the hacker knows. Daniel is being blamed, and nobody has turned up any evidence so far to prove someone else was responsible."

"And second?" Daniel asked.

"Simple," Mark said, giving the others a chance to figure it out. When no one said anything, he sighed and said. "From what I can tell, the hacker didn't get everything he wanted. Even though the break-in is being blamed on Daniel, it was still interrupted by the security at Net Force. The hacker didn't finish the job. Now that he knows his chameleon program works, he'll be back for sure."

"And maybe using one of our identities next time," Maj said, exchanging nervous glances with Megan. "So, how could we possibly go about trying to locate one of several hundred thousand hackers who are stupid enough to try and break into Net Force HQ?"

"Apparently this hacker wasn't that stupid," Daniel said. "After all, he got in."

"Or did he? Mark, you just said that whoever it was hadn't tripped the outer security alarms, right?" Megan asked.

"That's right," said Mark. "He was busted after failing to clear an internal security passwall. Why?"

"Maybe the reason no outside security was breached was because the hacker was already inside the Net Force site," Megan replied.

Mark thought for a moment, then looked up. "That would mean there's a mole at headquarters." He shook his head. "You've gotta be kidding."

"Think about it," Megan said. "In the past decade, no one, and I mean no one in hundreds of thousands of attempts, has been able to get inside the core Net Force programs and files. Now, suddenly, someone who can get through the outer encryptions like a ghost is downloading files from restricted areas? I may not know systems like you do, but I figure if he got inside that easily and without a trace, I can't see what would have stopped him from taking anything he wanted. And Net Force Security was onto him nearly right away."

"Good point," Daniel said. "Also, how would an outside hacker know to use my identity to try and gain access? Getting that information from the Net Force computers would be just as hard as getting the files he was caught trying to steal. He'd have been caught getting it, just like he was this time. So it has to be someone who knows I'm a Net Force Explorer." He frowned. "Or at least that I used to be one."

"And will be again," Mark said. "If someone wanted to find out about you being a Net Force Explorer, I'm sure they could dig it up. It's not exactly a state secret. But duplicating all your IDs and passwords—that took some looking. They had to get that data from either Net Force or your home computer. Still, what Megan said makes a lot of sense."

"Okay, let's suppose that someone inside Net Force is spying, and that they're likely to do it again. Our next question is, how do we narrow our suspects down to one out of five thousand plus agents?" Maj asked.

"Well, I think we can probably eliminate anybody who wouldn't normally be using the computers—that leaves out all the cafeteria workers," Daniel said. "The person we'd be looking for would be a full agent, and probably one who has had some contact with the Net Force Explorers, and especially with me. I'd bet my rep as a hothead means that I'm easier to frame than some of you would be. The hacker might have picked me for that reason."

"You're right. Otherwise, why use you at all? If this hacker is in Net Force, he'll want to stay hidden," Maj said. "And the best way to divert suspicion—"

"—is to plant it on someone else who makes a likely suspect," Daniel finished for her. "So you're saying that this run tested the chameleon program? And it worked, and that I took the fall? That leaves the real hacker free to try again. Frack, that really fries my boards!"

Maj nodded. "It's not all bad news. Now that all of the attention is focused on you, the mole should be feeling secure. He'll try again, and probably fairly soon. That gives us the opportunity to catch him and prove you are innocent."

"Which brings us back to our original problem: how do we find this hacker before he or she tries again?" Mark asked. "I mean, even with what little we know, I can think of at least a hundred people inside Net Force who know Daniel and are in a position to hack for those files."

"Well, they're probably in Washington, not launching out of some branch office," Maj said.

"Why do you think that?" Mark asked.

"Because they'd be more likely to know Daniel, for one thing. And if you're going to spy on the United States government, you'd want to go to the source," Maj said. "Most of the most notorious moles in this country have been caught in or around Washington. It's where the best agents and the richest targets are. So, where better than Net Force headquarters to set up your operation? Even with all the access over the Web, why take chances?"

"As if camping out in the place you're spying on isn't chancy enough. But all right, let's run with it. So far, here's my theory—this hacker is running around HQ, but he doesn't know his way around the veeyar site real well yet. He's still learning the ropes," Mark thought out loud. "Since this is a brand-new problem, maybe he's a recent transfer, or someone just assigned to Net Force HQ on a temp basis. We can certainly cross-reference the employee database of Net Force for newcomers in the last couple of months. That should narrow the field considerably. We'll check that list for any who've got reason to know or know of Daniel. So, what else can we check? What reasons would cause a person to sell out?"

"Remember your history. When it comes down to it, what's the one thing nearly every spy has sold out for?" Megan asked.

"Money," the other three choroused.

Megan nodded. "Any one of dozens of countries would pay handsomely for the secrets Net Force holds, not only their security programs, but the information they come across just in the everyday course of doing their jobs. Frack, it isn't just countries. There are probably hundreds of corporations who would also like that information."

"Yeah, like Techtronix," Mark said.

"Exactly," Megan said. "Now, if we could cross-reference the list of new employees around the time of the hack with their credit ratings and find out who's deep in the red or has been spending more than their salary should allow, then check that against the people who know Daniel, that would give us a short list of who's most likely to be lifting files from Net Force."

"The financial stuff shouldn't even be too hard to get. I can think of a dozen places where, with the right information and twenty bucks, you can get information on what someone purchased when they got their first allowance," Mark said. "Leave that to me. An hour online and I'll have what we need."

"That does bring up another point," Maj said. "Right now we're planning to snoop around Net Force, looking for a double agent. Shouldn't we let Captain Winters know about this?"

"Yeah, and how are we going to do that?" Daniel asked. "Waltz into his office and say, 'Hi, Captain, how are you doing today? Nice weather we're having, eh? By the way, did you know that we think one of the new agents in Net Force is a spy? We don't have a shred of proof; in fact, we're not even sure who it is. It doesn't matter, though, because we're going to catch them and clear poor old Daniel Sanchez's name so he doesn't have to grow up to be a sanitation worker in the inner city. Just wanted to let you know. Thanks and have a nice day.' Something like that, perhaps?"

Megan and Maj were chuckling at Daniel's earnest expression and the innocent voice he used to make his speech, but Mark had remained serious throughout the diatribe, smiling only toward the end. "Daniel's right, for the reasons he mentioned, but also for one other. Right now even Captain Winters is not above suspicion."

The other three looked at him. "Mark, do you realize what you're saying?" Megan asked.

"Of course I do. Look, we all know he's not the one, but someone's running around who can take anybody else's constructed persona and do whatever he wants with it, including attempting to break into classified files. The hacker could use Winters's ID next. Think about it—he has a handle on the Net Force Explorers like nobody else in Net Force. The point is, until we winnow that list down, we can't trust anyone at Net Force. Anyone—even Captain Winters. And that's why I put up that security dome in the first place," Mark said.

"Well, how secure are *we*, then? This is ridiculous, because we're all online right now, and I'm not going to get into a stupid discussion of 'Are you really Mark?' and 'Am I really Maj?' We've got to assume that we are who we say we are and go from there, or we'll never get anything done. Look, we know each other well enough that the minute we open our mouths, we know for sure that the real kid is talking. The hacker would know that, too. Our one advantage is that the hacker doesn't know we know about him. He still thinks he's safe, and that's going to be how we catch him, through overconfidence," Maj said.

"That may be true, but don't forget, our chameleon is also very good," Mark said. "Here's something we haven't tried yet, and should. This guy was able to backtrack his intrusion to Daniel's computer and, while he was at it, he changed Daniel's site logs so they showed the hacker's activities, not Daniel's. Maybe he left us some clues. You'd better let me run a scanprog on your system, Daniel. We know this guy's been messing with it. Maybe we can get a lead on our hacker that way. But Maj has a point. I'm not sure how safe the Net is. After this, I think we should try to meet in the real world as much as possible. Is this going to be a problem for anyone?"

Megan said, "Not for me, and Maj just about has free run of my house anyway, so staying over can be arranged if necessary."

"I'm near downtown, but my problem isn't geography. I'm just not sure if I can get away," Daniel said, shrugging. "My dad's not too happy with me right now. I don't know if I'm ever going to be let out of the house again."

"You live in Georgetown, too?" Mark asked.

Daniel nodded and gave his address.

"That's just a few blocks from where I live," Mark said. "Maybe I can come over to your house."

"Sure, I'd like that. Maybe after school sometime, you could run that scanprog in person. Heck, I could use the character reference with my folks."

"How about tomorrow?" Mark asked. "By that time I should have the information we need on our potential suspects, and we can start figuring out how to catch our chameleon."

"All right, that just leaves us with one more question. What's the easiest way to let each other know about new information, or call a meeting about this?" Megan asked. "With most of us on the Net, usually we'd use that, but now I just don't trust it anymore, or the landline phones. All of us have foilpaks, right?"

The other three nodded.

"We'll use those, then," Mark said. "The calls are encrypted and hard to intercept. It might be a good idea to give this project a name so we can talk about it in public if necessary. Some sort of code phrase."

"I hope you're not going to require secret handshakes and passwords, Squirt," Daniel said.

Mark smiled. "Not yet. So, does anybody have any ideas?"

The four kids thought for a moment, then Daniel looked up.

"I've got it, and this will work for virtmail as well. If you have anything new, just mention something about a report on Macbeth. Nobody's going to question that from a bunch of schoolkids. From there we can meet or do whatever to pross what our next step is."

"Macbeth—I like it," Megan said. "One of Shakespeare's

bloodiest characters, and a betrayer at that. Sounds perfect. 'O, what wicked webs we weave, when first we practice to deceive!' That quote isn't from the play, but it certainly summarizes our chameleon."

"Yeah, and he's already caught one of us. Let's try and make sure that no one else gets snared," Mark said.

Daniel, Maj, and Megan all nodded.

"All right, then we'll all talk tomorrow," Mark said, logging off with a flash. The girls said their goodbyes next and took off, leaving Daniel as alone as he'd been when he first arrived in the desert.

As he looked out across the flat landscape, a harsh smile creased his mouth. So far, everything was going better than he had hoped. *I've got to give the Squirt credit. He does not know when to quit,* he thought. *That's only gonna work for me, and it might even save my rump. Certainly couldn't appear too eager for his help, though. Got to have some pride.*

Daniel picked up his glider again and stepped to the edge of the cliff. He looked out across the endless desert, knowing that somewhere out on the Net, their quarry was lurking. *We're coming for you, chameleon, and I'm not gonna stop until I've nailed you to the wall.*

7

Early the next morning Mark woke up, got ready for
school, wolfed down two high-energy breakfast bars and a
glass of rice milk, and logged on to the Net Force site.
Checking to see if Captain Winters was available, Mark
discovered he was in a meeting for the next half hour.
Mark left a brief message for the captain to come and find
him if he had the time, then headed straight for the
general-use storage logs.

With Net Force being the governmental branch that it was,
the veeyar site was a simplified, no-frills version of the offices, with the general Netspace layout corresponding to the
real-world locations. Mark headed straight for what was com-
monly called "the morgue": compressed data files of non-
classified information that ranged from ancient cases to
expense reports to the current Net Force "Most Wanted" List,
and everything in between. Apparently some government
programmer had indulged a rare flash of humor when de-
signing this room, as the morgue was a long, dusty, low-
ceilinged room filled with endless rows of gray filing cabinets
that stretched off into the distance.

*Here's hoping what I want's in here. I've done enough
hacking into Net Force files for a while. Unlike Daniel, if*

they bust me *for hacking, I'll probably be guilty*, thought Mark as he scanned the hundreds of cabinets.

"Computer, collate report. Assemble all new personnel names with assignment or transfer dates from March first, 2025, to today."

As Mark watched, various file drawers began opening, with papers flying out and floating toward him. Within a few minutes there were several dozen sheets in front of him. Grabbing the papers out of the air, Mark wadded them up into a ball, activated his compression program, and threw the wad toward the door, sending the data off to his computer at home. The drawers had just finished closing when Mark heard the door open behind him. Turning, he saw Captain Winters walking toward him.

As the captain approached, Mark felt a shiver run down his spine. He hadn't done anything *that* wrong lately—so it wasn't the fear that Winters would bust him for hacking that was bothering him. Though he was perfectly safe at home, the thought that he might be speaking to the chameleon here in veeyar unnerved him. *Even if I scanned this man with my program, it would just tell me what construct this computer was originating from. And if it did say that this is coming from the captain's computer, it wouldn't mean a lot. If this chameleon is as good as I think he is, he could reroute his logon site through anyone's computer easily enough.*

"Mark, I got your message, but I only have a few minutes. What did you need?" he asked.

"I just wanted to tell you that we spoke to Daniel yesterday, and he's promised he's not going to do anything rash on his own," Mark said. *That part is at least true,* he thought. "I think he's going to wait until the preliminary investigation has concluded to see what Net Force comes up with before he makes an official response." *I hope by that time we'll have figured out who's really behind this.*

"Okay, just keep an eye on him for the next few days and make sure nothing happens. His father was very upset about the whole situation, and I'd rather not have the Secret Service mad at Net Force if I can help it," Captain Winters said.

"I don't suppose anything new has turned up yet?" Mark asked.

Captain Winters shook his head. "Sorry, Mark, but the links to Daniel are still our strongest leads so far. Of course, if anything does turn up, I'll let you know immediately." Captain Winters looked around as if seeing where they were for the first time. "By the way, what brought you down here?"

"I'm working on a report, and I needed to verify some dates. I thought Net Force might have more complete files than my school library for some Net stuff," Mark replied, internally wincing. Under normal circumstances he never would have thought of skirting the truth when talking to Captain Winters. This time, however, Mark was as close to the edge as he dared to get without actually lying. He *had* grabbed some information on the history of the Web and downloaded it to his home system, just so he could produce the documents in case he was asked about them later. And every word he'd said was the truth—though the report was for Daniel, rather than his school, as he'd implied. But even the omission of the real reason he was here bothered him. *This is the quickest way to get the information we need without anybody asking questions,* Mark thought. And if this wasn't the real Winters, then there was no harm done. He didn't mind misleading the chameleon, if that was what he was doing.

Captain Winters seemed to accept Mark's answer without question. "Speaking of school, isn't it almost time for you to be on your way?"

Mark grinned. *That* certainly sounded like the real Winters. "Right, sir," he said. He left the Net Force site, zoomed back to his home site to verify that the files were there, logged off, and headed out to catch the autobus for school.

For Daniel the day started out badly and just kept going downhill from there. The events of the weekend had left him feeling edgy and annoyed, and the burning anger in his stomach was always there now, simmering, waiting for something or someone to bring it to a rapid boil. Daniel knew he had to keep himself in check. Trouble at school was the last thing he needed.

Unfortunately, with all that he'd had on his mind, he had forgotten that a virtual simulation on the human circulatory system was due for Advanced Biology. Daniel had to endure a stern reprimand in front of the entire class. In physical education they had been studying football, and Daniel had been called for three fouls during the game, one of them personal, which he had been provoked into committing.

Finally, at lunchtime, Daniel had been eating alone when a boy plopped down across from him, flanked by two others. Daniel looked up and frowned. Sitting across from him was Marcus Connors, Bradford Academy's resident loudmouth and general annoyance. He was also the guy who had caused Daniel to draw the foul during the football game earlier. Daniel had always dismissed Connors as a guy with a chip on his shoulder, but if he was looking for a fight, it wouldn't take much to provoke Daniel into giving the chubby jerk a black eye.

"Hey, Sanchez, did you know you block like a girl? I'm glad I didn't have you on my team, we'd have lost for sure. Maybe if you didn't spend so much time with those cyber-nerds at that geek club you belong to, you might be in better shape."

Daniel set down his fork and swallowed the bite of food in his mouth. Even though every instinct in his body was screaming for him to deck the guy, he knew he couldn't afford to get into any more trouble. Instead, he kept his voice low. "Connors, you play so bad you couldn't even catch a cold, much less the football. The next time you hit me late, I'll do a lot worse than just clip you," Daniel said.

"The way you hit, I won't even feel it. It sure isn't my fault your offensive line sucked," Connors replied.

"That's true, but it would be a pleasant change for you to play by the rules for once," Daniel said. "You bore me as much off the field as you do on it. Now why don't you go find someone else to bother, I'm busy." With that, Daniel grabbed his fork and continued eating.

Connors stared at him for a moment, then looked at his two friends, who shook their heads. He slid Daniel's tray away just as he was about to take another bite.

"Connors, this is really getting old. Give that back," Daniel said through clenched teeth.

"Or what?" Connors sneered. "Come on, tough guy. What are you going to do about it?"

Instead of answering, Daniel reached out and grabbed Connors's thumb, squeezing the two phalanges together at a ninety-degree angle. Connors's face whitened with the sudden pain. His two buddies looked at each other, uncertain as to what to do.

"I'm going to ask you again, politely. If that tray isn't in front of me in three seconds"—Daniel squeezed Connors's thumb harder, causing the boy to gasp—"then I start asking impolitely. After the weekend I've had, you don't want that."

"Okay, okay! Just let go!" Connors scrabbled with his free hand and shoved the tray back to Daniel, who immediately released the boy's thumb and continued eating as if nothing had ever happened. Connors cradled his injured thumb and glared at Daniel, swallowing whatever threat he was going to make as one of the lunch hall monitors walked by. When he saw Connors and his friends' attention was focused elsewhere, Daniel quietly left the table. By the time Connors turned back, all he saw was the empty chair across from him and a tray with a half-eaten meal on it.

As Daniel walked away, he shook his head. *Frack, I sure hope Mark comes up with something today*, Daniel thought. *If I keep thinking about this, I'm gonna kill somebody.* He glanced at the clock as he walked down the hall. *One thirty-two. Only three more hours to go.*

Daniel turned down the hallway to his next class, only to stop and stare at the row of doors at the far end of the hall. On the other side a tall, skinny boy dressed in tattered jeans and a loud Hawaiian shirt peered in, his nose pressed up against the glass. When he saw Daniel watching him, his face lit up in an expression of exaggerated relief. The boy, who looked as out of place on the steps of Bradford Academy as a shark in a goldfish pond, crooked his finger at Daniel, beckoning him closer.

Daniel looked around to make sure no one had followed him out of the lunchroom, then trotted toward the doors. The high-tech security at Bradford ensured that no one who wasn't supposed to be there could get inside. Daniel swiped his ID card through the lock and pushed the door open.

"Jimmy, what are you doing here? I thought we were supposed to hook up after school?"

"Well, I got your message, so I decided to take today off and come check out this place. Man, so this is where the other half learns? I'll bet you guys get all the top-of-the-line gear," Jimmy said

Jimmy Cole had been Daniel's best friend since kindergarten. Growing up, they had always attended school together, but when Daniel's family moved to Georgetown, he'd had to leave Jimmy and the old neighborhood behind. They still kept in touch, however, and had been there for each other through thick and thin. In fact, Daniel had been going to the baseball game with Jimmy and some other friends from his old school when fate and his father had intervened.

"Yeah, it's twice as nice, so they work us twice as hard," Daniel replied. "How was the game?"

"Man, you missed an awesome show!" Jimmy said. "Top of the fifth, Rodrigo hammers one out toward our seats, I mean right to us. Everybody's scrambling to get under it, right? The ball starts coming down, and it looks like it's going to just miss the upper stands. So Gene leans out over the railing, holding his glove out, ready to make the catch. The ball drops, and it looks like he's going to miss it by inches. At the last moment he lunges over, just snagging it on his glove. Dude almost went over. Luckily, Rick and I grabbed him by the legs and hauled his butt back in. You should have been there. We got into the locker room when the game was over and had Rodrigo sign it. I guess the parents are still coming down hard on you?"

"Same crap, different day. But I'm glad you guys had a good time. Sure wish I could have been there," Daniel said.

"Yeah, would have been great to have you along. So what's up?" Jimmy asked.

"You still up for a little sneak-and-peek?" Daniel asked.

"Always. Just like the old days, huh?" Jimmy said with a mischievous grin. "Those were the nights."

During middle school, Daniel, Jimmy, and several other friends had always been getting into trouble in their old neighborhood. Jimmy, especially, had been a wild one. They used to go around and root through other people's garbage, not vandalizing or anything, just seeing how other people lived by looking at what they threw away. One night Jimmy had brought along an ancient fire extinguisher that still used pressurized water, and they had run around the entire evening squirting anything that moved, including passing traffic. As the years went by, their circle of friends had re-formed and gradually drifted apart, except for Daniel and Jimmy, who, as far as Daniel knew, was still up to his same old tricks.

"Nothing so memorable," Daniel said. "I need you to get two other guys from the old crew, guys you can trust."

"No problem. What's the job?" Jimmy asked.

"I'll just need each of you to keep an eye on a particular person Friday night. Possibly all night," Daniel said. "I'll have more information in a couple days."

"Just watch these people? That's it?" Jimmy asked.

"Yeah, I just need to know if they leave their house any time during the evening," Daniel said. "You guys could really help me out here."

"I think I know just the guys we need," Jimmy said. "What's going down? Anything I should know about?"

"I just got some people dogging me, that's all, and I want to make sure they stay off my back Friday night."

"Well, if you want to give them a more persuasive message, you just let me know. Me and the boys haven't mixed it up in a long time," Jimmy said.

"No, it's nothing like that, don't worry. I just need a couple extra sets of eyes that night," Daniel replied.

"All right, it's your neck," Jimmy said. Hearing the class bell ring, he gave Daniel a playful shove. "Sounds like you've got to put that big nose back to the grindstone."

"Yeah, don't remind me. I'll be in touch, and let you know how it's all gonna go down," Daniel said. "Next time we'll all catch the game together."

"Sounds like a plan. I've gotta run. Don't let this place make you too soft," Jimmy said.

"Never happen," Daniel replied. "I'll see you."

"Not if I see you first," Jimmy said over his shoulder as he headed down the steps.

Daniel watched him go, wishing for just a second that he

could follow right behind him. Then, with a sigh, he turned
around and headed back inside.

After school Mark took the shuttle bus over to Daniel's address. He rang the doorbell, and a woman Mark assumed
was Daniel's mother opened the door.

"You must be Mark. Daniel said you'd drop by. Please,
come in. Can I take your jacket?" Daniel's mom asked as
she ushered him through the wainscoted foyer into a hallway
with an ornate chandelier dangling from the ceiling.

"Thanks, Mrs. Sanchez. Is Daniel around? He and I have
a lot of work to do."

"Of course. In fact, he's been waiting for you. Go up the
stairs and turn left. His room is the doorway at the end of
the hall. Did you eat before coming over here?"

Mark grinned. *Moms.* "Yeah, I grabbed something on the
way here, but thanks anyway, Mrs. Sanchez."

"If you need anything, tell Daniel to let me know," Mrs.
Sanchez said.

"I'll do that," said Mark as he walked up the stairs. Once
out of sight of Daniel's mother, he trotted down the hallway
to the door at the far end. Light was coming from underneath
the door, but Mark didn't hear a sound. He knocked quietly.

A muffled voice from inside said, "Yeah?"

"Daniel, it's me," Mark said. There was a sound of things
being shoved aside or kicked out of the way, then the door
opened about eight inches, and Daniel's face appeared.

"Come on in," Daniel said.

Mark moved to push the door open wider but was stopped
by Daniel, who shook his head and moved out of the way.

When Mark slipped through the narrow opening, he saw
why. Piles of clothes covered the entire floor, and a mound
of them was wedged against the door. A mountain bike
leaned against the wall, with a pair of inline skates hanging
above it, right next to a chart of the periodic table. The
vaulted ceiling was covered with old crime movie posters,
everything from *Casablanca* to *Point Blank* to *Pulp Fiction*
to *Heat.* Shelves mounted on the walls held a dizzying array
of oddities, from a human skull with fangs instead of eyeteeth
to what looked like a half-formed fish suspended in a viscous

liquid. Mark squinted, trying to make out what it was.

"Shark embryo," Daniel said, noticing Mark's stare.

"Oh." Mark nodded as he kept looking around.

"Well, welcome to my prison," Daniel said, kicking shirts and pairs of jeans out of the way as he waded back to his veeyar system.

When Mark joined him, he let out a long whistle. "SOA Nakamura XS660 with a focused laser port. If this is prison, sign me up."

Daniel frowned. "You must have something like this at home. I mean, your dad's huge at Net Force, so he'd need the top of the line to stay ahead of the game."

"Sure, *he* would, but that doesn't mean that I have carte blanche to use it whenever I want. I get his hand-me-downs for my room. My system's clocked to the max, but it's still six months old. Nowadays, that's like working with dinosaur DNA, y'know?" Mark replied.

"Yeah, well, when it comes to education, nothing is too good for my father," Daniel said. "This is the one thing I persuaded him I needed for school. Not that I don't need it, of course, but I probably could have gotten by with a lesser model. I figured, what the heck, he can afford it. By the way, in case you run into my dad, we're working on a report sim for school. Macbeth, for instance."

"All right," Mark said. "Why don't we get started? I need to virtmail Maj and Megan and tell them to join us. As much as I dislike meeting online, it's still the most convenient way to get us together. In the meantime, we can finish up our data search and narrow the list of suspects."

"I take it you found something useful at Net Force?" Daniel asked. "By the way, I don't have a secondary veeyar setup for you to use. I hope that's not a problem."

"I figured you wouldn't. That's why I brought a veeyar collar," Mark replied, opening his backpack and removing what looked like a lightweight neck brace and a small black box. "All I need is a chair."

"Nopraw." Daniel went over to what looked like a three-foot-high pile of clothes and started shoving shirts and pairs of jeans aside. After a few seconds he pulled a chair out from under the mess and set it next to the veeyar hookup. "There you go."

Mark plopped into the chair and tossed Daniel the veeyar doubler module. "Plug this into any unused input port. It's wireless and will beam directly to my port," Mark said, putting the collar on. "Ready when you are."

Daniel sat down in the ergonomic chair of his system and flipped open a small panel, revealing several empty sockets. He plugged Mark in, then lined up his own implant. "Let's do it."

Mark settled back and blinked . . . and found himself standing on a large platform, a thousand feet above the ground. Below him he could see many levels of the building he was on spreading out beneath him, each one larger than the one above it, so the pyramid looked like it was composed of giant steps. The temple was surrounded by a verdant green jungle which stretched all the way to the horizon on three sides. On the fourth side, facing south, the foliage was broken up by several other smaller pyramids and the stone and wood frames of what looked like a city. A warm breeze ruffled Mark's hair, bringing with it the smells of the jungle, dark earth, and blooming flowers, as well as a cacophony of animal calls—birds, monkeys, and once the snarl of a jaguar.

"Daniel, I'd never have figured you for something like this. Where are we?" Mark asked, not taking his eyes off the incredible landscape stretching out for miles around him.

Daniel was standing beside Mark now, also looking out across the ocean of green foliage that stretched out before them. "The Yucatan peninsula, circa early 1400s. It's an alternate history sim I like to play around in. By the time Columbus, Cortez, and Pizarro get here, I plan to have Central and South America united in one huge empire. I figure, with just a few alterations of history, like having them immunize themselves against smallpox, I should be able to repel the invaders while pushing up into North America. I hope, if I can influence the East Coast in time, I can stop all the Europeans from gaining a foothold anywhere in the Americas, and control both continents while I'm at it."

Mark nodded. "Multiplayer game?"

"Yeah, it can be. It's got something like fifty thousand

players worldwide. I don't join them, though. I prefer to make my own policies and destiny. I like the down-and-dirty chaos of real history more than the alternate worlds of fantasy or science fiction," Daniel said. "While you were taking in the view, I virtmailed Meg and Maj to meet us here."

"Great, while we're waiting, I'll run that scandoc and see if anything abnormal shows up in your system," Mark said, pulling a red cross from his pocket and tossing it into the air. The program activated, expanding into a screen that began listing the programs the doc was looking at while Mark and Daniel watched. After a few minutes a soft chime announced the scandoc had finished its sweep. Mark brought up the summary in front of them.

"Well, I can't find anything that would suggest someone co-opting your system, which means that no one has or—"

"—they're so good you can't find any trace of them," Daniel finished for him.

"Um, yeah," Mark said. "Although for what it's worth, I'd say it was the former."

"Of course you would." Daniel smiled. "But that's unimportant right now. You don't think the chameleon used my station, correct?"

"Not that I can tell," Mark said, frowning.

"So somehow he managed to fool the Net Force computers into thinking that his signal, disguised as mine, also came from my computer. How would he do that?"

Good question, Mark thought. "There are several ways to disguise a transmission as someone else's. But our chameleon didn't have to do that. All he had to do is make sure that his logon signature matched yours and bounced through yours while he was hacked into Net Force's core. Then, before Net Force checked them, he had to hack in to your system and alter your site logs to match his actions. That way he's in the clear, and you get blamed." A series of loud drumbeats sounded in the distance. "Sounds like Maj and Megan are here," Daniel said. "Enter."

A second later both Megan and Maj appeared beside them.

" 'So foul and fair a day I have not seen,' " Megan said with a smile. "*Macbeth*, Act One, Scene Three. This whole Macbeth thing put me in a mood to read the play again."

"I hope our little drama will have a happier ending than Shakespeare's," Maj said. "You two better have made some progress since yesterday, because we've barely had time to *think* about this, much less do anything about it."

Mark and Daniel exchanged glances, and Mark replied, "As a matter of fact, we have." He took another icon, a folded sheet of paper, and threw it into the air, activating it. The paper unfolded into a list with more than two dozen names on it. "This is the list of all the personnel who have transferred or been temporarily assigned to Net Force HQ in the last two months, listed by date of arrival. For our convenience, I've already sorted out the people who would have had access to the computer systems as well as the expertise to execute something like this." Mark nodded at the paper, which resorted itself into two columns, a smaller list on top, followed by the larger list. "Now we take the names with unexplained cash flows, collate the names on both lists, and from there we pick the ones most likely to select Daniel as the patsy for the chameleon program.

"The top five names on this list are sysops or people in records or maintenance, one in operations, two in records, one in security, and one in maintenance. Now, let's cross-reference this list with the credit reports." Mark took another sheet of paper and tossed it up. The paper unfurled beside the first list, revealing three names. "Looks to me like these are the ones with both motive and opportunity."

The four teens crowded around the lists. Daniel was first to speak. "Isn't that interesting? Ryan Valas's name pops right out at you, doesn't it?"

"Surely you don't think he would be foolish enough to try something like this in his position?" Maj asked. "He'd risk going against both the CIA and Net Force. And he's an outsider at Net Force. That would make it harder for him to crack into the system."

"On the surface I would agree with you," Mark said. "But who better to take that risk than a person who nobody would suspect? And he's been spending money like water the past couple of years. He owes a ton to his creditors."

" 'A gentleman on whom I built/An absolute trust,' " Megan said. "Still, if you ask me, one of these other two, Carter

Donley or Sheila Devane, is more likely. They're better able to conceal their actions if they're up to something shady, being in the more autonomous areas of Net Force. This Donley guy in maintenance—well, every computer system would have to be serviced and checked sooner or later. What better time to insert your own trapdoor?"

"Personally," Daniel said, "my money would be on Devane. She works in security, and her employment record includes work in casino security, electronic and online. Even if she didn't pick up the gambling bug, no doubt she's learned a lot of tricks. And she met me when she came and spoke at the Net Force Explorer meeting a few months back."

"The fact is, these three people all have financial motives and the opportunity to be doing this," Maj said. "And at least two of them have spent enough time with Net Force Explorers to pick one as a handy target. Until we have enough evidence to either identify the real culprit or clear them, I suggest we treat them as our main suspects."

"True, and the log records show that all of them were online when the hack occurred," Mark said. "That's another arrow pointing at them as suspects. We'll start our search for the chameleon with these three."

"Okay, now that we've narrowed down our preliminary list, how do we go about finding out which, if any, of them is behind this?" Daniel asked.

"How about we just go to each of them and ask?" Mark said.

The other three stared at him as if he'd just grown another head. "What?" Maj asked.

"Remember, our one advantage is that the hacker doesn't know we know. We've got the perfect cover to ask seemingly innocent questions. We're kids, remember?" Mark said.

"Speak for yourself, Squirt," Daniel said. Megan and Maj grinned at that.

"Yeah, but you know what I mean," Mark replied, grimacing. "A lot of the personnel at Net Force don't really take us seriously, which in this case works to our advantage. We've got the perfect opportunity and the perfect cover right at hand. Captain Winters said we could choose any person we wanted to work with within Net Force. I think we should use the shadow program to get one of us assigned to each one of our prime suspects. Then we can plant the idea we've got a program the chameleon would go for. My lurker program, for instance," Mark said.

"If we give them the idea that it would be valuable enough, they might try to lift it," Megan said. "You may be on to something. We'd have some idea when and where the bad guys would strike if we did that."

"And that's when Net Force would nail them," Maj said. "I like it."

Daniel shook his head. "No, not Net Force. We have to catch them."

Now it was his turn to feel three pairs of eyes staring at him. "Remember, we don't have a bit of real evidence pointing to these guys. We're taking action on this because I know I'm innocent and you guys believe me. Net Force thinks they've already got their hacker—it's me. As the Squir—Mark—said, no one will take us seriously if we run to Captain Winters with a wild story about setting a trap for a Net Force mole. We can't convince Net Force to do this, so we have to do it ourselves. Look, all I propose is that we set the trap and watch to see who takes the bait. If the hacker truly doesn't suspect anything, it should be easy to record his activities. Then we've got the evidence we need to get Net Force involved. We take the log and any other evidence we've got to Captain Winters and let him handle the rest. No muss, no fuss, and everyone's happy, except the chameleon, who gets busted and goes to jail, preferably for a few decades."

"Gee, that sounds good in theory, but what if we get caught while doing this? I don't need to remind certain people here of what happens when we go behind the captain's or my dad's back, do I?" Mark said, looking hard at Megan and Maj, who both suddenly found the jungle landscape infinitely more interesting than returning his gaze. "After all, some of us have more to lose than you do."

A flash of anger crossed Daniel's face. "And some of us are trying to get back a reputation that might be gone forever. But if you're getting cold feet—"

"All right, you two, stop it," Maj said. "Mark, if you don't

want to be involved, then you can leave right now, before
this goes any further."

"I just want everyone here to be aware of the risks involved in what we're doing. Ultimately, we're trying to get
enough evidence to accuse a high-ranking member of a government agency of what amounts to treason. Even though we
have no evidence yet, we know that someone who can get
into Net Force framed Daniel. We know he was trying to get
hold of classified information. The bad guy's out there
whether Net Force knows it or not. He's got to be stopped.
And Daniel has to be cleared. I'm not saying our reasons to
do this aren't good enough. I just want everyone to know
what we're getting into here."

"All right, you've laid it out. So, guys, are you in or out?"
Daniel asked.

"I'm in," Mark said.

"In for a penny, in for a pound," Maj said. "Count me in.
What about you, Megan?"

" 'If it were done when 'tis done, then 'twere well/It were
done quickly.' *Macbeth*, Act One, Scene Seven," the brown-
haired girl said. "The sooner this chameleon is caught, the
better. Like Mark said, he's got to be stopped. And the next
time he tries something, he could use one of us for his shield.
I'm in."

"All right. Now, who gets whom?" Mark asked. "Here's
our top-suspect list so far. There's three of us, and three of
them. I'd like to shadow Valas, mainly because he's dealing
in programming for international security and Web monitoring. Since I've done my share of that kind of work, I'd be
best at speaking his language." He waited for any sign of
protest from anyone, and when he heard nothing, went on.
"That leaves Donley in Systems Maintenance and Devane in
Security." He looked at the two girls. "I'll leave you two to
figure out who's going to tackle each of them."

Megan and Maj looked at each other.

"Any preference?" Maj asked.

"I'd rather take Security, if it's all the same to you," Maj
replied.

Megan sighed. "I was afraid of that. Rock, paper, scissors?"

Maj nodded and the two girls each extended a fist.

"One, two, three," they both chanted, hammering their fists in the air. On the third time Megan's hand was flat, showing paper, while Maj's hand had two fingers extended like the blades of a scissors.

"It's Security for me. To the dungeons with you," Maj said with a triumphant grin, referring to the lower levels of Net Force headquarters.

"This time, at least," Megan replied. "All right, I've got Donley."

" 'When shall we four meet again/In thunder, lightning, or in rain?' " Megan asked.

"I thought there were only three witches in Macbeth," Maj said.

"There are, but there are four of us, so I thought it would be better to be accurate rather than true to the Bard," Megan said. "Regardless, it's going to take some time and finagling to get these assignments out of Captain Winters, so when do we meet again?"

"I think for now we should get into the shadow program as quickly as possible, and start getting to know our contacts. I don't think there will be any problem getting assigned to each of our people, do you?"

"I'll bet no one will be requesting a look at Maintenance any time soon," Megan replied with a sigh. "So I shouldn't have any problem getting set up. They'll probably be surprised to see me down there."

"Well, just try to act as interested as possible," Mark said.

"Easy for you to say. You'll be up top where all the action is. I'll be stuck watching solder harden," Megan said.

The sound of a throat being cleared made the three of them turn. Daniel stood a few feet away, his hands behind his back. "I . . . just wanted to thank all of you for going to bat for me on this. I know none of you really has any stake in this besides wanting to catch whoever's doing this, but you're risking a lot to clear me. I appreciate it."

The other three looked at him, then Mark grinned. "Hey, we're all Net Force Explorers here, right? To quote another literary classic, 'All for one and one for all.' We're going to bust this chameleon and make him regret he ever tried to crack into Net Force."

"Or her. And we're especially going to make the jerk regret using one of the Explorers to do it with," Maj said.

"Let's virtmail our requests to Captain Winters right away." Mark consulted his schedule. "I'm going to see if I can start working with my target as soon as possible. If anyone comes up with anything interesting, let all of us know; otherwise, it's business as usual."

"And that means school," Daniel said. "Frack, I've got to finish that circulatory-system simulation before tomorrow or I'm a goner. Mark, I'm sure my mom can give you a ride home."

"Nopraw, I'll walk. Thanks, anyway, for the offer," Mark said. "Until we meet again."

The four teens winked out of existence in the veeyar site, leaving only the loud virtual jungle and silent stone temples behind.

8

Mark was busy most of the next day at school, but the minute the final bell rang, he was out the door and heading to a silver minivan, where his mom was waiting for him. She was working the night shift that evening, and Mark had asked if he could go in with her, since his shadow program also started that evening.

No one could have been more surprised than Mark when his foilpack had beeped before he'd even gotten home from Daniel's house, signaling an e-message from a source he'd tagged as urgent. When Mark checked his mail, he discovered that Captain Winters had approved his request for the shadow program exactly as he'd requested it, beginning as soon as possible. According to Winters, Ryan Valas would be working at Headquarters that evening and would love to have Mark watch over his shoulder.

Definite advantages to being the commander's son, Mark thought as he trotted to the bullet-shaped Dodge van, a make and model not too uncommon on the Bradford Academy grounds.

When Mark's parents had realized just how bright their son was, they had petitioned for him to attend the exclusive prep school early. The administrators had scheduled an appointment for Mark and his parents, and requested that he take their admissions test. When asked when a suitable time would be, Mark had replied, "How about right now?" Four hours later Mark had aced the test, and he'd been a Bradford student ever since. He had lived up to everybody's expectations—including his own—ever since by posting the highest grades in all his classes, despite being the youngest student in them by far.

The van's door opened and Mark got inside, nodding to his mom. "Hey, how's it going?"

"Fine, Mark. How was school?" His mom glanced up at her son from her computer screen.

"About the usual. I handed in my extrapolation sim in Military Theory on how the Axis powers could have won World War II," Mark said. "Another day, another A."

"You know, I never worry about your confidence level," his mother said as she shut down her computer and started the van. "I may worry about a lot of other things, but never that. What are you up to at headquarters tonight?"

"I'm starting the shadow program. You know, where we pair up with a senior Net Force officer and take a look at his job and how he does it? I'm scheduled to meet with Ryan Valas, our CIA liaison, and go over the latest in computer security." *And hopefully begin setting a trap for a chameleon*, Mark thought. "It ought to be interesting."

"Why aren't you doing this online?" his mom asked.

"Cool computers and cooler company, that's why. I love being at headquarters, and you know it. I figured I might get a better feel for things face-to-face. Also, I thought I'd get a look at Mr. Valas's role both in real time and on the Net," Mark said. "You don't always get both levels online."

"I can understand that. You'll like Ryan. I worked with him on a security issue for a conference in Belgium," his mother said. "I think you'll find him interesting."

"I'm sure I will," Mark replied. His mother returned her attention to the road, and Mark's thoughts returned to what he was going to do this evening, which brought a question to mind. "Mom?"

"Yes?"

"Has there been any news on that hacker problem yet?" Mark asked.

"You mean the one with Daniel Sanchez?" she replied.

"Yeah," Mark said. "Do you or Joanna have a handle on who really did it?"

"I wish I had better news for you, but it's looking like we may have to consider Daniel as our only suspect. If something doesn't turn up soon, we're going to have to book him. Joanna and I have not been able to find a single other lead. No one's been bragging about this, even on the underground usenets, and you know how much hackers love to talk."

"Yeah. Is there any chance that this might have been done by someone inside Net Force rather than Daniel or another random hacker?" Mark asked. *What the heck, it can't hurt asking a Net Force honcho what she thinks of our theory.*

"By someone inside Net Force?" She shook her head. "That's not possible. Your father and Joanna are positive that the hacker's signal originated outside the Net Force mainframe. And I'm sure it's a hacker, even if your friend didn't do it. Your father and I and many other agents review the dossiers of everyone assigned to headquarters. Plus, there are extensive background investigations conducted on all staff members. Usually we request the people we want for the organization, which makes it easier to pick people who are right for the job, since we've already had an eye on them for some time before they become a part of Net Force. I would say that, unless we have somehow gotten a deep-cover mole in our midst, it's very unlikely this is an inside job."

Mark nodded. "That's one way to look at it." Inwardly his mind was racing. *She's so confident. Could it be that our hunch is wrong? Maybe someone outside Net Force has figured out a way to copy DNA tags.* Mark pondered that thought for a while. *I think we're right. Until something better comes along, I'm sticking to the game plan.*

When the minivan pulled up to the Net Force headquarters, Mark and his mom both got out and headed through the checkpoint at the entrance. After having their retinas scanned and matched, and passing through the weapons sniffer, Mark and his mother headed inside to their respective destinations.

•　　•　　•

When Mark reached the corridor that lead to the main operations room for Net Force, he found Ryan Valas waiting for him outside the doors. The tall man smiled when he saw Mark approaching.

"I'm certainly impressed by your enthusiasm, Mark. I thought you'd drop by online later this evening. But here you are in person. How long do you plan to stay tonight?"

"As long as possible, if you don't mind."

"Are your parents okay with that? And don't you have school in the morning? When do you find the time to sleep?"

"I catch a nap here and there. My dad says I've got too much energy, so he tries to make sure I stay busy. His theory is that if I pack enough stuff into a day, I'll be exhausted when I go home and fall right asleep. So far, it hasn't worked worth a darn," Mark replied.

"I'll bet. Would you like to get started?"

"Absolutely, Mr. Valas," Mark said.

"Please, if we're going to be working together, call me Ryan. I plan to call you Mark, after all. Fair enough?"

"All right," Mark said. *He certainly seems friendly*, Mark thought. *And he sure doesn't act like a spy—of course, a good spy wouldn't, I guess.*

Valas produced his key card and ran it through the slot beside the doors. He then stared at the small screen beside the door as the retinal scan program activated. A green light flashed on, and the doors slid silently open.

"Normally I'd give you more of a presentation on the workings of the operations room, but I have a feeling you probably know more about it than I do."

"I doubt that. My dad's brought me in here a few times, but usually only when it's slow," Mark said.

"Then you should enjoy this. Of course, I'm not on the front lines like most of the other guys here. As a representative of the CIA I usually only assist in an advisory capacity."

"What is it exactly that you do with Net Force, Mister—I mean, Ryan?" Mark asked. "I thought the Central Intelligence Agency primarily concerned itself with policing the activities of foreign countries as they impact the United States. Net Force exists to monitor Web crime as it pertains to the United States. Where do the two come together?"

"Good question, Mark. I'll start with the simple answer. The Net doesn't really have national boundaries, so the CIA and Net Force often run into similar problems and similar problem causes as we're policing the Net. My position here is to work with people—like your mom, for example—to develop more secure ways of transmitting sensitive data," Valas said. "Normally that would be a job for the security sysops at Net Force, but my agency is also interested in breaking codes and communication pipelines from other aggressive foreign powers, several of which are actively anti-American.

"If we could track and shut down all terrorist Web activity at the source, before it's even initiated, the lives we'd save could be countless, not to mention the site damage we'd prevent and the dollars and headaches we'd save legitimate Net users and suppliers.

"That's where the Net Force–CIA partnership comes in. You guys have the technical know-how, and I provide access to the CIA's resources on possible sources and kinds of terrorism. Together, the CIA and Net Force create online security for America."

If that's his simple answer, I don't know if I want to hear anything more complicated, Mark thought. "So you're always on the lookout for programs to decode or track people who try to remain unseen on the Web, right?" he asked.

"Absolutely. The more ways we can discover who's lurking on the Net and how, the more opportunities we have to stop them if they are up to no good," Valas said. "And that's especially true for the people who don't want to be seen. The first step to fighting an enemy, any enemy, is to learn as much as you can about them."

"Sun Tzu, right?" Mark asked.

"Paraphrased, certainly. But, yes, he advocated intelligence gathering and preparation before every battle. Are you interested in martial philosophy?" Valas asked.

"A little, but I just dabble," Mark said. "You know, I've been working on a program that sounds right up your alley— it actively seeks out lurkers on the Web. I ran a successful beta test on it, and Joanna's pretty excited about it. I can't show you the program itself, but I've got a copy of the beta test with me, if you'd like to see it."

"Sure, let's have a look at it now. I'm free for the next twenty minutes or so, then I've got a virtconference in Japan regarding security for their multinational corporations. Why don't you come along as a ghost, then you can get more of an idea of my role here?" Valas said.

"Sounds great. Won't going to a virtconference violate access protocol, though?" Mark asked. "I don't want to do that."

"No, this is basically a preliminary strategy meeting. It shouldn't have anything going on that you couldn't find in a good Netzine. We won't get down to the nuts and bolts of the actual security details until later, but I thought it might help you to see just how far Net Force's influence, even unofficially, can go. But first, since I've got the time, let's bring up that beta test of yours. Why don't you launch from that console?" Valas pointed to the seat next to his terminal, then sat himself down in the console chair and jacked in, with Mark right behind him.

"This test I did a few days ago looked pretty promising to me. I really think Net Force is going to be able to use it," Mark said, bringing up the hide-and-seek game. As he watched Valas link into it, Mark was aware of how long ago it all seemed. *Two days ago everything was fine,* he thought. *Now I can't walk down a hall in Net Force without wondering who the traitor is.*

After the file was done, Valas turned to Mark. "You've got an incredible detection suite here, Mark. Does your father know what you're working on in your spare time?" he asked.

Mark nodded, and Valas resumed his inspection of the file. "Fascinating, a program that scans all spectrums to locate the user in any configuration. Have you given any thought about scanning crosswise in various transmission fields, perhaps for particular bandwidth modulations?"

"I hadn't gotten that far yet. I was trying to work out the basic platform to spot lurkers by locating the data stream, no matter how it was hidden or configured, from their computer to whatever site they're in," Mark replied.

"Yes, but take a look at this," Valas said, stopping the

action where Mark caught Megan. He reached for another icon and scanned Megan's form with something that looked like a stylus. A viewscreen popped up beside him, listing all of the technical data on Megan's login record. He then fiddled with a few numbers, making it appear as if Megan was running her connection through a compressed variable frequency modulation program, then ran the video again, filtering it again through Mark's detection program. This time, when Mark scanned the section of the wall she was at, nothing appeared. As the file played back, Mark still spotted Megan, but now it looked as if he was looking at and talking to empty air.

Valas closed the file and turned to Mark. "See, there are a lot of different ways, some of them very simple, to fool electronic eyes. What if your lurker is piggybacking on another data stream, using someone else's system while the first person is online as well? There are a lot of ways to infiltrate a system, and your program needs to operate on the broadest possible detection spectrum, so you can find the hacker before he can do any damage."

"Which is why you said this should be a suite of detection programs," Mark said.

"Exactly. Like Navy AWACS planes loaded with equipment to monitor just about every conceivable form of communication, your program should contain just about every type of scanning subroutine that exists. Then you run them concurrently and one of them will, hopefully, detect any intruders."

"Looks like I've got my work cut out for me," Mark said. "You've made me think about a bunch of stuff I hadn't considered before this."

"Yeah, but that's half the fun of it," Valas said. "Look, right now, we've got to make that meeting. But after it's over, maybe we can work some more on this. Is there a copy of this program on file here? If I get some time, I can give you some more pointers on what detection areas you're weak in."

"I'd love to work with you on this, but I promised Joanna I'd keep this under wraps until she's seen it," Mark said. "I was hoping to show the beta test to Joanna, but she's been really busy, due to the, uh, security problems you guys have been having. And I haven't loaded the program onto the computer here."

"Have you got it at home? I'd be happy to download it and look it over," Valas said.

"After I talked to Joanna about the program, she had some suggestions for me to incorporate, too. Actually, it was pretty flattering—she's so sure the program is useful, she asked me to work on it on my dad's secure system, the one that isn't connected to anything. So I can't download it for you right now. Besides, I want the chance to work on it at home some more before I show it to anybody. And Joanna's got first crack at it. I really did promise her I'd keep it under wraps until she's seen it. But I want your input on this when she's done. How about this? I'll send you a virtmail when I'm through working on it and it's on the secure site here, and then you can talk to Joanna about looking at it."

"Did Joanna say when she was going to take a look at it?" Valas asked.

"Probably not until the weekend, so I'll be sure to have the file ready by then. She mentioned something about using it Saturday on some old cases in the secure files, so that's where the program will be located on the server. I think she was going to run the data from those recent Net Force intrusions through it, to see if it could come up with anything," Mark replied, watching for Valas's reaction. *Did he just flinch, or was that my imagination?* "How long is this meeting we're attending going to last?"

"Well, with the Japanese fondness for protocol and formality, it could stretch a couple hours at least. Still up for it?"

"Sure," Mark said. "But I may have to duck out a bit early. Homework and all that, you know." *The man didn't even pause for an instant when I told him Joanna was looking more closely at the intrusion,* Mark thought. *If he is our chameleon, he sure is a cool customer.*

"I understand. I used to be a student once, a long time ago. But try to stay for as much as you can of the meeting. I think it'll be a good experience for you to see a little of what we do in other parts of the world. We'll just set you up as a ghost, so you can leave whenever you want. Ready?"

"Let's go," Mark said.

"Nippon Technologies Consolidated meeting, go," Valas said. The Net Force offices faded out of sight, to be replaced with an austere corporate meeting room decorated in black lacquer and marble. The walls were the traditional paper and wood *shoji* screens, giving the room an aura of peace and calm. The only thing that marred that sense of peace was a finely detailed set of *samurai* armor standing in the corner. Valas slipped out of his shoes, walked to the low table in the middle of the room, and sat down. Mark stood behind him, invisible and inaudible to all except Valas.

"When in Rome, you know," Valas said.

Mark nodded. "Do you speak Japanese?"

"Unfortunately, no. I have to rely on a translation program. I'll lose a bit of face because I can't speak to them directly, although they'd never tell me that," Valas replied.

"What is this meeting regarding exactly?" Mark asked.

"Industrial espionage," Valas answered.

Just then the mirror-polished black doors at the end of the room opened, and three immaculately dressed middle-aged Japanese men walked in, followed by a younger Japanese woman. Valas bowed and spoke to them, introducing himself, and the meeting began.

While Mark found the discussion interesting, his mind kept wandering, as he thought about the man in front of him. *Valas certainly doesn't fit my idea of a spy*, he thought. *Then again, that's the idea. Spies wouldn't be very good at their jobs if they stood out. But like Daniel said, to be useful, a good spy would have to be highly placed, someone with a lot of access, but also someone that wouldn't attract suspicion.* Mark took a moment to tune back into the discussion. Valas was demonstrating various general security measures that could be integrated into corporate systems. All four of the Japanese listened intently. Valas spoke easily, apparently not intimidated at all by the language barrier. His manner was polite and deferential, yet firm. It was obvious who was running the show.

Well, from what I've seen, I sure hope the spy isn't him, Mark thought. *I like him, and he seems good at his job. Still,*

I've baited the hook. I'll cast the line on Friday. Then we'll reel in our catch and see who came to dinner.

Mark looked up and saw that the three Japanese men were conferring among themselves. It was a good time to bail out and actually get some schoolwork done. Saving Daniel was really cutting into his lesson time. He touched Valas on the sleeve and motioned that he had to go. Valas nodded and waved. Mark popped out of the conference hall and back to Net Force's virtual headquarters.

Once there, Mark logged off and stretched until he felt his bones creak. No matter how good the equipment, he always felt stiff after an extended session in a veeyar couch. Mark looked over at Valas, still sitting immobile, immersed in his virtconference, and tried to picture the man selling out his country. It was a tough fit.

Come Friday, we'll find out just which side you're on, pal, Mark thought as he headed out of the command center doors.

Daniel came home right after school. He had little choice in the matter. Since the whole Net Force situation had exploded, he'd been pretty much under house arrest, going only from home to school and back again, which had not helped matters between Daniel and his father. Ramos thought that his son should let Net Force handle the investigation, while Daniel had adamantly tried to convince his father to give him enough freedom to let him clear his own name.

Which is hard to do when you're stuck at home, with the computer nearly locked up, he thought as he trotted up the front steps. *Besides, Dad goes ballistic every time I bring it up. I think he's convinced I really did it, and that I'm going to go out there and try to bury evidence to convict me rather than search for evidence to clear me. He won't even believe me when I swear I'm innocent.*

Cut off from Net Force headquarters, Daniel felt as if they were building a case against him and he wasn't even being allowed to defend himself. *You know, if Mark, Megan, and Maj weren't helping me, there is no way I'd be able to clear myself,* he thought. *I'm a prisoner here in my own house, locked in physically, and locked out of most of the Net.*

Entering the house, Daniel smelled the wonderful tang of

spiced beef in the air and wandered down the hall to the kitchen, where he found his mother preparing dinner.

"Hi, Mom. Anything I can help with?" Daniel asked as he kissed her on the cheek. *At least she believes in me*, he thought.

"As a matter of fact, grab a knife and start slicing those bell peppers I've set on the counter," his mom replied. "How was school today?"

"Good. I finished that circulatory simulation report and turned it in. We have to start thinking about what classes we want to take next semester, so I'm going over the list tonight," Daniel said as he washed and cored the peppers, then sliced them into strips. "Fajitas for supper, eh?"

"Yes," she said. "I hate to bring up a sore subject, but have you talked to your father recently?"

"About what?" Daniel asked, delaying his answer.

She rolled her eyes at him. "You know . . ."

"Not if I could help it. Our last two conversations didn't accomplish much, so I thought I'd stay out of his way for a while, let him cool down."

"And what about you? Have you cooled down as well?" She drained the strips of cooked beef and put the pan back on the stove to warm.

"Yes, I think I have. But how can I talk to him when it feels like I'm talking to a brick wall? He never even hears me. It's like nothing I say gets through to him," Daniel said.

"Funny, that's the exact same thing he said to me a few days ago about talking to you. Maybe the problem is that both of you are trying so hard to get your own points across that you're not taking the time to listen," his mother said. "Daniel, you're in serious trouble right now, and your father can help you. You need to work together on this. Sometimes you two remind me of my class at school. I thought dealing with twenty kids who each want their own way is difficult, but that's nothing compared to you two."

Daniel frowned. "But—"

"I'm not done yet," she continued. "Just listen for a change." She warmed the flour tortillas as she continued talking. "Your father is a proud man, and you've inherited that pride. You use it as a shield, which isn't a bad thing most of the time, because it gives you self-esteem. Without it, people might try to use you, but you're too smart and confident to let that happen. Unfortunately, where your father is concerned, you've let your pride become armor. Your successes so far have made you overconfident, and you think you can handle anything. You enjoy being as independent as possible, and you feel that your father is too restrictive.

"In his mind, he's just as proud of you as you are of yourself. He wants you to accomplish all that you can, even if it means pushing you sometimes."

Daniel took a breath, letting his mom's words sink in before he answered. "I see your point, but how can I make him understand that things aren't the same today as they were when he was younger? Talk about a generation gap. Sometimes when I talk to Dad I feel like we're standing on opposite sides of the planet."

"You're right. But your father has a good point. He thinks that although the world may change, some people stay the same. And he's right. There are people who haven't changed with the times. A racist with a computer and Web access is still a racist, but now he's able to link with other racists around the world, and together they can hold their hate parties online. The issue of race can cause problems, even now. And that's why your father wants you to be well prepared for the real world. He doesn't want to see you hurt the way he was. He loves you." Daniel's mom took some dishes from a cabinet and handed them to her son. "And I love you, too. Enough lecturing. Go set the table, please."

"Is Dad home?" Daniel asked.

"He called just before you got in and said he was on his way. I'd like to have a nice family dinner with all of us here at least one time this week, so if you have anything you need to do before dinner, go and take care of it now," his mom said.

Daniel finished setting the dining room table and hurried upstairs. Pausing only to sling his backpack and jacket into a corner, he jacked in and checked his virtmail, breathing a sigh of relief when he saw a message from Mark. Opening it caused a life-size image of Mark to appear in front of Daniel.

"Hey, Daniel," the recording said, "the bait's been planted. Call me when you get this message. By the way, have you ever actually read *Macbeth*? Great story! I could really get into this Shakespeare stuff. Catch you later."

Daniel headed to Mark's veeyar address, but Mark wasn't online. That was weird—Mark pretty much lived online. Knowing it was just a matter of time until his friend showed up, Daniel left a message and then patched into the security cameras outside the house. Selecting the one over the garage, which gave him the best view of the driveway, he shrank the camera view and embedded it in a corner of his site. There. His dad wasn't surprising him this time. . . .

He had just finished when Mark appeared in his veeyar environment.

"Hi, Daniel," he said. "I take it you got my message?"

"Yeah. How'd it go with Valas?" Daniel asked.

"Just fine, although I've gotta say he seems like a stand-up kind of guy. I find it hard to believe that he's the one behind this."

"Well, somebody inside Net Force is behind it, and if it *is* your stand-up guy Agent Valas, I'm not going to shed any tears for him," Daniel said.

"All right, all right. I was just making an observation, not questioning your innocence," Mark said. "For what it's worth, I heard from Megan and Maj as well. Maj is meeting with her shadow assignment tomorrow, and Megan is still setting up her appointment."

"Great, just great. What if the chameleon hits Net Force again? If we're not ready, he'll slip through our fingers," Daniel said.

"I don't think so. Remember, our chameleon doesn't think anybody's on to him yet, so he's confident he can pull this off as often as he needs to. Why would he worry? Everybody's still looking at you as the suspect," Mark said.

"Thanks for reminding me," Daniel replied.

"Anyway, the way we're setting the bait up, we're virtually guaranteeing that he'll hit headquarters Friday night if he's one of these three suspects. We'll be waiting, and we'll nail him," Mark said. "If the guy doesn't go after the bait Friday, he's probably not one of our original suspects. So then we dig a little deeper and find who else might be behind the information thefts, and set the trap again. One way or another, we'll get this guy in the end."

"I sure hope you're right. I'm getting tired of living under house arrest. That reminds me—as long as I've got you here, Mark, there's something I need to ask you," Daniel said. "When we set up our mole, I need to get out of the house for it. I'd like to see our guy go down in person. The way things are going, I may not be able to. Could you make me a trapdoor in my home security system so that I could get out if I needed to? All I'd need is a five-minute window."

"It's not bad enough that you're already in trouble, now you want to make it worse?" Mark asked. "And maybe drag me into the doghouse with you? I told you before, some of us have more to lose than you do in all of this. Circumventing your father's security system would not only be poking my nose in where it doesn't belong, it's also sure to be noticed right away. Besides, why would you need to get out of the house for any of this? I thought we were only going to watch for electronic intrusion at Net Force. That's veeyar all the way, man."

"I've got to head downstairs for dinner, so I don't have time to go into it right now, but I wouldn't ask you to do it if it wasn't important. I'll explain it all later, I promise, but I need to get it set up. And I'll take the rap on it if it goes bad. I swear your name will never come up. Look, I'm hoping it won't have to be used, but I'd like a backup plan in case I can't get out of the house on my own," Daniel said.

"Frack, Daniel, I don't know. The last time I did something like this, I got caught big time. I was offline for three weeks, and that's like solitary confinement for me," Mark said.

"Come on, it won't even be hard. The system is a HomeGuard F-600 series," Daniel said. "It's got a simple trapdoor password for one exit and one entry with a self-erase subroutine built in, no problem. My father will never even know I'm gone."

"If it's so easy, why don't you do it?"

"Aww, Mark . . ." Daniel said."

"All right, but you'd better work really hard at getting

permission to do whatever it is you're planning to do," Mark said. "And if you're caught, I'm going to make certain that every indicator on that trapdoor program points squarely at you. Got it?"

"Don't worry, Squirt, I've got everything under control," Daniel said. "Tell Megan and Maj that we'll be meeting tomorrow morning before school to set everything up. I'll need that trapdoor before Friday night, all right?"

"You sure don't ask for much, do you?" Mark sighed. "Okay, I'll see what I can do."

Just then Daniel noticed his father's car pulling into the driveway on the security camera. "Uh-oh, dinner's on. I've gotta run, Mark. I'll talk to you later." With that Daniel signed off and headed downstairs.

His father had just come in through the garage door, and Daniel could hear his parents talking as he walked into the dining room. His mother had set everything on the table, and Daniel sat at his usual place and waited for them to come in. He heard his mother laugh at something his father was telling her, and he smiled ruefully, aware that he hadn't heard laughter like that for the past few days.

The parents in question walked into the dining room and sat down.

"Hello, Daniel," his father said.

"Hi, Dad," Daniel replied. Neither he nor his father ventured any small talk. Daniel didn't want to start another fight, which he seemed to do lately every time he opened his mouth around his dad. Maybe his dad felt the same way. . . .

Daniel sat silently, waiting until his father had served himself before constructing his own fajita. Finally the silence became too much for him. "How was work?" he said.

"About the same," his father replied. "You know, a lot of people think that guarding the White House is a glamorous job, but the truth is it's rather boring. I find myself wanting to be out on the road again, running alongside the President in a parade or something. Even tracking counterfeiters was a lot more exciting than this."

"Ramos, you know why you took the White House detail when it was offered to you. It's one of the top assignments in the Service, and it looks good in your file. And the biggest plus is that we get to see you just about every day, which certainly wasn't the case when you were on the road," his wife pointed out.

Maybe you feel that way, Daniel thought. *There are times when I wish he was gone more often.*

"Yeah, those sure weren't the best days. Traveling across the country for weeks at a time, sometimes so deep undercover that I couldn't call home, eating fast food or room service three meals a day, and never getting enough sleep. Still . . ." Ramos looked almost wistful for a moment, and Daniel smiled to himself. *Only my dad could consider a promotion to the White House a negative thing,* he thought, *But as long as he's feeling nostalgic . . .*

"Dad? I have a favor to ask. I know I'm grounded until the whole Net Force thing is resolved, but I really need to get together with Mark Gridley on a project we're doing. I want to know if we can work out something that would let me take the zoomer for the evening to go to his house," Daniel asked.

For a moment, there was dead silence in the room. Then Daniel's father asked, "What's the project?"

Well, at least he didn't say no right off the bat. So far, so good, Daniel thought. "We're working on a comprehensive report about the security of the Web. You know, electronic privacy, and encoding transmitted data, and all that?"

"Yes, I'm familiar with it. Why can't you get together over the Web and work that way?"

Why can't we, indeed? That very question had haunted Daniel when he had first tried to create an excuse to get out of the house. With the creative powers of the Web available to him, anything from researching the gravity of Saturn to examining the political state of twelfth-century Scotland was only a download away. *Sometimes the Web is just too damn useful,* he thought. It was also why he wasn't bothering to use Macbeth as the cover story. His father wouldn't buy that one for a minute. "Well, we're interviewing Mark's father, Jay Gridley, the commander of Net Force, and we thought it would be better to conduct the interview in person. You know, maybe take him out to dinner somewhere to thank him for taking the time."

Ramos's brows knitted together, and Daniel could almost feel the scrutiny his words were coming under. "So you want to wine and dine the head of Net Force while you pick his brain about security issues? Why not just meet him in an online café?"

"Dad, that would be like asking you questions about your guard detail while you were still on duty at the White House. Besides, you know the food at an online café is virtual—it's hardly the right way to say thanks. Jay works around computers all day, I'm sure he would welcome the break from virtual life," Daniel said.

Ramos thought for several seconds, which Daniel took as a good sign. Then his father looked at him. "Son, I'm sure Mr. Gridley would appreciate the time you both would put into this, but I'm afraid that I can't allow an exception to your punishment, even if it is school-related. I'm sure Mark can work something out with his father that will allow you to get the information you need."

"But, Dad, it would only be for a few hours—"

"Daniel, I said *no*. You could have done this if you had gotten the straight A's I expected of you, but now it's not possible. You're grounded, just as I warned you'd be. The subject is closed," Ramos said with a frown.

He is so unreasonable! Daniel felt a small spark in the pit of his stomach, which he clamped down on. *No reason for me to get pissed off. I knew he was going to say that. Well, at least I tried to do it the easy way,* Daniel thought. Aloud, he said, "Yeah, I guess we'll work something out." He took a deep breath and concentrated on relaxing. *I'll just have to implement my backup plan. Good thing I had Mark go into action early. Looks like I'll need that trapdoor after all.*

"Of course you will, son. How is school going? Any luck on improving those marks?" Ramos asked as he refilled his plate.

"Oh, some. I'm leading the class in most of my subjects. And the ones that caught me off guard when I switched to the tougher course load are getting easier. I think you'll be much happier with my report card at the end of the next semester," Daniel said. *After all, it's not like I have anything else to do in my room but work, work, work. Most parents*

*would be ecstatic over the kind of marks I got last semester
from a school like Bradford. But not my dad. Oh, no, only
straight A's for his kid. I wonder what kind of grades he got
in high school?* His father's next words, however, were almost enough to make him forget that thought.

"Good, a sharp mind is your best defense. Oh, I almost
forgot, I had written the wrong date down for that two-day
seminar on terrorist psychology. I've got to go to Langley
tomorrow and Friday, instead of next week," Ramos said.

I can't believe this! I've finally caught a break? Daniel
thought. *With Dad gone, getting out of the house will be
easier than I imagined. If Mom goes to bed early, I could be
on my way by ten.*

"Well, honey, if that's what they want. I'm sure Daniel
and I will be just fine," Carol said, looking at her son.
"Right?"

Daniel looked at both of his parents, and a wide smile
slowly spread across his face. "Right."

9

After school Maj hopped on the autobus and sat down, tapping her foot with each stop that went by. Even though her appointment with her target was online, she still felt butterflies in her stomach the closer she got to home.

It's nothing to worry about, she thought. *As far as anybody else is concerned, I'm just a Net Force Explorer who wants to see how the security staff at Net Force police their domain. After all, trying to protect one of the most heavily hacked sites on the Web can't be easy. All I have to do is just remember that and everything will be fine.*

Maj leaned back in the padded bus seat and took a deep breath, trying to relax. *I wish I knew what Daniel had in mind. Maybe I should drop Captain Winters a quick note and let him know what's going on.* She started to reach for her foilpack, but hesitated. *If I do call, I can't let him know anything about what we'll be doing, just in case the chameleon is listening. Darn it!* She stopped reaching for the phone. *When Net Force goes wrong, is anything safe?*

Finally, she pulled her foilpack out of her fashionable, hand-woven natural hemp purse and flipped it open, activating the phone mode as she did so. "Net Force, Captain Winters's voice mail," she commanded. A few seconds later she heard Winters's voice in her ear. When the beep sounded, Maj said, "Captain, this is Maj Green. We caught up with Daniel, and he's all right, although he still protests his innocence every chance he gets. We're staying as close to him as possible. I'm meeting online with my shadow-program security operative, Sheila Devane, this afternoon. Just wanted to keep you up-to-date. I'll try to reach you after my meeting."

Maj clicked the phone closed just as the autobus pulled up to the stop closest to her home. A walk down the long driveway brought her to the front door of her family's rambling house. One palm scan and voice scan later, she walked in, closing the door behind her.

"Hello! Anybody home?" Maj said as she slipped out of her jacket and hung it on the rack near the front door. Her mom's career as a computer site designer usually kept her online at all hours of the day, but this time she was apparently out of the house at a real-time appointment. Maj remembered that her father, a professor at Georgetown University, had mentioned a budget conference for his department. He hadn't looked exactly thrilled with the thought of it when he'd brought it up at breakfast this morning, which probably meant he expected the thing to drag on forever.

Even Maj's siblings, her older brother, Rick, and her five-year-old sister, Muffin, were apparently out of the house, leaving only silence to greet her.

Good, thought Maj as she rummaged through the cabinets of the L-shaped kitchen, searching for something to assuage the rumbling hunger in her stomach. She came up with a vacuum-packed self-heating package of tofu-spinach lasagna and a ginger soda from the refrigerator. Maj activated the entrée's heating unit, popped the gel-pack open, and took a long drink while waiting for her meal to cook. A few minutes later she was digging in. What did people do in the bad old days when it took hours to put a meal on the table? She'd starve to death without self-heating prepacks!

When she finished, she cleaned up and left the kitchen, heading through the cavernous dining room, down a long corridor past various bedroom doors and into the family room, where, surrounded by overflowing bookshelves, an implant chair sat.

Maj looked at her watch, wondering if she should just head over to Net Force now. The message she had gotten from Sheila had told her to drop by any time, particularly in the afternoon or evening. *Nothing ventured, nothing gained*, she told herself as she slipped into the chair. *Heck, if she's not there, I can Net surf . . . it's not like I've got something better to do right now.*

Maj lined up her implant and dropped into veeyar with a blink. The family interface was set up to look like their house, except now the exits from the family room led to wherever the user wanted to go on the Net. And she'd added a special touch that still made her laugh every time she saw it. The interfaces with the Net looked as if they were attached to her space with duct tape. Her father had sworn often enough that everything in the house was held together with the stuff. In veeyar she'd taken him at his word. Maj headed out toward Net Force headquarters, and within seconds was standing at the place where she was supposed to meet her Net Force shadow-program contact.

The face of a handsome bearded man in his mid-twenties appeared on a screen floating before her—the security officer in charge of this part of Net Force's firewall. "Yes, can I help you?"

"Maj Green of the Net Force Explorers to see Sheila Devane. I have an appointment," Maj said,

"Just a moment." The man ran an ID check, looked to see that she was expected, then turned around and spoke off-screen. "She's here, Sheila."

"Send her in."

The man turned around and smiled, motioning Maj forward with his hand. As he did so, the screen he was on grew larger, until it was taller than Maj herself. "Come on in."

Maj stepped forward, passing through the screen directly into the virtual security room itself.

Unlike most rooms on the Net Force virtual site, which matched their real-time counterparts when they had them, the security site couldn't possibly be duplicated in the real world. Every square foot of the massive room was in use, with operatives on the floor, all four walls, and the ceiling. As Maj watched, one man got up and walked across the ceiling, down the wall and over to a door, which disappeared after he stepped through. All of the operatives were staring at the viewscreens surrounding them, monitoring who knew what. Although just about everyone seemed to be talking, Maj couldn't hear a word they were saying. Experimentally she took one small step on the wall, then another. As soon as her feet touched the wall, gravity oriented itself under her, so it felt as if she was now standing on the floor. Everyone else reoriented as well, so the agents that had been on the far wall were now on what was Maj's ceiling. Maj looked up—and saw a sight that took her breath away.

Overhead, spinning silently, was the Earth in all its glory, from the green and brown of its continents to the vast dark blue oceans. Hundreds of satellites orbited the globe, along with the two space stations that had been built during the past decade. As Maj watched, she saw thousands of thread-like multicolored lines crisscrossing the seven continents, from major cities to the middle of nowhere and everywhere in between. They disappeared after a second, and a new set bloomed all across the world. This pattern repeated itself several more times while Maj watched.

"Kind of takes your breath away, doesn't it?" a voice beside Maj said.

"Yeah," Maj said, still mesmerized by the repeating light show. Blinking, she turned to look at the person beside her.

The speaker was a short, rotund woman in her mid-forties. A smile played around the corners of her mouth, showing bright white teeth against her tan skin. Her gray-streaked black hair was pulled back in a simple ponytail. She was clad in a white blouse and forest green slacks. She looked . . . well, nice. Friendly. Not like a spy at all. Or even like a Net Force internal security guru. "Hi, I'm Sheila Devane, and you must be Maj Green," the woman said, holding out her hand.

Maj automatically took it. "That's right."

The older woman looked Maj up and down, appraising her. "You're lucky. Due to the sensitive nature of our department, security is not officially part of the shadow program. However, when we saw your request, Captain Winters and I decided to make an exception this time. It's a pleasure to have you here."

"Thanks, a part of me still can't believe I got so lucky. I mean, security is one of those departments that you hear about, but never see," Maj said.

Sheila chuckled. "Good, that's just the way we try to keep things. I'd hate to think we weren't doing our job. We want the operations side of the department to be as secret as possible, except from those with the proper clearance. It's not that we're paranoid, it's just that the less anybody knows about us, the better we can do what we need to do to keep Net Force, and the Net itself, safe and secure. Actually, this isn't even the 'real' security site. To ensure that you don't accidentally see any classified material, I had a couple of the boys record an average duty night and change all of the data. The activity on the globe is real, but it's from several months ago."

"I understand. I'm glad you did it. Now I don't have to worry about inadvertently giving away government secrets. What do the lines on the globe represent?" Maj asked.

"Each one of these lines is the trace of an attempted hack," Sheila said. "When all the lines disappear, ten seconds has passed. Then the traces start all over again. What you're seeing is the basic view that every security operative works from. Of course, some of us modify this view to suit our own preferences. Let me show you mine."

With a wave of her hand, the room and globe disappeared, and the two women were standing on one of thousands upon thousands of gossamer lines, stretching off in every direction. From time to time one of the lines would tremble slightly and change color, from a soft blue or green to bright red. As Maj looked around, she could see a definite pattern to the formation, with crossbars supporting each layer of lines. Reaching out to touch one, Maj found it slightly sticky, as if it was a strand in a three-dimensional—

"Spiderweb!" she said, grinning.

"Exactly," Sheila said. "When you've been at this kind of thing as long as I have, you tend to pick a certain template and stick with it."

"How long has that been?" Maj asked.

"I got started in online security about fifteen years ago, when the online casinos were just coming into their own. I designed several secure site-to-site money transfer programs that are still being used today. After being responsible for the transfer of up to fifty billion dollars at one time, I thought I was looking for something with a little more peace and quiet. Instead, Net Force came calling, and here I am, back in the thick of everything Net-related. No peace in sight, or even quiet."

As Maj looked around, she saw movement in all corners of the web. Hundreds upon hundreds of spiders scuttled along the strands, darting brown recluses, graceful black widows, garden spiders, and several varieties she had never seen before, from relatively tiny ones the size of her hand to huge spiders as large as she was.

"Beautiful, aren't they?" Sheila asked. "I hope they don't bother you. Arachnids are a hobby of mine."

"They're certainly impressive," Maj replied. Although she personally had nothing against spiders, the sheer number of them here made her feel a bit squeamish. She shrugged it off and continued. "What's the difference between security's role at Net Force and the main operations room? Don't you both track down hackers?"

"One part of our work, our primary job, is to protect the information and people in Net Force, and to keep our external firewalls up, which allows the folks upstairs to do their job, tracking down those people who try to break in. We're more watchdogs than law enforcement in that sense," Sheila said. "Naturally, on many operations we work hand in hand with the ops room to supply data, and, when necessary, we testify against suspected hackers."

"I realize the questions you can answer are limited by the security protocols you have. So if I ask anything that you feel is out of line, please tell me. But maybe you can show me an old attempted break-in, from first contact to apprehension?" Maj asked.

"I'd be glad to—" Sheila started to reply when the web all around them suddenly started flashing red.

"What's that?" Maj asked. Before Sheila could answer, the bearded man appeared before them.

"Sheila, we've got a code one-five red in the classified files. He's five seconds in," the man said.

"Lock the perimeter down and seal off whatever sector he's in. I'm on my way," Sheila said. She turned to Maj, "Sorry about this. Stay here. I'll be back."

"Wait, how do I—" Maj started to say just as the older woman vanished. "Get out of here? Never mind, it's clear I don't. Okay," she muttered to herself and sat down.

With Sheila gone, the dozens of spiders scurrying around her seemed a bit more menacing. Maj tried to watch them for a moment, but meeting their predatory multi-eyed stares caused a shiver to run through her body.

So much for that idea, she thought. *Classified files. I wonder if our chameleon is back again? If so, whose identity is he using? If he is hacking now, that would mean that Sheila can't possibly be behind this latest intrusion, right? Unless she was simultaneously talking to me and hacking into those files? It would be a pretty good alibi.*

Maj caught a blur of movement out of the corner of her eye. *Did that spider just move closer to me?* She turned her head to regard the large black widow she thought she had seen move. It *did* seem closer now. As she watched, the spider took a few more steps toward her, its mandibles waving in the air. The black widow was followed by several garden spiders, and a couple of dozen more that Maj couldn't identify.

Time to move, Maj thought. She got up, ready to retreat to give the spiders more room, only to discover that they weren't the only ones taking an interest in her. Looking around, she found herself surrounded by an army of eight-legged soldiers, covering her from all sides, including above and below.

"I think I've got a little problem here," Maj said, staring at the arachnid ranks all around her. "Freeze program," she commanded.

A soft tone sounded. "User not authorized for site commands." A request to leave the site yielded the same results.

"Sheila? I think I may need your help!" Maj yelled.

No response.

"Security? Anybody?" No human help appeared. The spiders merely moved closer.

Great, not only can't I leave, but my guardians are something out of The Hobbit, *Maj thought. Now I know exactly what a trapped fly feels like. A really unlucky fly!* She tried to slow her rapid breathing. *What's going on? Is the chameleon doing this? Where's Devane?*

At that thought, all of the spiders trembled as one, then slowly began moving toward her, scuttling across the web strands on all sides, dropping by the dozen from the ceiling on gossamer threads. Maj swatted a few out of the air but quickly realized that there was no way she could stop all of them.

It's only virtual, she told herself. *I'm perfectly safe.*

It didn't help. She curled into a tight ball, her shoulders hunched, her eyes closed, waiting for the first light touch of their legs, a scream building in her throat and about to explode. . . .

"Freeze program!" a voice commanded behind her. Maj opened her eyes and looked to see Sheila behind her, her face grim. "I don't know what you think you're trying to pull, but you've got a lot of explaining to do."

"What are you talking about?" Maj asked. "I haven't done a thing! I've been held hostage and nearly mobbed by your spiders ever since you left!"

"Our program recordings just told me a different story," Sheila retorted. "According to our system records, that hacker in the files was you."

The next morning Daniel followed his grim-faced father and worried-looking mother as they walked down the hall to Captain Winters's office.

Daniel's heart hammered in his chest as his father stood in front of the door and waited.

It's all over. I'm done for. Net Force has completed their case, and they're kicking me out of the program.

When his father had told him earlier that morning of this meeting with Captain Winters and Commander Jay Gridley, Daniel's hopes had sunk. He hadn't had any time for his plans to clear his name to come to anything. They hadn't given him time to prove he was innocent. Now it might be too late! Stunned by the announcement, he had numbly accompanied his parents to Net Force headquarters. What had hurt Daniel the worst was that all during the trip, his father had seemed to avoid looking him in the eye. *He's already found me guilty, too. He'll never believe another word I say. I will never be free of this.*

The door slid open, and Daniel and his parents entered Captain Winters's office. The captain was behind his desk, and he got up to shake hands with Daniel's father and Daniel himself. Jay Gridley was there as well.

Man, it must be bad if they've got the head of Net Force down here to dish out the news. They must think I'm some kind of criminal!

Daniel was surprised to see that Winters actually give him a small smile and a nod.

That's weird. If he is going to kick me out, he's sure getting a lot more pleasure than I'd have expected out of it, Daniel thought. *Or maybe this is about something related to the case?* He looked around, watching Commander Gridley greet his parents. Daniel had only seen Gridley once or twice in the flesh, usually when he went to visit Mark. The man looked like an older version of his son, a relaxed Thai-American with an easygoing confidence. He, too, had a small smile on his face, making Daniel even more confused. *What the frack is going on?*

"Good morning, and thank you for coming here on such short notice," Captain Winters said once they all sat down. "I'm sorry I couldn't brief you on what's going on here when I called, but we felt that the matters we're about to discuss were too sensitive to relate over unsecured lines. So we had to ask you to be here in person."

Maybe that's not it at all. Maybe they want me here because they're going to lock me up and throw out the key like I'm some international criminal!

"And what is it that we are here to discuss, Captain Winters?" Daniel's father asked. Looking at him, Daniel saw he was sitting ramrod straight in his chair, and his tone, although polite enough, was curt.

At least I'm not the only one fracked off about being here,
Daniel thought.

"I can assure you that we will answer all of your questions
in due time, Mr. Sanchez. Commander Gridley just wants to
talk to Daniel first. Jay?"

Gridley leaned forward in his chair.

Here it comes, Daniel thought. He wanted to cry out, to
declare his innocence right there, but he knew they'd never
listen to him. Nobody ever did. The words remained trapped
in his suddenly dry throat. Daniel gritted his teeth and waited
for the man to speak.

Instead of accusing him, Commander Gridley merely
asked him a question. "Daniel, were you online between the
hours of four and six P.M. yesterday afternoon?"

Daniel stared at the Net Force commander as if Jay had
just asked him a question in Thai.

What does that have to do with anything? he thought as
he mentally reviewed what he had done yesterday.

"No, I wasn't. As my mother can tell you, I came right
home from school and worked for a few hours to finish up
some math problems for my calculus class. It was purely
pencil and paper stuff. I hit the books until about five-thirty,
had dinner, then studied for the rest of the evening online,"
Daniel said, watching Jay and Captain Winters exchange a
quick glance. "But I don't think I got online until after seven,
and I never left the school's virtual library. My parents have
grounded me from just about everywhere on the Net."

"So you weren't near the online Net Force headquarters
at any time yesterday?" Jay asked.

Daniel kept his gaze leveled on the eyes of the man who
held his future in his hand. When he spoke, his voice was
clear and steady. "No, sir."

Jay leaned back in his chair and nodded. "That's what we
thought."

"Will someone please tell us what this is about?" Daniel's
mother asked.

"I was just getting to that," Jay said. "Yesterday, at four
fifty-three P.M., we had an intrusion of our main site, similar
to the one that it appears Daniel was involved in previously."

Dammit, I was not! Daniel thought, but kept silent as Commander Gridley continued.

"The hacker was able to download several vital files and escape," Gridley said. "When we traced the online identity, it came up as—"

If he says my name, I might as well send in my résumé to the local burger stand, because that's where I'll be working for the next fifty years, Daniel thought.

"—Maj Green," Jay continued, "who was actually online and at Net Force headquarters at the exact time of the break-in."

Of course she was. She was meeting with her shadow-program person yesterday, Daniel thought. *That means—* "There's your proof that I'm not behind this!" Daniel said. "If I wasn't online during that time, and Maj was here, that means that someone else is taking our online identities and using them! Don't you see? Surely you don't believe that two Net Force Explorers are trying to access the exact same classified files just for kicks!"

Captain Winters held up his hand. "No, we don't. We've got a serious security breach on our hands, not a childhood prank. It's obvious that someone is far more interested in these files than we originally thought. But as to clearing you, Daniel, I wish it was that simple. I can't absolutely rule you out as a suspect in the second break-in. As we all know, it would have been possible to program a proxy to co-opt Maj's identity and attempt to hack into Net Force, and then plant it in Maj's computer, waiting for her to go online. You had the access. Now, one of our agents has been monitoring your Net activity since this whole thing started, and we're almost positive that it wasn't you this time. But we still don't have a better lead for the first intrusion. For the time being, at least as far as our investigation goes, you're still a suspect there, just as Maj is a suspect in the second break-in. The two of you are no longer our primary suspects. But until we turn up something better, we can't just close the case on you two, as much as I'd like to."

Daniel's anger surged, and he started to protest, but something in Captain Winters's gaze told him it would be best to keep quiet. His temples throbbed as he reined in his emotions and bit off what he had been about to say. *The captain has never steered me wrong. I'd better give him the benefit of the doubt, even if no one else is doing the same for me,* Daniel thought. He tuned back in to the conversation to hear his father talking.

"—whole situation is ridiculous. My son did not work this hard to get into your program, only to be labeled a criminal when he's clearly innocent. If you have charges you wish to press, then do so, and I will refer this matter to my attorney," Ramon said.

Daniel's eyebrows knitted in surprise. *First he asks me how I've been breaking the law in my free time, then he's sticking up for me to senior Net Force officers? When did I enter the Twilight Zone?*

"Mr. Sanchez, at this time there has been no formal accusation of your son, and we hope there won't ever be. Absolutely none of this is on record yet. However, whenever any agent of Net Force is suspected of illegal activity, our standard policy is to remove him or her from active duty until the investigation is complete," Jay said. "We can't do any less with our Net Force Explorers. I know how this must look to both of you, seeing this happen to your son—"

How it looks to them? What about what it's doing to me? Daniel thought, watching his parents shake their heads.

"—but we cannot take the risk of putting national security in peril for the sake of one person, however much I believe he might be innocent. I hope you can understand our situation. I am confident that this matter will be resolved, and hopefully resolved quickly, to everyone's satisfaction, except the person responsible for the breaches."

Ramon and his wife exchanged a long look. Something passed between them without words. Then Daniel's mother turned back to Captain Winters and Jay. "Of course we understand. And we're sure you're doing everything you can to help our son. Is there anything we can do to assist you?"

"I think the most important thing to do right now is to keep Daniel offline unless it's absolutely necessary," Jay said. "This will keep our hacker from adding any more ammunition to the evidence against you. Assuming someone else is behind this, if the attacks continue when you're not online, that will strengthen the case for your innocence, Daniel."

"So I just have to stand here and take this? Let somebody try to ruin my life, and give up everything that matters to me while he does it?" At a stern look from James Winters, Daniel swallowed the worst of his anger. "Right. Okay. It seems that's about all I can do," Daniel said. "Are you any closer to getting a handle on how this is happening? I always thought that the online signal from a user was unique, impossible to fake. Now it seems that's all a crock."

"We thought so, too. This is something new to us. We're checking into several leads, but so far we haven't found anything concrete yet," Captain Winters replied.

Or you have, but since I'm still a suspect, you're not going to tell me, Daniel thought.

"Do you agree with what we've proposed, Daniel?" Captain Winters asked.

Daniel nodded reluctantly. "I'm for doing anything that will solve this mess." *Including finding the chameleon myself, if need be.*

"That about does it, then. Thanks again for coming in on such short notice. I'm sorry it had to be under these circumstances," Captain Winters said as he rose. The Sanchez family also rose, with Ramos shaking hands with Jay and Captain Winters. Jay excused himself, and headed for the door. Daniel's parents followed him, with Daniel behind them.

As Daniel headed toward the door, he was intercepted by Winters. "Don't give up yet, Daniel. We're going to find whoever's behind this. You know that, right?"

Not if I find him first, Daniel thought, then nodded to Captain Winters.

"Right," he replied, then hurried out the door to catch up to his family.

"Dad?" he called trotting down the corridor after them. His mother and father turned when they heard him, stopping to let him catch up to them.

"Everything all right, Daniel?" his mother asked.

"Oh, yeah, just fine," Daniel said. "Dad, I just . . . wanted to say thanks. I really appreciate you standing up for me in there."

"No matter what, you're still my son," Ramos said. "From what I heard in there, it sounds like these Net Force people don't even know what's going on themselves. I'm not sure what to believe anymore. They'd better get to the bottom of this, and soon, or I'll start making some noise about improper procedure myself. I know several people on Capitol Hill who would love to hear how Net Force is screwing this up."

"Now, Ramos, I'm sure Net Force is doing everything it can to help. They must want to stop this even more than we do. We just need to give them a little more time," his wife said.

And give me a little more time to implement my plans, Daniel said. "Yeah, Dad. Captain Winters told me they're doing everything in their power to find out who's doing this."

"The one thing I do agree with Captain Winters on is that you're restricted from accessing the Net until this thing is over," Ramos said. "If you want to start earning my trust back, this is as good a way as any to start."

"But I never broke trust with you! I'm innocent!" A look from his father silenced him. "Yes, sir," Daniel said. He kept his expression neutral as they all walked down the hall. *The more things change, the more they stay the same. Winters and Jay practically admitted they didn't know who was behind this second attack, and I still get punished for it. I've gotta nail this guy, and fast, before the rest of my life is gone before it even starts. It's gonna be a long rest of the week.*

Maj sat in her room, still fuming over the events of the previous afternoon.

It's bad enough they thought I was behind that latest intrusion, but to grill me for three hours like a common criminal? It's a good thing they called Captain Winters or I'd probably still be in veeyar sweating under the lights.

Then, when I'm cleared, they say, "You're free to go. But we'd like you to restrict your Net access to essentials until you're cleared." Cleared! Like I did this! No apology, no explanation, nothing. All I know is that our chameleon took my identity and apparently got somewhere he shouldn't have. Frack, when I catch up to this guy the only surfing he'll be doing is in the prison washing machines!

Maj's foilpack beeped, signaling an incoming call. She reached for it and flipped it open. "Hello?"

"Maj, this is Captain Winters. How are you doing?"

"Oh, about as well as can be expected, considering what I went through yesterday."

"I know, I know, but I won't make any excuses for Security. They *were* doing their job," Winters said.

"Maybe so, but I got the impression that some of them take it a little too personally," Maj said.

"Well, how would you like it if you're supposed to be the best in the world at what you did, only to be apparently shown up by a seventeen-year-old kid?" Captain Winters asked.

"If I'd actually done what they thought I had, I'd feel pretty smug. And they should feel a little threatened by a break-in. It's their job to stop them from happening. We're all supposed to be professionals, right? But what about the phrase *innocent until proven guilty,* which they obviously don't know?" Maj said. *Ooops.* She took a deep breath and relaxed. *I can't believe I just said that,* she thought. She waited for a reply. After several seconds she heard a low chuckle over the line.

"Feeling better?" Winters asked.

"Yeah," Maj replied. "Before I forget and go off on another rant, thanks for stepping in last night."

"No problem," Captain Winters said. "When I heard what had happened, I knew it couldn't have really been you. Sheila, Joanna, and I talked, and we've come to the conclusion that it was definitely not you, although the signal says it was."

"But how is that possible?" Maj asked. "Ever since veeyar became possible, no one individual signal has ever been perfectly copied. The safeguards in the Net make that impossible."

"You're right. As far as we know, the signal is still not copyable," Winters replied. "I don't think I need to tell you that this goes no further. Joanna's current theory is that, somehow, the hack involving you was done by piggybacking onto your signal when you were already online, then diverting part of it, in effect making a proxy of you for that time, and using it to try to access the place the hacker wanted to go."

Just like Daniel tried to do against Mark in the hide-and-seek game, Maj thought. *Only this time the second proxy is controlled by the hacker, not by the signal owner. Mark should know about this. We may need to scan Daniel's hard drive to see if he has any programs that could do that. Great, now I'm thinking of him as a suspect. But he still is a suspect, no matter how he protests his innocence. And so am I.*

"Maj?" Captain Winters asked. "Are you still there?"

"Yes, Captain, sorry, I was just bytegathering for a moment. What were you saying?"

"I just had a meeting with Daniel and his parents. They've agreed to voluntarily restrict Daniel from the Net. And that goes for you, too. I want you to watch him even more closely now, in case he tries to log on from a remote site. We've still got agents watching him, but if he's behind this, it's conceivable he could lose them. I know how good he is."

"You still think he may be involved?" Maj asked. *Frack, I think he still may be involved.*

"No, I don't. Daniel has always been up front with me from the beginning, so I find it hard to believe he would do something like this now. But the nature of these attacks make it impossible for Net Force to clear Daniel, or you, for that matter, since you were at online headquarters when the second attack occurred. The only way I can prove you're innocent is make sure you are both offline and under observation when the next attack comes. We're going to catch this guy. Both Joanna and Sheila are confident about that."

As am I, since I'm going to do it with my bare hands if necessary, Maj thought.

"I'll keep track of Daniel as closely as I can," she said. "May I tell Mark and Megan about this? I'd like somebody from my side watching my back, if you don't mind. I may need them in the loop."

"I don't think that will be a problem. Good luck," Captain Winters said.

"Thanks, Captain," Maj replied, then signed off. She tossed the foilpack on the bed beside her and stared out the window. *The only thing I'm sure of is that I'm not the one behind these attacks. I don't know if Daniel is or not. But I do know who can find out.* Maj ran downstairs to the veeyar chair and started looking for Mark Gridley.

10

The next morning Daniel got up early and called Mark on his foilpack. Quickly summarizing why he couldn't meet with everybody on the Net, he asked Mark to go online and patch the others to his foilpack. Within a few minutes everyone was connected.

Maj, too, patched in with a foilpack. Once she was connected, she didn't even give Daniel a chance to speak. "I've got a bone to pick with you. This little scheme of yours to catch the chameleon nearly got me busted last night. Whatever your plan is, we all need to know everything from this point on. I don't know about how the rest of you feel about Daniel's silence on this plan of his, but after being blindsided and then interrogated by Net Force Security for three hours last night, I was pretty darned ticked off. Now I'm a suspect, just like Daniel. I've got every bit as much at stake as he does. And that chameleon may get any one of you next."

"What? What are you talking about?" Mark asked. "Daniel just told me that Captain Winters and my dad were going to keep him off the Net. Is there something you haven't told us, Daniel?"

"Yes, but I wanted to get everyone together before I explained the situation," Daniel replied. "If you'll just give me a minute—"

"Everybody stay calm and shut up," Megan interrupted. "For the sake of clarity. All right, Maj, tell us what happened."

Maj filled in the others on her meeting with Sheila Devane, what she knew of the break-in, and her subsequent questioning.

"That's what I was going to tell you guys," Daniel said. "The stakes have been raised for all of us now, and the clock is ticking. The sooner we nail this guy, the less chance there is of him swiping anybody else's identity."

"At least we agree on that," Maj said. "Besides, we've eliminated one of our three initial suspects. It can't be Devane. She was much too involved with me at the time of the hack to be our chameleon."

"Exactly. That leaves us with two of our initial suspects, Valas and Donley, both of whom have been given the info they need to bait them into striking tomorrow night. I took care of Donley myself, so I know that was done right. And Mark tells me Ryan Valas was set up like a duck in a shooting gallery. If either of them is guilty, they're going to go for it. So, we'll find out soon enough if we've managed to identify our chameleon," Megan said. "With luck, we'll get enough evidence to put this guy away for good."

"Right," Daniel said. "We just have to be ready for them. Now, does anyone have a problem getting free tomorrow night?"

The other three shook their heads.

"Good," Daniel said. "Maj, can you arrange to stay at Megan's house tomorrow night?"

Megan and Maj looked at each other, and nodded.

"Nopraw," Megan said, "We've got an open-door policy anyway."

"Good, but you won't be staying there all night, so, Megan, don't tell your mother any more about this than you have to."

"What?" Maj said. "I don't lie to my parents, not for you or anybody."

"Whoa, whoa, nobody said anything about lying," Daniel

said. "Just tell your folks that a friend from the Net Force Explorers is picking you up, and you'll probably end up staying at Megan's house. That way you're covered."

"Why? Why all the sneaking around and three-quarters truths, Daniel?" Mark asked. "What are you planning?"

"Because I'm going to need some help doing surveillance on the Net Force grounds, and I'd like Maj there with me. We're both suspects, so we can watch each other's backs and make sure we've got alibis for the night," Daniel said.

"Maybe it was just me, but I could have sworn you just said 'surveillance on the Net Force grounds'? What the frack are you talking about?" Mark asked.

"Look, we think this is an inside job, which means that the perp is someone who has access to Net Force. With Mark and Megan telling everyone that Mark is turning his program over to Joanna on Friday, and that she's going to use it Saturday to try and track the guy that's hacking Net Force, the chameleon *has* to go after it, or he may be discovered."

"You're sure about that?" Megan asked.

"Nobody's sure about anything here. But the only opportunity our bad guy has is Friday night, since the program is going to be on Mark's dad's isolated home system until then. That computer's not connected to the Net, so no matter how good this guy is, he can't get at it there. With any luck, and if we've picked the right suspects to bait, we should flush the hacker out of the woodwork while we're watching."

"Watching online—that's what we're talking about here, isn't it?" Mark asked.

"Sure, we'll watch the Net. That's what Megan and you will be doing. But Maj and I can't help you—we've been told to stay offline. That's okay. It may even work in our favor. I think we have to take into account the possibility that the chameleon may be too good for us to catch. Net Force hasn't managed to catch him yet, have they? I think it's because they're looking in the wrong place, but he may just be that good. I want a backup plan in case he slips through your fingers. If Maj and I stake out Net Force's HQ, we'll be watching not only on the Net, but in the real world as well. Anyone coming or going, we'll see them," Daniel said. "If the chameleon really is somebody doing this from within Net Force, we'll at least have a record who was on-site during the hack. We can use that list to refine our suspect list if we don't catch our guy on Friday night."

"So you want us to actually stake out Net Force headquarters?" Maj said. "Are you crazy?"

"No, it makes perfect sense—just listen. . . ." Daniel said. "If our chameleon goes in, wraps the program up, and slips it past Mark and Megan—no offense guys, I'm not saying it would be easy to do—then the recordings of who comes and goes during odd times on this Friday night might be the only lead we have to catch our hacker. Net Force has records of who is on-site at any given time, but we don't. Since they're looking for an outside hacker, Net Force won't use that info. We will. This is the only way I can figure to get a list of who is at Net Force HQ during a hack without breaking into Net Force's computers. We're already in too much trouble to try that, don't you think? This way it's not like we're doing anything illegal. We all have clearance for the HQ parking lot. We'll just be parked somewhere inconspicuous, watching who comes and goes. We'll even be following orders—Maj and I will be offline."

"And what if we do spot one of our suspects leaving in the wee hours of the morning, just as Mark and Megan spot an irregularity on the Web or Net Force announces a hack? What do we do then?" Maj asked.

"You'll tail the suspect and see where he goes, make a note of it, and leave, just as Megan and I will follow the hacker's signal to its origin, make a note of it, and leave. Under no circumstances will we do anything else," Mark said. "Am I making myself clear?"

"I couldn't have said it better myself," Daniel said. "So, what do you say? Are you all in?"

"In for a pound, in for a ton," Maj said. "I'm ready to put this guy out of business, not matter what. I really don't like being used, especially by somebody who's committing treason."

Daniel looked at Mark and Megan. "What about you guys? If you're having second thoughts, I don't want to hear about it on Friday night."

"You already know the answer to that," Mark said.

" 'I am in blood/Stepp'd in so far, that, should I wade no more/Returning would be as tedious as go o'er'," Megan said. "We've come this far. Let's finish it."

"Thanks for the wonderful imagery," Mark said. "All right, let's go over the plan one last time. I will set up the program at HQ Friday evening and virtmail Valas that it's there. Megan, you're in charge of virtmailing Donley. Friday night, Maj and Daniel are staking out headquarters. You two work out the details about meeting and getting there. Megan and I will be watching Net Force online at the same time. Whoever spots anything suspicious first, contact the others. We'll play it by ear and follow our leads wherever they go. Under no circumstances are we to engage anyone or try anything stupid. This guy could be dangerous—and I don't want anybody to do anything to provoke him. This is about getting evidence, not about putting ourselves at risk. Are we all clear?"

"Clear," the other three said.

"Great, I'm happy we've got this all ironed out," Megan said. "Frack, I've got to get going. I'm going to be late for school."

"Me, too. I'll catch you guys later," Maj said. "I can't believe I'm doing this."

"Well, just try to get through it," Mark said. The two girls said goodbye and broke their connections.

After the girls were gone, Daniel broke the silence. "I trust you have something for me?" he asked Mark.

"Pushy, pushy. I'll have you know this wasn't exactly easy to do in one night, thank you very much," Mark grumbled. "I've sent it over to you already. You've got two uses, then it's done. Bring up the security program, point the thing that looks like a remote at it, and zap away. When you want to come and go, just punch the code on the side into your system. Don't forget it. It also erases any log notation of anyone coming or going, and will delete itself from your system after the second use. Don't mess it up," Mark said.

"Don't worry, I won't," Daniel said. "Your decoy program is ready, right?"

"It'll be there, waiting for the chameleon," Mark said. "I'll uncover it Friday, all nice and tempting."

"Good. I'm not expecting another hack attempt until then. After this latest hack, the chameleon will probably lie low for a while, gauging Net Force's response. Oh, don't forget to bring your foilpack tomorrow. We'll need it to keep in touch with you."

"Don't worry, I'll have everything we need," Mark said.

Daniel noticed the odd tone in Mark's voice. "You cool?" he asked.

Mark was silent for a moment. "Yeah, I'm down, but, I don't know, I just wish there was a better way to do this."

"You got one? I'd love to hear it. As much as I want to clear my name, what I don't want to do is take anybody else down with me," Daniel said. "That's why all we're going to do is watch, I promise. I'll talk to you Friday. Later."

You bet we're only going to watch. That's the only reason I haven't told Captain Winters or my dad about this whole idea, Mark thought after Daniel was gone. While he agreed with Daniel's logic about getting the evidence, he'd also seen the consequences of Net Force Explorers going off and doing things on their own. One of them, Matt Hunter, had even been taken hostage. Mark himself had suffered the consequences of Netsnooping where he shouldn't have. Maj and he had been infected with a nasty real-time virus coded to their DNA on the Net by a disturbed teen who was out for revenge on some friends of his. They'd both ended up in the hospital after that little adventure. Mark was prepared to scratch this whole operation if it looked as if Daniel was going to get out of hand. *But as long as we're just watching, it should be all right. I hope.*

11

The time until the trap was sprung crawled by. Daniel found it almost impossible to concentrate. He was repeatedly warned by his teachers to snap out of it during his classes. His mother even asked him if he was coming down with something. To keep a low profile while he was waiting to clear his name, he nodded when appropriate, shook his head when appropriate, and as soon as the people talking to him turned their attention to something else, he resumed thinking about Friday night.

By Friday afternoon, he found it impossible to sit still. He mapped out his route through the house, practiced it a few times, and set aside the special gear they would need that night. Most of it was actually his father's, but Daniel figured he could return it before his dad noticed that it was missing. He installed Mark's trapdoor program to bypass the security system, a process that only took a few minutes, not nearly enough time for a good distraction. Daniel was itching to get started, but he had two hours to kill before he could leave the house.

Flipping open his foilpack, he dialed a familiar number. "Jimmy? Yeah, it's Daniel. You guys in place? Okay, you know what to do right? No, there's no messing around this time, it's important. Yeah, I should be checking in with you around three or four this morning. Yeah, good luck to you, too. Later."

He flipped the phone closed and sat there for a moment. *This has to work. And it has to go off without a hitch. I can't drag Mark, Maj, or Megan into something dangerous.* Despite his commitment to clearing his name, he felt responsible for making sure none of the other three got into trouble or hurt trying to save him. *If anything happened to them because of me, that would be worse than me being banished from the Net Force Explorers. We've got to find this guy. I just wish I could get started right now. But there's no point. Mark hasn't even got the trap in place yet.*

To take his mind off his problems, he busied himself with cleaning his room, making an enormous mound of dirty laundry in the corner of the room, and then practicing his jump shots by tossing wadded balls of clothes into the laundry chute. His accuracy was running about twenty-five percent, which sucked.

After what seemed like days of waiting, he heard the grandfather clock in the hallway strike. It was finally time. He activated Mark's trapdoor program, noting with satisfaction that it worked perfectly. He slipped into his jacket and out of his room, closing the door behind him. Softly creeping to the second-floor landing, he peeked down the darkened stairway into the dining room. Seeing no lights, he stole down the stairs and padded through the house to his father's study.

Daniel quickly stowed the things he needed in his backpack, checked to make sure he had his driver's license with him, then went back to the kitchen. He opened the door leading to the garage and flipped on the light.

In the farthest space of the three-car garage, a small, low, bubble-shaped car sat. A thick cord ran from its fender to an outlet in the wall. This was the "zoomer," a short-range battery-powered vehicle. It could seat two, with a practical range of 500 kilometers and a top speed of eighty kilometers per hour. It was energy-efficient, nonpolluting, and quiet. You just had to make sure it didn't run out of juice on you in the middle of nowhere, because it took forever to recharge.

Daniel's parents used it for short errands and the occasional night on the town.

Daniel closed the door behind him, walked over to the car, and unplugged the cord, coiling it neatly in the trunk. He got into the car and activated the power system, listening to the almost inaudible hum of the motor. Daniel hit the garage door opener button and waited for the door to fully retract. He made sure the car was charged to the max while he waited. When the door had stopped, he put the car into gear and eased it out of the garage, closing the door behind him.

A light rain was falling as Daniel pulled up to Maj's house in Alexandria. The air smelled fresh and sweet as the moisture washed away the dust and dirt of the day.

Daniel got out of the car and trotted up the front steps of Maj's home, shielding his eyes from the automatic security light that came on when he approached. He rang the doorbell and waited, zipping up his jacket as he scanned the front of the house. A few seconds later the door opened and Maj appeared.

"Are you ready?" Daniel asked.

"Yeah, let's go," Maj said. The two teens walked out to the zoomer. "Cute," Maj said when she saw the car. "Do you use it when you play with your action figures?"

"Hey, it'll get the job done," Daniel said, "just as long as we don't get involved in a high-speed chase. A motivated kid on a Big Wheel could probably beat this thing. But we're just watching, remember? No crazy stunts. It'll be fine for tonight."

"Megan asked me to tell you that she just sent the virtmail about Mark's program to her suspect," Maj said. "He got it— she got a reply."

"Good," Daniel said. "Did you talk to Mark?"

Maj patted her backpack. "Yeah. He says we're all set up." She smiled as she got into the electric car. "Let's get going."

Daniel slipped into the driver's seat. He buckled his seat belt and made sure Maj had fastened hers. The car wouldn't start if the passengers weren't fully secured in their seats. He pushed the ignition button and eased the car out into the street.

At this time of night, traffic was sparse, and they made the drive to Net Force Headquarters in less than half the time it normally took. Both Maj and Daniel were quiet, each thinking of what they were about to do. A few blocks away from the parking lot, Daniel pulled the zoomer over and turned off its headlights.

"Why'd we stop here?" Maj asked.

"You have to take the car in. I'm not exactly well liked at Net Force right now, even if Jay Gridley and Captain Winters don't really think I'm responsible for the hacks.

"Like I'm in any better shape after my adventures?" Maj pointed out.

"Yeah, but you were here virtually when it went down. Nobody really thinks you're a suspect."

"Sheesh," Maj said. "Okay. I'll drive if it makes you happy."

"You do know how to operate one of these?" Daniel said as he got out.

"Of course, I have my license, too, you know. This," Maj said, indicating the simple controls, "is nothing." She slid into the driver's seat, but Daniel didn't get into the passenger seat. He was fiddling with something at the back of the car. "So what do you think you're doing?"

"See that lever on the floor between the door and your seat? Push down on it."

Maj did so, and heard a metallic thunk. She looked in the rearview mirror and saw the trunk of the car opening. "I'll be in here." He slid into the trunk.

"You're letting this cloak-and-dagger stuff go to your head," Maj said. "Why do you need to hide?"

"Because I think it will look suspicious if both of us turn up together," Daniel pointed out. "I don't want anybody to take notice that we're here, or it might alert our hacker. Now, if the guard asks you to do anything, just go along with him. I'll handle whatever needs to be done," Daniel said.

"I don't like the sound of that," Maj said.

"Relax, hiding's not illegal. And I'm not going to assault the guy or anything if he finds me. I'm in enough hot water here as it is. Just don't panic or anything and do whatever he asks, okay?"

"All right," Maj said, "We'd just better not get caught."

"Trust me," Daniel said with a devilish grin. "Let's go."

Maj waited until Daniel was in the trunk with the cover closed, then flicked the lights on, shifted the car into drive, and pulled away from the curb. She kept her eyes glued on the checkpoint as she approached, trying to drive casually. Pulling into the Net Force headquarters driveway, she rolled up to the guard post.

Maj knew that the first checkpoint was relatively simple. There was an armed guard on duty twenty-four hours a day. There was a system of pop-up concrete and steel barricades and metal tire spikes to stop a possible terrorist attack. She didn't think she was in any danger from those, however.

She stopped between the white lines, like the sign said, and waited for the Marine guard to come over to her. It took him longer than she expected, and she started to worry. *Is he scanning the car? What's going on?*

Finally the guard ambled over. "Identification, please?"

Maj handed over her passcard, which he scanned into his electronic datapad. A soft chirp later, he handed the card back to her. "Miss Greene, would you turn off the vehicle and step out, please?"

Maj felt cold fear lance through her chest. *Was she barred from Net Force because she was a suspect in that second break-in attempt? If she was, was she going to get in trouble for trying to visit the Net Force HQ? And if she was in this much trouble already, what were they going to do to her if they found Daniel hiding in the trunk?* "Is there a problem, sir?"

"Please turn the car off and step out of the vehicle," the guard requested again.

Maj opened the door and got out, grabbing her jacket and slipping it on to ward off the light rain that was falling. The guard produced a hand-held retina scanner. "Would you please look into the eyepieces?"

Frowning, Maj did so. Okay—this is normal procedure. *So far, so good,* she thought. The scanner would match her retina patterns with what was on file at Net Force, so that wasn't a problem. The machine beeped again, and the guard looked at it, then nodded. He took a device, which looked like the mirror dentists used to check hard-to-reach teeth, only it was six feet long, and equipped with a powerful light on the end. The guard used it to look under the car on all sides, walking around the vehicle until he was satisfied.

Just as Maj was about to relax, the guard said, "I'm going to have to ask you to open your trunk."

For a moment, Maj's heartbeat stopped. But even if her body was frozen, her mind was still working. "May I ask why?" she heard herself say.

"Sure. We have no record of this car ever being on the Net Force grounds. An inspection is mandatory for all new vehicles entering the base."

Oh, no! Maj thought. *We're busted, just because Daniel had to play spy guy!* "Just a moment, I have to find the trunk release," she said loudly, bending over and fumbling around on the car floor. She thought she heard a rustling noise from the trunk, but she couldn't be sure. *But there's nowhere else to hide in there. Where's he going to go?* After Maj had stalled as long as she dared, she said, "Ah, here it is!" and hit the release lever.

When she straightened up, she noticed that the guard had taken a few steps away from her, and that his hand was much closer to the butt of his holstered pistol than she remembered it being a minute ago.

"Step to the rear of the vehicle, miss," the guard said.

Maj walked around to the back of the small car and waited. She could feel the guard's presence behind her, and it did not fill her with reassurance.

"Please open the trunk, miss."

Taking a deep breath, Maj put her hand on the trunk hatch. *This is it, any chance of me having a career with Net Force is over. I'll be sweeping halls in a junior high school somewhere for the next sixty years in my glorious new position as a maintenance technician, or maybe I can rise to exalted heights in fast-food management. No, they use too many computers, too. Oh, I'm going to look horrible in baggy neon orange! I'll bet they don't have Hilfiger in prison. Darn that Daniel Sanchez!* Closing her eyes, Maj opened the trunk.

For a moment there was absolute silence. Maj felt a bright light shining on her face, and she waited for the handcuffs to be slapped on her wrists. She started when she heard the

Marine's voice again. "Miss Green, are you all right?"

Maj opened her eyes and looked at the guard, who was watching her with concern on his face. "Yes?" she squeaked.

"You just looked a little pale for a moment. I thought you might be ill," the Marine said. "Would you like to sit down?"

Maj couldn't take it any longer, and she looked into the car trunk. Except for a "doughnut" spare tire, a jack and handle, and a small tool kit, the space was empty.

Maj's head snapped up. "Of course, I'm fine. Was there anything else you needed, sir?" she asked, feeling her heart start to beat again.

The guard's demeanor had relaxed visibly. "Nope, that'll do it. You can go on in, and have a good night," the guard said.

"Thank you, sir," Maj said with every ounce of sincerity she possessed. She forced herself to calmly walk to the driver's side, open the zoomer's door, and get in. She fastened her seat belt again, trying a few times before her shaking hand could insert the belt into the lock. She started the car, waved to the guard, who nodded and raised the gate for her. Maj drove into the parking lot and headed for the far side, all the while wondering, *Where in the hell is Daniel?*

Suddenly a hand clutched her shoulder, causing Maj to scream and jump. She involuntarily twisted the steering wheel, causing the car to swerve.

"Easy there, Maj, we're not driving in the Indianapolis 500," Daniel said, laughing as he clambered over the passenger seat and sat down.

"Sanchez, you creep, you almost gave me a coronary! Where in the name of Houdini were you?" Maj asked.

"Oh, there's a space between the seats and the trunk. It holds the ragtop if you've got a convertible model, but we've always used it as storage space. I used to hide in there when I didn't want my parents to find me. Funny," Daniel said as he rubbed his back. "It's a lot smaller than I remember."

"For a minute there I thought we were going to be the only Net Force Explorers who would finish the program from prison," Maj said. "You owe me for this, Daniel, big time."

"If we get the evidence we need to clear ourselves, I'll have paid you back for the scare in full. How was I supposed to know they would inspect the car? Besides, you handled it like a pro. Maybe we should team up and go into the spy business together?" Daniel asked, winking at her.

"No, thanks, I don't need any more stress than I already got tonight, thank you. Okay, here we are. A nice secluded corner with a view of both the parking lot checkpoint and the main entrance, yet out of sight of the guard post," Maj said, stretching her shoulders. "Frack, am I tense."

"You should learn to relax," Daniel said, then howled as she punched him on the arm. "What was that for?"

"Don't even go there. All right, you've brought the car and I got us inside. I'm gonna get the connection set up with Mark and Megan. So what kind of gear did you decide to bring to this stakeout, spy guy?" Maj asked as she dialed up her friends in conference mode on her foilpack phone.

Daniel reached behind his seat and started pulling out objects and handing them to her. "Binoculars with night vision. Night-vision scope. Digital camcorder with telescopic night-vision lens. Medium-range hands-free communicators. And this," he said, pulling out a small black box and a small flatscreen datapad.

Maj was too busy looking through the binoculars to notice what he was holding. "Wow." She set the field glasses down and looked over at Daniel. "What's that?"

"This is for if we get a solid fix on our chameleon," Daniel said, switching the datapad on. Maj saw a visual of a map with a small red light blinking in the corner. "It's a homing beacon and tracker, so we can follow him."

"I thought you said we were only going to watch," Maj said.

"We *are* only going to watch. We're going to watch the guy leave, follow him at a safe distance with this tracker, and after we get the address of where he's gone, the next thing we'll be watching is his name on the news when he gets arrested," Daniel said. "We discussed this. You said you were in. Don't be getting cold feet on me now."

"I'm not, I just want to be sure we follow the plan, all right?" Maj said with a touch of annoyance. For a moment each of them examined the parking lot on their respective sides of the car, saying nothing.

"I meant what I said earlier, you know," Daniel said after a minute.

"What was that?" Maj said.

"That you handled the guard like a pro. I heard the whole thing. A lot of people would have cracked under that kind of pressure, but you trusted me enough to know that I wasn't going to be in that trunk when you opened it. That takes a lot of courage, and I want you to know I appreciate it," Daniel said.

"Thanks. I don't mind telling you that I was scared spitless when he asked me to pop the trunk. I wasn't sure you had anywhere to hide."

Daniel nodded. "I don't blame you, I probably would have been worried, too. We'd better get set up. Contact Mark and Megan and make sure they're ready as well," Daniel said.

"Right," Maj replied.

Daniel turned on the power pack for the night-vision goggles and slipped them on. Maj and the scattered vehicles in the parking lot turned an eerie glowing green as the goggles gathered and amplified the available light over 40,000 times. With the goggles on, Daniel could see his surroundings like it was daylight. He looked at Maj, who was examining the cars in the parking lot very closely, then checking a hand-written list she'd pulled from her pocket.

"One piece of advice," Daniel said. "Do *not* look directly at a bright light source, such as the headlights of a car. The light amplification will blind you." He saw Maj put the glasses down quickly. "Don't worry, it wouldn't be permanent."

"Thanks for the warning. Anything else I should know before burning out my retinas?" Maj asked as she gingerly raised the binoculars to her face again.

"No, that's about it. What are you looking for?" he asked.

"I had Mark get the license plate numbers of our suspects, and I'm cross-checking them with the cars in the parking lot. So far, no matches."

"That means our bad guy hasn't shown up yet," Daniel said, upset.

"Or that he's in a row I haven't checked yet." Maj put the binoculars down beside her. "Don't be so impatient. I want to check all the cars before I get hold of Mark." She picked up the binoculars and resumed her careful search. Daniel waited, so wound up he was hardly able to breathe.

When Mark got home that Friday night, he headed straight for his room. He did this so he could minimize the chances of seeing his father, who otherwise might ask potentially uncomfortable questions about what he was doing that evening. Mark had never lied to his father, didn't intend to start tonight, and he knew a simple answer like "surfing the Net" would only lead to more questions. Mark figured the best way to avoid that trap was to stay out of his father's way for the evening.

Settling into his chair, he jacked in and checked his virtmails, discarding most of them and reading the rest. One of them in particular caught his eye. It was from Ryan Valas. Mark activated it and sat back.

"Hi, Mark," the recording said. "I got your virtmail about the program. Let me know what Joanna thinks of it, and if you come up with anything new, all right? Take it easy."

Mark studied Valas's face while the message was playing. He couldn't help liking the guy. *I sure hope it isn't you, man,* he thought. *Still, the bait is set. Now let's see who comes to call.*

The message ended, and Mark archived it. He then looked to see if Megan was online yet. She was. Mark darted over to where she was and found her exiting a virtual fantasy gameworld.

"Hey, Megan, you ready?" Mark asked.

"Hi, Mark. Yeah, I'm set. I was just chatting with some friends back there," she replied.

"Okay, here's what's going on so far. Since Daniel and I think our chameleon might try to shoot whatever he steals out over the Net this time, our job is to set up a dragnet around Net Force headquarters to monitor outgoing electronic traffic. I've spent the last two days setting up sneak-a-peek programs that will let us know if the program we're looking for comes out," Mark said.

"And we just follow it to wherever it's going, right?" Megan asked. "What if it's camouflaged?"

"That's why I brought these," Mark said, taking out two pairs of sunglasses and handing one pair to Megan. "Put them on."

When Megan slipped the sunglasses over her eyes, the world around her took on a geometric quality. All detail and color was gone, with the Net Force site and other nearby data nodes looking like huge skeletal frames of buildings, outlined in glowing blue lines. It was as if the two teens were looking at a world where everything was built by connecting the dots.

"This is the other thing I've been working on," Mark said.

"Why does this look so familiar?" Megan asked.

"Did you ever see an old flatfilm called *Tron*?" Mark asked. When Megan shook her head, he continued. "It's not bad. Anyway, this is kind of what they thought the Net would look like back in the early days of computer, when the Net barely even existed. They were wrong, of course, but I liked the look and I appropriated their visuals. Cool, huh? Now, when my program is downloaded, it will broadcast a signal that will be visible to us as a bright streak of light, which we can track from above. That's why I've made the buildings transparent. My program will stand out like a star gone nova in this scenario. When we see it come out of Net Force, we trail it to its destination and head back to report. Simple enough, eh?"

Megan nodded. "Mark, are you sure that Daniel won't try anything out there? He's a little out of control, I think, since this accusation came down on him. Maybe you should have gone with him to headquarters."

"Maybe, but I'm better in here than out there. Besides, if Daniel did want to try something crazy, how would I stop him? He's twice my size, and I bet he fights dirty. Maj has all that martial art experience—she can take him if she has to. And she's got enough common sense for three kids her age. She's a victim of this hacker, too. She'll keep Daniel focused on the matter at hand. Don't be so uptight. His plan sounded reasonable to me. I'm sure Maj and he have everything under control."

"Maybe, but back in Captain Winters's office even you said he's a hothead. So where does he want to go? Right to

Net Force headquarters. He's up to something—I just know it. Something he's not telling us about. I don't want him getting into worse trouble than he's in already. And I especially don't want him getting Maj into more trouble," Megan said.

"Look, will you just relax? Daniel knows how important this is, and I know he won't do anything to screw it up. Besides, that's why I agreed that Maj should be out there with him, and you in here with me. Maj will be a rational influence. She'll keep Daniel in check." *At least that's what's supposed to happen,* he thought. He shook his head, disturbed by the nagging doubts Megan had planted. "Let's just concentrate on getting the data we need, okay?"

A soft chime, signaling an incoming message, interrupted him. "That must be them now," Mark said. "Hey, Daniel, Maj?"

"We're here. Just a minute, I'll bring us up onscreen." A second later Daniel and Maj appeared in front of them. The foilpack visuals weren't the best, but Mark and Megan could see enough to tell their friends were in the Net Force HQ main parking lot.

"I take it you and Megan are in position, Squirt?" Maj asked.

"We are cocked, locked, and ready to rock. The nanosec my program hits the Net, we'll be on it like sharks on a blood trail," Mark said.

"Just as long as the blood's not your own. We'll be leaving the foilpack on standby, in case you need to reach us. Good hunting," Maj said.

"You, too. Let us know if anything happens," Megan said.

"You got it," Maj replied.

Megan shrank the image until it appeared as a small icon floating in their virtual world. After Daniel and Maj were iconized, Mark looked at Megan. "Come on, we might as well get a better view." He pointed to a cloud drifting by in the night sky and rose into the air. The little icon followed him.

After a second so did Megan. She found Mark stretched out in a puffy white reclining chair, a satisfied grin on his face. He was undulating strangely, and when Megan looked closer, she saw that parts of the chair were moving, rolling up and down his back.

"What the heck are you doing?" she asked.

"Cloud chair with Shiatsu massage option. You should try it, it's fantastic," Mark replied. "Come on down, grab some vapor, and make yourself at home."

Megan dived back down and landed gently on the cloud a few feet from Mark, who was now absorbed in monitoring the world he was floating through. Reaching down, Megan found that the cloud was malleable to her touch, like clay. Within seconds she had fashioned a free-floating hammock, and settled in with a sigh. The cloud hammock molded itself to her body, soft and warm. She could learn to like this scenario. From here they had a clear view of the entire Net Force site, the skeletonized buildings rising like half-finished skyscrapers. Megan guided her hammock over beside Mark, who was staring at a small window inset into the cloud in front of him.

"What's this?" she asked.

"I needed a way to figure out when the chameleon is going to go for the program, so I installed a peek program right at the node my decoy program is sitting in," Mark said. "I'll be able to see everyone who's trying to access that node, so we can hopefully let Daniel and Maj know exactly when they should be looking for the chameleon in real time."

"Great. If you can see who is doing this, we'll have enough evidence to go to Winters," Megan said. "Then Net Force can clear Daniel and Maj, and lock the real hacker away."

"Maybe, but don't forget, the chameleon has always used another Explorer's identity to hack. We're only going to know when he attacks, but not necessarily who he is. Even if it is someone on the inside, he's still not going to be himself," Mark said. "He's probably going to be disguised as a Net Force Explorer who is online when he does his hack."

"But we're Net Force Explorers, and we're online," Megan said. "That means that the hacker could appear to be—"

"—you or me," Mark said, his face grim. "And all we can do right now is wait and see if he uses one of us when it happens."

12

Maj stared at her short list of license plate numbers. Not one of those plates was in the Net Force parking lot. She'd looked everywhere. Daniel was scanning the parking lot with the camcorder.

"Recording the cars' plate numbers?" she asked. "I told you our suspects aren't here yet."

"Maybe, maybe not. If we're wrong about our suspects, if it's someone else, Mark wouldn't be able to give you a plate number. I want to make sure we have a full surveillance on the lot, and a record of everyone who comes and goes tonight. Even if we're right about our suspects, it's possible they've got another vehicle stashed that Net Force doesn't know about."

"No, Mark would have known that. None of our suspects has more than one vehicle registered to them," Maj replied

"Maybe they've only got one company car, which doesn't narrow it down much, because half these vehicles have government plates," Daniel said, "But if *you* were spying, would you want anyone to see you coming and going in the car you drive everyday? If I were a spy, I'd have a car nobody knew about stashed somewhere."

"Maybe, but a spy's entire purpose is to blend in, to do

the same things he does every day, not attracting suspicion,"
Maj said. She picked up the binoculars and slowly scanned
around the parking lot. "That means not showing up at Net
Force in a strange vehicle. Speaking of being a spy, where
did you get all of this stuff anyway? Don't tell me you're a
Peeping Tom in your spare time."

Daniel chuckled. "Hardly. I got the stuff from my dad. My
father started out in the Secret Service chasing counterfeiters.
He used to kid me all the time about going on a stakeout
with him, not that it would ever happen. Now that I get my
chance, he's not here. Anyway, I 'borrowed' all this from
him. He's out of town this week."

"Borrowed, eh? Does he even know you've got it?" Maj
asked.

"No, he doesn't, which is why neither of us is going to
drop and break anything," Daniel said. "Look, it's nothing
you have to worry about. It's my responsibility, all right?
Besides, I know if I had asked, his answer would have been
no. He's sure I'm guilty—I know I'm innocent. I'm doing
what I have to do to prove I'm right."

The headlights of a car entering the parking lot distracted
both of them. Daniel snatched up the camcorder and trained
it on the car and its driver, while Maj looked at the license
plate and compared it to her list.

"Nope, not this one, either," she said.

Daniel kept the camcorder running. Maj looked through
the night-vision binoculars at the glowing green driver as he
got out of his car. He was dressed in what looked like a
shapeless jumpsuit, with a small bag at his side.

"Looks like part of the night maintenance staff," Maj said.

"Yeah," Daniel said, following the man with his camcorder. "Best not to take chances, though."

The man entered the building, and Daniel lowered the digital recorder. "Like my dad always told me, now we come
to the exciting part."

"What's that?" Maj asked.

"Sitting on our butts for several hours hoping something
happens," Daniel replied.

"Oh." Maj reached for her backpack on the floor and

pulled out a foil container. "I brought some drinks. Would you like one?"

"Yeah, thanks. I was so busy getting everything else, I forgot about bringing anything to eat or drink." Daniel took the gel-pack and tabbed it open. "Cherry-lime-tangerine, my favorite. Thanks."

"I've got some granola bars as well, if you'd like," Maj said.

"Not right now. I'm too keyed up to eat," Daniel said.

Maj took a long swallow of her drink. She cracked her window a bit, feeling the cool wet air waft over her face. The rain had turned into a light mist that drifted in through the open window. Looking back at Daniel, she saw he was staring intensely at the parking lot.

"You and your father don't get along very well, do you?" she asked quietly.

Daniel didn't look at her. "What makes you say that?"

"Just the way you replied to my question about how you got the gear. I mean, it's really none of my business, so I'll just drop it if you want," Maj said.

"Why are you so interested? Do you think my dad's right? That I'm just a screwup?" Daniel said.

Maj turned in her seat to face him. "Daniel, you know that's not true. I'm here, aren't I? If we're caught, I've got just as much to lose as you do." The tension that had been simmering in her since the incident at the guard post suddenly boiled over. "Do you think I'd put my status as a Net Force Explorer on the line if I didn't believe in you? I need to clear my name, sure—but this is your plan, not mine. I'm here because I believe you can pull this off. Mark, Megan, and I are trying to help you, and we're letting you tell us what to do here. Would we do that if we didn't believe in you? Frack, why can't you just see a helping hand for what it is!" Maj crossed her arms and stared out her window at the parking lot.

For a few seconds the only sound in the car was the light patter of rain on its rooftop. Maj didn't look at Daniel when he first spoke.

"Sorry, you're absolutely right. Apparently, this just isn't my week for keeping friends on my side," Daniel said. "I shouldn't have jumped all over you when you were trying to be there for me. I can't do this alone. Besides, it would be a long walk back to your house in the rain."

Maj looked over at him, keeping her face stern. "So who said I'd be the one walking back? I'm the one in the driver's seat."

"Are you telling me the guard wouldn't believe you came to Net Force headquarters for a haircut, a gender change, and a tan?" Daniel asked, grinning. "He's probably so bored I could drive this zoomer out of here and he wouldn't notice."

"Let's not find out," Maj said, cracking a smile. "No more head games, eh?"

"Right," Daniel replied.

"So," Maj said, shifting back around in her seat, "what's going on? I mean, your home situation is clearly eating at you, but it hasn't gotten so bad that you've been booted out onto the street or anything, right?"

Daniel fiddled with his drink, then looked out his side window. "No . . . I don't know. We're just . . . I haven't talked about this with anyone except my mom."

"Perhaps a different point of view might help. I promise it won't go outside this car," Maj said.

"I'll hold you to that," Daniel said, looked at her for a long moment. Then he shrugged. "Why not? I've gone over it in my head a hundred times and I haven't gotten anywhere."

Daniel leaned back in his seat and looked at the zoomer's ceiling. Maj just waited. Finally he spoke. "Simply put, my father and I don't see eye to eye on a lot of things. He's constantly trying to mold me into a junior version of him, and, although I respect him for what he's done, I don't feel that I have to live my life the way he lives his."

"What do you mean 'mold you'? Is he trying to persuade you to join the Secret Service?" Maj asked.

"No, he's told me I could do whatever I want, well, as long as the career involved graduate school and a suit. The real problem is that he pressures me so much about school and career and the future, sometimes I feel like a lump of coal he's trying to squeeze into a diamond," Daniel said. "And right now I'm not sure I want to be a diamond. I mean, sure, I want to succeed at whatever I eventually decide to do, but I'm not going to head out into the career grind just yet. I need more time to explore the world, try things out, and see if I like them."

"So let me see if I've got this straight," Maj said. "You feel that your father is pressuring you too much about school and your future, whereas you just want him to lay off and let you find your own way."

"Exactly," Daniel said. "Yeah, that's it exactly. But no matter how hard I try to make him understand, he still feels compelled to treat me like I'm six years old. I've waited for years for him to realize that I'm not a kid anymore, but nothing changes. That's why I had to do this, to prove to him that I can take responsibility for myself. Otherwise I feel like I'm waiting for something that might never happen."

"Kind of like the situation we're in now?" Maj asked.

"What do you mean?" Daniel asked.

"Well, we're here because we think the chameleon might be pulling another infiltration, right? But we're not sure, so we're waiting to see if it happens. It sounds like you feel that your father will never give you the freedom you think you deserve. But you haven't taken off yet, because you're still waiting to see if he'll come around, right?"

"I guess so," Daniel replied.

"Do you feel that your father only wants what's best for you?" Maj asked.

"Yeah, he tells me that all the time," Daniel said. "Usually, right about the time he starts imposing impossible standards for me to live up to."

"Then why don't you accept what he says and get on with making him proud of you?" Maj asked.

"Because I can never do enough," Daniel said. "I bring home a report card with top marks, I don't get praised, I get moved into tougher classes. If I get a 'B' in any of those tougher classes, I'm grounded for life. I can't play on any of the school sports teams or have a part-time job, because according to him, that would be a 'distraction' which would interfere with my schoolwork. Frack, he even sees the Net Force Explorers as just something else I can add to my résumé. It seems every decision in my life hasn't even been made by me, but by him."

"You feel trapped by your father making decisions you should make?" Maj asked.

"Sometimes I'm amazed I can breathe without asking his permission," Daniel said. "And before you start, I have tried to talk to him about it, a lot of times. But he just ignores my arguments or sidesteps them, saying that he knows what's best for me. Well, unless he's suddenly become a mind reader, he doesn't have any idea what's best for me, because only I know that."

"That's very true," Maj said. "Now all you have to do is convince your father of that fact."

"Yeah, but how can I do that, when he won't even listen to me?" Daniel asked.

"There has to be some way," Maj said. "There must be some thing that your father would automatically respond to, some event or trigger that would guarantee him snapping to and paying attention. You've just got to figure out what that trigger is."

"Humph, you'd think me getting suspended from the Explorers would be enough to make him listen to me, but even then, he shut me out. He's convinced I'm guilty," Daniel said. "Maybe now you can see why finding out who did this is so important to me. It's not just because of what I would lose if I got kicked out of the Net Force Explorers, but so that I can prove to my father I'm capable. It would show him that I *can* handle any trouble I get into myself, and that I can make my own decisions."

"Maybe that's the silver lining in this whole mess. If you can bust this chameleon, and *show* your father that you're worthy of more responsibility, he's bound to recognize your accomplishments."

"Yeah, or else he'll ground me until I'm fifty," Daniel said. "I hope it's what you just said, otherwise I don't know how I'll survive being grounded until college. I'm sometimes afraid I'll just bust out, run away . . ."

Just then the glare of approaching headlights caused both Daniel and Maj to look out the windshield, grabbing camcorder and binoculars as they tracked another car into the parking lot. It pulled into a space a few yards away from the janitor's car, and a figure clad in a black trench coat got out.

"Can you see his face?" Daniel asked, thumbing the zoom on his camcorder.

"No, his back is to me now, so I can't get a good visual on him," Maj said. "His license plate doesn't match our list, either, but it's a government vehicle, so, like you said, anybody could be driving it."

"Well, that's two possibilities for our chameleon who aren't on our suspect list, plus everyone who was already here when we arrived," Daniel said. He lifted both the transmitter and datapad off the floor near his seat and put them on the dashboard. "I figure our chameleon will go for the program and then probably split soon after. So all we have to do is wait for Mark and Megan to signal when the program has been activated, watch for the next person to come out, and trail them."

"Sounds great, but how are you going to plant the bug on the right car when you don't even know which one the chameleon came in?"

Daniel hefted a pair of small foam devices that looked like hearing aids with tiny microphones attached. "When Mark notifies us of what's happening, I'll get out and hide in between those cars over there. If it's one of the two guys who just arrived, that'll put me within striking distance of both their cars. As soon as you see the target come out, whisper who it is to me, and I'll plant the bug."

"And if it's not one of the people we've seen so far?" Maj asked.

"The chameleon may have been here for a few hours before we got here. I agree that this is a long shot. But I know Mark's watching his own program. With any luck, Mark should be able to figure out who it is, and give us the right plate number in time. But if not, then I'll just have to improvise," Daniel said.

"That's fine, as long as you don't do anything stupid," Maj replied. "I don't want to be dragged down into a nasty mess of *your* making.

Daniel looked at her. "You don't pull any punches, do you?"

"Not when it's my butt on the line. You're not the only one involved in this, you know." Maj looked at the silent foilpack next to her.

"I hate waiting around. I wish it would happen already," Daniel said.

Just then the foilpack beeped insistently. Both Daniel and Maj stared at it for a moment.

"Be careful what you ask for, you just might get it," Maj said as she picked it up and flipped it open.

Up among the clouds, both Mark and Megan were bored stiff. After a half hour of absolutely nothing happening, their attention had started to wander. The major distraction had started when Mark had scooped up a handful of cloud, molded it into a ball, and tossed it at Megan. The cloud ball had disintegrated upon impact, bursting in thousands of tiny chilly droplets on her face and arms.

"Squirt!" Of course, Megan had immediately retaliated, grabbing her own handful of cloud and hurling it at the smaller boy. Soon balls of water vapor were flying through the air, making the area look like a giant cotton candy machine had exploded.

"Hold it, hold it," Megan said, dropping the massive cloud ball she had been about to throw. "Shouldn't we be watching for the program to come out of Net Force HQ?"

Mark wiped off several wisps of cloud and shook his head. "I already told you, I've got peek programs set up all around the site as well as on the program itself. If anything even twitches down there, we'll know about it."

"But what if the chameleon camouflages his signal in a way you don't expect?" Megan asked.

"Why would he?" Mark asked back. "First of all, if he is here, he's under the guise of someone else. Second, he thinks he's safe from detection, so there's no need for him, as Joe Anonymous, to disguise an innocuous package he datadumps."

"I'm glad you understand the criminal mind so well," Megan said, frowning. "I'm going to watch anyway." She flopped down on the cloud and focused on the Net Force site, which was nearly deserted.

"You're just mad because I kept pegging you, that's all," Mark said, but he sat down beside her and studied the Net Force site as well, idly playing with the last handful of cloud he had grabbed.

"What are all those different colored glowing lines radiating out from Net Force HQ?" Megan asked.

"Oh, those are the monitoring systems Net Force uses to scan and track the various major networks across America," Mark said. "The green is financial, military is blue, industrial yellow, government red, etc. The specialized subroutines process data all the time. That's why it looks like they're spreading out from under the building in all different directions."

"Why couldn't the chameleon be using one of those pipelines as a conduit to transfer his information?" Megan asked. "I would think that would be a perfect cover."

"Two reasons. First, these are highly encrypted monitoring systems, and any attempt to download actual data through them would appear as a big red flag. Second, if he had, I'm sure Jo would have found the access point and put a houndbot prog on it. Our guy's too smart for that."

"How do you know so much about what this guy is or isn't going to do?" Megan asked.

"Simple," Mark replied. "He's really good. And that's how I would do it."

"Oh," Megan said. She returned her gaze to the Net Force site, and from there she looked out at the vast virtual horizon and the hundreds of lights that studded the landscape, each one illuminating its own web portal. Below, tiny lights crisscrossed the empty space as night-shift web commuters traveled from site to site. Above them, those who chose to fly soared through the night sky, using everything from dirigibles to the backs of pterodactyls.

"Funny, it looks peaceful from up here," Megan said, looking down at all the lights.

"Yeah, too bad that can change in the blink of an eye," Mark said, nudging her and pointing. "And speaking of blinks, I think we've got something. Data dump at six o'clock. My program warning just went off."

Megan looked at the Net Force site, which had suddenly grown a small dot of light on its southern wall. As she and

Mark watched, the dot zoomed out across the landscape, leaving a glowing, easily visible white trail behind it.

"That's it! Call Maj and Daniel and tell them to be ready," Mark said, frantically activating programs on his screen while trying to keep an eye on the white dot. "He's going in on a maintenance system, not even using a main access line like he did before. If he's impersonating someone else, then I'll bet he's not going to stay in HQ very long. Whoever it is, this guy's really good. I'm almost through his proxy. Come on, come on, who are you?"

"Mark, let's go," Megan said.

"Just a second, I've almost got him," Mark said, tossing program icons onto the screen. "There, it's . . . Harry Jameson? Who the frack is that?" Mark asked. "Where's the Net Force database when I need it! Name: Jameson, Harry. Show file."

Mark and Megan waited for the nanoseconds the system took to spit out the information. It seemed like years. But finally—

"A janitor? Our hack is a janitor?" Mark's face lit up as comprehension dawned. "A janitor! Where is— He just logged off!"

Mark leaped off the cloud and into the air in pursuit.

"Tell Daniel and Maj to watch for the janitor!" Megan yelled to her foilpack connection as she followed Mark. "Maj, we just spotted a dump. We're following it now. We think it's a guy named Harry Jameson, a janitor. Watch for anyone leaving the headquarters dressed like a janitor or maintenance person in the next few minutes. Call you later." She faintly heard Maj reply as she sped to catch up with Mark. Together the two flew faster and faster, gaining on the speeding point of light in the distance.

13

"I got it, Megan. Thanks, and good luck," Maj said. She closed the foilpack and grabbed a headset, inserting the foam plug into her ear. "They're following the signal now. Megan said to watch for someone leaving dressed like a janitor in the next few minutes. The ID on this hack was a guy named Harry Jameson, and that's what he does here at Net Force."

"It would be useful if our guy in the jumpsuit is the guy. We already know exactly where his car is." Daniel had already slipped on the other headset and was adjusting the microphone. He grabbed the transmitter and datapad from the dashboard and glanced at Maj. "I'm going to head outside and test our reception." He flipped the switch that turned off the overhead dome light, opened the door, and stepped outside, quietly closing the door behind him.

"Testing, one, two. Maj, do you copy this?" Daniel whispered as he looked around, then slowly started walking toward the cars in the parking lot.

"Loud and clear. Hey, what if Net Force is monitoring radio communications?" Maj asked.

"Don't worry, the Secret Service wouldn't be any good if it didn't have some secrets, right? Our communications are scrambled, translated only between your set and mine. Any eavesdropper will just hear static," Daniel said as he eased over to a minivan at the far end of the lot. "Okay, this is the best I can do. From here I should be able to reach just about all of the cars in the lot fairly quickly. Keep scanning the entrance and let me know who comes out. From there I'll bug the car and then we'll just follow him home."

"Okay," Maj said, snatching up the binoculars from beside her. She focused them on the main doors of the building and watched. The rain had stopped, but a fine mist still filled the air, making the parking lot seem shrouded in gloom. Maj steadied her hands and kept watching the doors, waiting for something to happen.

"Anything yet?" the voice in her ear made Maj start.

"I'll let you know. It'll take him a few minutes to get out of the building if he's going to leave, you know," Maj said. "Now keep quiet and stay alert."

After that the two teens fell silent, watching and waiting. A car pulled into the lot and parked, and a woman got out and headed inside.

Several minutes after that the doors swung open, and a figure dressed in a jumpsuit carrying a duffel bag walked out. Maj grabbed the digital camera and zoomed in on the man's face, but it was obscured by a billed cap.

"Daniel, it looks like a janitor is coming out. He's coming your way," Megan said.

"Is it the guy we saw coming in? Is he going toward his car?" Daniel's insistent whisper came in her ear.

"I can't tell, it looks like he is ... no, wait, he's heading toward a different one, farther away from you," Maj said. "This must be a different janitor than the one we spotted."

"That's just great! Which car is it? I can't see, so I'm moving forward," Daniel said.

"Keep low, you don't want to be spotted," Maj said as she saw Daniel bend over, ducking behind the cars as he crouch-walked toward the jumpsuited janitor. She tried to keep one eye on him and one on the approaching man at the same time "I think he's heading toward the maroon sedan at the end of the row you're on. Be careful."

Daniel trotted, still bent over, toward the end of the row. "I think I see it. Where is he now?"

"Daniel, that's the car. He's almost there. Slow down or he'll see you," Maj said, following the janitor with the digital recorder. She panned over to see Daniel one car over, about to creep around to the rear of the janitor's sedan.

The janitor walked to the driver's door of his car. He kept going however, heading toward the trunk. Daniel was just about to round the corner of the next car.

"Freeze, Daniel, don't move!" Maj whispered. "He's heading toward the trunk."

Daniel shrank back into the shadow of the vehicle he was hiding behind. Maj saw him reach into his pocket and bring out what she assumed to be the transmitter.

The janitor opened his trunk, slung the bag inside, and closed the lid, pushing down hard to make sure the trunk locked. He then went to the driver's door, opened it, and got inside.

"Go, now," Maj whispered. She watched as Daniel duck-walked to the rear of the car and reached underneath. The car's lights came on, and a second later the engine started. It must have been a gasohol-electric hybrid, because after a few seconds the noise of the engine died off to almost nothing.

By this time Daniel had finished fiddling underneath the car and was trotting, still bent over, to the vehicle on the other side of the janitor's car. The janitor turned on his headlights, and the car slowly moved out of the parking lot toward the gate. As soon as it was far enough away, Daniel ran back to the zoomer and motioned to Maj to start it up.

"Pop the trunk and let's go," he said.

"You think this is the guy?" Maj asked.

"He's leaving at the right time, and he's dressed for the part, right? Until Mark works his magic, nothing we do is certain. But it can't hurt to trail the most likely suspect we've got out here in the real world, can it? Now let's get going before we lose him," Daniel said as he headed for the trunk. A second later Maj felt the car sway under the added weight, and then the trunk lid slammed down. She started the zoomer and headed for the checkpoint, her fingers tightening on the steering wheel.

* * *

Mark and Megan had pulled up to the racing dot of light. So far, it was following a fairly simple path, staying on the main information lines, not pulling any evasive maneuvers.

"Why can't we just follow the trail it leaves?" Megan asked.

"Because," Mark said, "I want to keep track of it the whole time, in case our chameleon tries to switch signals on us."

"I thought you said he didn't suspect anything," Megan replied.

"Even if he doesn't, a good hacker is always careful," Mark said. "And this guy is very good. I'm recording this whole thing, so we can all go over it later."

Even as he spoke, the light dot suddenly veered off directly toward a large corporation's Web site, heading straight for the side of the Net building. Mark followed, diving down toward the skyscraper wall. Megan was right behind him, her heart pounding. Even though Mark had turned off the wind, she still thought she felt a breeze wash over her face and hair as she rushed closer to the ground.

"Um, Mark, isn't that a building?" she asked as they flew closer to the site the program had passed through.

"Yeah, it's a common hacker technique, called laundering the program," Mark called back to her. "Data is fed through another site, usually one with a lot of high-volume data streams, to confuse any potential traces. The hacker is hoping the program will get lost in the massive data shuffle. Some hackers tag their breaks to do this automatically, like this guy did. Fortunately, he didn't count on me following him."

"That's great, but won't they discom us if we go in through the wall?" Megan asked.

"Nopraw. When you fly Gridley Air, you fly prepared. Watch carefully," Mark said, taking what looked like a small piece of black felt and throwing it ahead of him. The felt expanded into a circular hole about three meters across. "Fly through," Mark called, aiming himself straight for the hole.

Megan looked down just in time to see the program hit the side of the building and enter. Sucking in a breath, she flew toward the inky blackness.

A second later they were inside. Megan looked around, scanning the skeletonized code of the building for Mark.

"Meg, hurry! Down here," Mark called from below. Megan looked down to see Mark standing next to what looked like a brightly colored manhole. As she flew down and landed neatly beside him, she also noticed that the light trail led up to the hole and disappeared into it.

"Just in time. The program's entered the data stream leading out of this site. We're going in after it."

"What about your vaunted tracking program?" Maj asked, hands on her hips.

"Hey, who knew he was this much of a 'noid? Even I'm not right all the time, although if you tell anybody else I said that, I'll deny everything. Now jump!" Mark said, leaping into the hole. Megan stepped forward as well, and was sucked into the data stream, both of them vanishing from the site as if they had never existed.

Maj slowly approached the guard post, trying to keep an eye on the janitor's car, which had just turned the corner onto the highway, and the guard, who was watching her approach.

"Evening, Miss Green," the guard said as he took her passcard and scanned it again. Maj flashed what she hoped was a smile at him.

The Marine handed her card back and activated the gate. "Have a good evening."

"You, too," Maj said, and this time her smile was genuine. The gate opened, and she pressed the accelerator pedal, easing the zoomer out of the drive and onto the highway.

Once they were out of sight of headquarters, Maj thumped on the passenger seat as she floored the pedal, sending the little car speeding forward. A few seconds later Daniel extricated himself from the trunk area, and climbed into the seat next to her.

"Where is he?" were the first words out of his mouth.

"Relax, he's just over the next hill," Maj said, leaning back and letting the car coast down into the valley. "We don't want to get too close. After all, it's not like there's a lot of traffic to blend into at this hour."

"Yeah, you're right," Daniel said, not even glancing at her. All of his concentration was focused on the tiny taillights of the car ahead of them. "I hope you recorded that whole thing in the parking lot."

"Yeah, I got him. Got you, too," Maj replied with a tight smile. "Nice moves."

"Thanks." Without looking, Daniel reached for the small tracker datapad and turned it on. Immediately the car was filled with a soft beeping noise, and Daniel showed her the pad with a small red dot slowly moving toward a map of Washington, D.C. "Looks like he's heading into town."

Maj nodded. "And we're right behind him."

Except for the two cars, the road was deserted. Their target was driving leisurely, staying around the speed limit, like he didn't have a care in the world. Maj was careful to stay pretty far behind him. Neither of them said anything, each too intent on what they were doing. Daniel in particular kept looking at the hacker's car as if he thought it might disappear if he took his eyes off of it, glancing only occasionally at the data-pad in his lap.

They continued like that for a while, a two-car convoy heading into the city. After a few minutes Maj and Daniel could see the glow from the lights of Washington, D.C. The hacker's car kept going, up Highway 95 into the outskirts of Alexandria. There he got on the I-495 interchange and headed north.

"Keep following, but keep a few cars behind him," Daniel said as they sped up to merge with traffic.

"All right. You still tracking him?" Maj asked.

"Yeah, the transmitter has a ten kilometer range, and we'll never be that far away. Here's our exit," Daniel said, pointing.

Maj took the off-ramp and turned onto the interstate. Even at this hour, traffic was still fairly heavy here, with massive freight-hauling trucks jockeying for position with the passenger vehicle traffic on the road.

"Let's get closer. You can speed up. The police almost never patrol here," Daniel said.

"How do you know?" Maj asked.

"My parents and I got stranded out here about midnight last year. It took the police almost forty minutes to get to us," Daniel replied. "They said then that they rarely patrol this area."

"Didn't someone come from Annandale?" Maj asked, noting the exit sign for the suburb they were coming up on. The car they were following wasn't currently visible, blocked from view by a couple of the big trucks.

"The cop that finally arrived *was* from Annandale," Daniel said.

"Oh. I can't see anything here. Check the transmitter and tell me how our boy's doing," Maj said.

"He just passed Braddock Road, heading due north," Daniel replied.

"Good, like he doesn't have a care in the world," Maj said. "I hope Mark and Megan are doing as well."

"I'm sure they're fine. Frack, they've got the easy part," Daniel said with a shrug. "If they run into trouble, they can just log off. We're the ones following the suspected spy all over hill and dale. I'd switch places with them any day."

"That's about the smartest thing you've said all night," Maj said. "But let's concentrate on what we're doing now." Maj glanced around. "I've already bent or broken enough parental rules tonight to last me for the next several years."

"All right, all right, fair enough," Daniel said, checking the datapad again. "Wait a minute, this can't be right," Daniel said, looking closely at the small screen. "According to this, we just lost him."

Megan fell through the manhole and landed on a large rubber raft floating in the middle of the coursing stream of data. Looking around, she found that the pipeline had turned into a steaming rain forest, with tall jungle trees forming an unbroken canopy of green overhead. The noises of strange jungle animals filled the lush foliage around her. Mark was already sitting at the bow of the boat, paddle in hand.

"Grab one of these and I'll get us going," Mark said.

Megan saw a paddle at her feet and picked it up. By the time she had it, the raft was already swiftly moving down the multicolored information river. "Why do I need this if we're following the current?"

"You'll need it for those," Mark said, pointing ahead of

the raft. A few yards ahead, the water seemed to boil and churn as dozens of something moved angrily under its surface.

"What did you expect from a travel agency specializing in jungle tours? Hang on, here we go!" Mark said as he rose up on his knees and held his paddle like a baseball bat. Megan followed suit, and then the raft entered the area of frothing water.

As soon as it did, dozens of small round fish erupted from the river and began flying around them, swooping in to attack one of the two kids. When Megan got a closer look at them, she saw that their gaping mouths were filled with needle-sharp teeth. Mark immediately began swatting them out of the air. Megan gasped and began swinging wildly, cutting through the scores of hungry flapping fish.

"What the frack are these?" she yelled to Mark as she slammed another scaled monstrosity back into the water.

"Security tags. If one bites you, they're like a homing beacon to the company's security systems, letting them know exactly where you are whenever you're on the Net. They're usually very hard to dislodge. Look out!"

Megan turned, just in time to see one of the fish heading straight for her face. Her martial arts reflexes kicked in, and she swung her paddle, connecting solidly with the scaled creature and sending it careening away from her.

"That's what I need, balance," Megan said. She spread her knees apart and waited for the fish to come to her, using the paddle like a staff to block and slap the flying horrors away. Another few seconds and they were out of the roiling water.

"Nice," Mark said, scooping up an errant fish that had landed in the raft near him and flipping it over the side. "But we're not out of the jungle yet."

"What would have happened if we hadn't been on the raft?" Megan asked.

"We'd be swimming, of course," Mark said, wincing at the thought. "Until we were eaten alive, anyway. Is it just me, or is the wind picking up?"

Megan looked around and saw that the tree trunks around them were starting to sway back and forth. She brushed her hair out of her face, only to have the wind blow it right back over her eyes. "Is there any way we can get this thing to move faster?"

"We could actually paddle, but I don't think that will help. Wait a minute, I think we're coming to the exit point," Mark said, craning his head to try and see what was ahead of them.

Megan crawled to the front of the raft as well. "The wind's died down now," she said.

"Yeah, but what's that roaring noise?" Mark said. "Uh-oh."

"That doesn't mean what I think it means, does it?" Megan asked.

"Hold on *really* tight now," Mark said, grabbing the safety ropes on the raft. "We're going over—"

By this time the roaring noise was so loud that Megan couldn't hear the rest of Mark's sentence. She didn't need to, however, because she could see what was coming up.

The falls were about fifty yards ahead, and approaching fast—too fast to avoid. The river seemed to disappear, dropping off into nothingness as the water poured over what looked like an endlessly churning white-water death trap. Megan barely had time to grab a rope of her own and open her mouth to scream before the raft shot out over the falls and plummeted wildly into the cloud of white spray at the waterfall's bottom—

—And like that they were out of the jungle simulation and standing on a featureless gray plain.

"That was certainly one of the strangest security programs I've ever seen. Give me your standard anti-intruder missiles and houndprogs any day," Mark said. "Can you pross that some of the lubefoots actually datasurf stuff like that for fun? They just ride along and hold contests by picking a certain point on the Web and seeing who can pipeline surf closest to it."

Megan slowly nodded her head. "Yeah, like you've never done it yourself. Hey, why aren't we following the blip anymore?"

"Because I know where it went, and I'm not even going to try and follow it," Mark said. "I stopped when I saw where it was headed. Don't worry, you can't miss it. Come on, I'll show you."

Mark and Megan rose into the air. A few seconds later they were following the glowing trail again, flying toward what looked like a massive wall of mirrors that stretched across the horizon as far as the eye could see. The mirrors stretched upward as well, a solid, unbroken wall of virtual glass. Mark and Megan saw their reflections, first as tiny dots, then slowly growing larger as they approached. Web traffic was nonexistent here, as if no one dared to violate the awesome monolith of silver and glass. Mark's program faded into nonexistence a few yards before the mirrors.

"What is this place?" Megan asked, looking all around. "And why isn't your program affecting it?"

"Honestly, I don't know why my program isn't working. This," Mark indicated with a sweep of his arms, "is the virtual headquarters of Techtronix. From here, employees with the proper clearance can access data on any one of TT's dozens of manufacturing plants, factories, businesses, and other information, depending on who you are. I don't think they need all this space, but they like to show off. And, you have to admit, it *is* impressive."

"Yeah, it is at that," Megan agreed. "You're sure the program went in there?"

"Yeah, I'm sure. All data going into and coming out of Techtronix is shielded automatically with some of the best encryption code money can buy. That's why it seems so quiet here. We can't see any of the data coming or going," Mark said. "Even a houndprog couldn't follow that program in there. I'd rather try to break into Net Force HQ over a foil-pack than attempt to hack that sec wall."

"So our hacker at Net Force is working for Techtronix," Megan said.

"That's what it looks like so far," Mark said. "Unfortunately, this is as far as we're going."

"Really?" Megan asked. "But I thought you were good?" she said with a sardonic smile.

Mark, still staring up at the great wall of mirrors, didn't seem to notice. "Good, sure. Suicidal, no way. I've heard rumors . . . nothing official, understand, but there are whispers on the Net that Techtronix goes after hackers who try to break into their sites in a nasty way. They're not content with stopping intruders. They want them rubbed out, off the Net forever. Site wipeout viruses, data corrupters, that kind of thing."

"That's illegal. Those are just Netrumors flying around," Megan said, although she looked around uneasily as she did so.

"Maybe it's illegal—but so is treason. From what we've seen tonight, that doesn't seem to bother them. I'm not going to find out what else they're capable of the hard way," Mark said.

"So what now? Our search just ends here?" Megan asked. "No real results?"

"Well, my program is supposed to broadcast its location back to Net Force headquarters whenever anyone tries to access it, but I doubt that's going to happen. The Techtronix programmers will have it isolated six ways from Sunday. All we know for sure is that it's stopped here. I've been monitoring the perimeter, and nothing resembling it has come out in the past few minutes."

"Assuming you'd even recognize it," Megan said.

"Of course I would, there wasn't enough time to change it that much. No, it stopped here. Come on, let's fly, and hope that Daniel and Maj had better luck," Mark said, taking off and hovering in the air for a second. Megan took one last look at the silent, towering mirrorwall, and flew up to join Mark in the air.

"What? What do you mean, we lost him?" Maj asked.

"I mean," Daniel said, showing her the datapad, now blank and silent, "We've lost him. He's not on the tracker screen. See if you can get around those trucks and get a visual."

Maj took her eyes off the road for a second and glanced at the small screen. Sure enough, there was no small red dot that marked the janitor's car on it. She sped up and passed the trucks which had blocked her vision. There was no maroon sedan anywhere in sight.

"How could this happen? Is that thing working right?" Maj asked.

"Yes, it was fine up until a minute ago. Then he just vanished," Daniel said. "Look, there're two exit ramps he could have taken, so let's backtrack and take one and hope it's the right choice."

"Yeah, and then which direction do we go, right or left?" Maj said.

"All right, you've got a point. Let's not panic just yet," Daniel said. "This could be just a temporary lost signal. Let's keep going and maybe we'll pick him up again."

"You hope," Maj said, but she got off at the next exit, turned around, and hit the first of the two possible roads their hacker could have used. The silence in the car grew longer and longer, neither Daniel or Maj daring to make a sound in case they might drown out the beep of the tracker.

After many minutes, and after trying both possible roads for miles in either direction, Maj sighed. "Face it, Daniel, we lost him."

Daniel was still staring at the datascreen.

"Daniel?" Maj said, thinking, *Oh boy, he's lost it. He's gonna freak*!

Then she heard it.

The tracker was beeping again.

"Yes!" Daniel said. "We got him!"

"Where?" Maj asked.

"He's about two kilometers behind us. There, there's a cross lane coming up. We can turn there," Daniel said.

"I see it," Maj replied, cranking the wheel over. The zoomer made the turn, and Maj quickly merged with the traffic. She pushed the accelerator to the floor and sent the car speeding down the road, both of them searching for any sign of their target.

"We're just about parallel with him, so he's on a surface road, heading in the same direction," Daniel said.

"Which way?" Maj asked.

"Go right at the lights," Daniel said. "We're about a half-kilometer away from him. Wait, he's stationary now. Be ready to park and look inconspicuous if we get too close to him."

They drove on in silence for a couple of minutes, each searching the road intently. Suddenly Daniel pointed. "There it is. Right there!"

Maj immediately pulled off the road and shut off the engine. Daniel had the digital camera up to his eye and was scanning the dark car ahead of them, sitting off the road next to a park-and-ride lot.

"No lights, and the engine's not running. I can't see any movement in the front or backseat. I think he's out of here. But I don't like this," Daniel said as he put the camcorder down, pulled a pair of leather gloves from his pocket, and began slipping them on.

"Why? So he gave us the slip and grabbed another car," Maj said. "It's annoying, but at least we're not going to get killed by a mad hacker out here in the dark. Why are you so worried?"

"Why would he leave this car here, where it's sure to be found, ticketed, and towed, rather than in the park-and-ride lot? He wants this car found. But why?"

"Shouldn't we call someone?" Maj asked.

"Who? The police? Maybe, once we know something's really wrong, other than that we've lost our guy. You want to tell them we've been tailing a car that we think, though we've got no evidence that'll stand up in a court of law, might hold a world-class hacker, and then we lost it, and now we've found it, and it's parked and empty and we're worried?"

Meg shook her head. "Not when you put it like that."

"Me, neither. I don't want to call the cops unless I have to. We're certainly not going to call anybody at Net Force, either," Daniel said, "until we know there's something really wrong here, something more than our guy getting into a nice, prepared getaway vehicle in this lot, and driving away and losing us."

"What are you going to do?" Maj asked.

"The only thing I can think of," Daniel said. "Check out the car." He slipped a small black object that resembled a flat flashlight with two tiny gleaming metal prongs on one end out of his pocket.

"What's that?" Maj asked.

For an answer, Daniel pressed a small button on the side of the device. A blue arc of electricity crackled between the prongs.

"Stun gun—60,000 volts here, more than enough to drop someone twice this guy's size," Daniel said.

"I thought you said we were only going to follow him," Maj said. "We were just going to see where he goes, then report back."

"We did follow him. And I don't think he's here. Don't worry, I'm not going to try and take him on or anything. I carry this around all the time for self-defense. Got mugged and assaulted once, and my folks wanted to make sure it didn't happen again. But it also comes in handy for times like this," Daniel said. "When I'm not sure what I'm gonna find."

"You're not going to go out there, are you?" Maj asked.

"Yes, I am. I'm going to find out what I can about this guy, one way or another," Daniel replied, cracking the door open. "That car's evidence."

Maj did the same on her side. "Then I'm coming with you. My reputation's on the line, just the same as yours."

Daniel looked at her for a moment, then shrugged. "Fine. It's your neck. After all that martial arts training, you're probably more dangerous in a fight than I am, anyway. Come on."

The two teens eased out of the zoomer and softly closed their doors. Maj looked across at Daniel, who pointed to the rear of the sedan, then himself and pantomimed walking over. She nodded.

Daniel crept along the side of the road to the rear of the other car, then waved Maj to follow. She did so, staying as low as possible. Once at the back of the car, Daniel pointed to the passenger side, then to her, then to his eyes, indicating she should watch that side from where she was. Maj nodded, feeling sweat break out on her brow. Her heart was hammering in her chest, and it was suddenly much harder to breathe.

Daniel gripped the stun gun tighter and crouch-walked toward the driver's side door. When he got there, he took a deep breath and reached for the door handle. Maj tried to divide her attention between Daniel and the passenger side of the car, her gaze flicking back and forth.

Daniel seemed to mentally count to himself for a few

beats, then wrenched the door open and looked inside, his stun gun raised and ready to zap anything that moved. Maj held her breath, waiting for the sounds of a struggle, a yell, anything. When several seconds passed without any noise whatsoever, she cautiously peeked her head over.

Daniel was standing outside the car, looking at her. "He's gone. He's really gone! Damn it!" he shouted, slamming his fist on the roof of the car.

Maj straightened as well, feeling the stiffness as the long night of sitting finally caught up with her. "Hey, all's not lost yet, Daniel. We've got the license plate of this vehicle, and I'm sure Mark can trace who it belongs to. We're not beaten yet, not by a long shot. Trust me on that, okay?"

Daniel looked at her, the angry gleam in his eyes slowly fading. "Yeah, maybe you're right." He held up his hand, his thumb and forefinger a centimeter apart. "But we were *this* close to him, and he got away. He must have had a second vehicle here at the park-and-ride lot to use once he dumped this one."

"Our chameleon is good, I'll give him that," Maj said. "Come on, maybe we'll get lucky, too, and he left something behind. Are the keys in the ignition?"

Daniel bent over and looked. "No, but I've found the trunk release. Maybe he left that bag."

Maj looked back in time to see the trunk lid pop up. "You don't suppose—"

"What, that he's hiding in the trunk? Please," Daniel replied, walking and meeting her behind the car, reaching for the lid, and pulling it up.

The interior of the car trunk was a mess, overflowing with books, blankets, cleaning supplies, papers, jumper cables, and boxes. Every inch of space was filled right to the top in a disorganized jumble.

"Some janitor, he can't even keep his own car clean. Backseat's the same way," Daniel said, putting the stun gun away and reaching down to sort through some of the mess. He started rooting through the stuff while Maj watched for oncoming cars. She heard a grunt from Daniel, then a startled yelp, and she looked back in time to see him drop a large flat box and backpedal away from the trunk, groping for the stun gun in his jacket.

"What's in there?" Maj said, and before he could answer, she peered into the trunk.

There, nestled among the brushes and spark plugs, was what looked like a human hand. Working carefully, Maj pulled a couple of more things out of the trunk, exposing first the arm, then the rest of the man it belonged to.

Daniel and Maj had just found their first body.

14

Maj's hand flew to her mouth, and she backed away to stand beside Daniel, who had stopped several feet away from the car. Neither of them spoke for a minute, unable to take their eyes away from the trunk and its contents.

"Did you touch anything?" Daniel asked.

"What?" Maj asked.

"I said, did you touch anything?" Daniel asked. "I need to know if you left any fingerprints."

"How can you ask me that after what we just saw?" Maj asked incredulously.

He turned and grabbed her by the shoulders, making sure she was looking directly at him. "Because right now, thinking about anything *but* that is the only thing that's keeping me from screaming, all right?"

"All right. Now let go," Maj said, her voice rising.

Daniel relaxed and released her. "I'm sorry. You see a thousand dead bodies on the Holovids or in virtual, but it's nothing like the real thing."

"Yeah, and it's not something I want to repeat any time soon," Maj said.

"Remember what I said about not calling the police," Daniel said, getting his foilpack out and flipping it open. "Well, I was wrong."

"I thought they'd be the last ones you'd call," Maj said.

"Maybe before this, but we're in way over our heads here. We're up against a killer, and we need all the help we can get. If we don't tell anyone, then he's free to come and go at Net Force as he pleases. Besides, if they don't believe this evidence, I might as well give up," Daniel said, dialing a number.

"I hope you're calling Net Force, too," Maj asked.

"Don't worry, I am. I'd like Captain Winters to get here first if possible. I'm going to need to lay out what we've found so far so he can stick up for me—us—when the police arrive. I'm not going to let you get into any more trouble on my account."

"How are you going to get ahold of Winters at this time of night?" Maj asked.

"By calling the one person whose father can contact him anywhere," Daniel said. "Hi, Mark? Yeah, it's me. You're not going to believe what we just found. . . ."

Four hours later the only thought on Daniel's mind was *I wish I'd never made that phone call.*

He was sitting in a cramped interrogation room at the Annandale police station with a scowling Captain Winters and Detective Robert Mercer, and he was heartily sick of the whole thing. He was also dreading the prospect of having to face his father over this. His mother had gotten through to his father at Langley, and he'd stopped by and picked her up on the way here. They were probably burning rubber to get here just to yell at him again, maybe this time even boot him out of the house, if he was lucky. *At least things can't get any worse*, Daniel thought.

"Daniel, let's go over this one more time," Detective Mercer said.

Whoops, wrong again, he groaned inwardly.

"Remember that you're not under arrest or being charged with anything at this time, so anything you say is completely voluntary," Detective Mercer said. "Do you understand?"

Daniel nodded. "I understand. So . . . from the beginning . . .

Madeline Greene and I had been following the driver of this car because we suspected him of illegally downloading classified documents from Net Force. We followed him to the freeway exit, where we lost him for a few minutes. After picking up his signal again, we found the car parked where you saw it on the side of the road. While we were trying to learn what had happened to the suspect, we opened the trunk and discovered the body," he said, watching his spoken words automatically transcribed on the monitor on the far wall.

"After you 'picked up his signal'?" the detective asked.

"Yeah, I had placed a tracking device on his car so we would be able to trace him without too much trouble. I didn't want to get too close to him. I was afraid he might be dangerous."

"When did you first suspect somebody inside of Net Force of removing classified data?" Detective Mercer asked.

"After my online identity was used to facilitate a hack I had no part in at Net Force Headquarters," Daniel answered. *How many times do we have to go through this?* he thought. He had always believed that long, drawn-out interrogation scenes were just fiction dreamed up for the HoloNet. After tonight, he would never make that mistake again.

"You say you weren't responsible for hacking into Net Force, that this man you were following was the hacker, but you don't know his identity?" Detective Mercer said.

"Correct. We set a trap for the hacker, and the trap was sprung. I've got footage of this guy leaving Net Force right after the most recent hack. It's on the digital camera I was using to record who came and went in the parking lot," Daniel said. "We were staking out the parking lot, waiting for a hack, and waiting to see who came out after the hack to figure out who was responsible. The Net Force guys took the vid feed back to the lab."

The detective looked at Captain Winters, who said, "The boy is correct. That information is currently in Net Force's possession. After we've looked at it and determined that it doesn't pose a threat to security at headquarters, we'll send you a copy. At the very least, we'll send you every usable shot of the perp."

"Thank you for your cooperation," Detective Mercer said, his mouth twisting. Daniel looked at Captain Winters's grim expression. *It's obvious these two don't like each other much.*

"Daniel, you say that you had never seen this dead man before?" Winter said.

"Yeah, I guess so. I mean, from what Mark said, he was a maintenance person at Net Force. You just . . . don't notice those people, you know? As far as I can tell, I don't remember seeing him on the headquarters grounds. I'm not there much late at night, when they do most of the maintenance work."

"So we have a firm ID on the body? And has it been verified that the deceased did work at Net Force?" Detective Mercer asked Captain Winters.

"Yes, Mark's ID of the identity used by the hacker matches the identity of the dead man. He had been an employee of ours for the past five years," Winters said.

"And in your earlier statement you claim that you were never able to see the face of the man you were chasing, the man who was driving and abandoned the car with the body in the trunk, is that correct, Daniel?" Detective Mercer asked.

"Yes. I've said that twice before," Daniel said.

Detective Mercer looked at him for a few seconds before speaking. "Just a couple more questions, and we'll be through here. Now, you said you were trying to learn what had happened to the suspect, so you investigated the car?"

"Correct," Daniel replied.

"What exactly did you look at?" the detective asked.

"I opened the front door, looked to see if the keys were in the ignition, and they weren't. I then looked at the front seat, which held no clues obvious to me, and then I activated the trunk release. I then went to the trunk, where I discovered the body," Daniel said. "Maj can verify all of this." The fear and nervousness had burned out of him during the past hour, leaving only resignation. *At least, I'm not having any difficulty sticking to my story. The only problem is I may change it out of sheer boredom. After my father, jail certainly can't be any worse.*

"All right, Daniel, as of right now you're free to go," Detective Mercer said as he stood up. "We've got your state-

ment for now. We also have Maj's. We may need to follow
up on some more details of this case, in which case we'll be
in touch. Your parents are waiting outside for you, Daniel.
Mr. Winters, if I could speak with you for just a moment."
The detective nodded at the captain as he opened the door
to let Daniel out.

When Daniel stepped out into the hallway, he saw his
mother and father waiting by the main desk. He also saw
Maj sitting and talking with her parents, who were on the
other side of the room. When she saw him, she raised her
eyebrows in a quizzical expression.

Daniel nodded to her and walked over to his mother and
father. "I need to talk to Maj for a minute and maybe Captain
Winters, then I'll go wherever you want me to," he said
quietly.

Ramos had the strangest expression on his face. Daniel
couldn't tell if his father was so furious with him that he
couldn't say anything or if he was so surprised at what was
going on that he couldn't speak. Finally something coherent
came out of his father's mouth. "Are you all right, son?"

"Yes, Dad, I am," Daniel said.

"Captain Winters filled us in as much as he could when
he called, including what you had found," his mom said.

"I know this is a mess," Daniel said. "Look, we need to
talk more about this, but I think Maj is waiting for me over
there. I'll just be a minute, I promise," Daniel said.

Ramos nodded. "We'll be here," he said, the strange look
still on his face.

*What is with him? I mean, besides the phone call he got
at three* A.M. *telling him that his son is at the police station
after finding a dead body,* Daniel thought as he headed over
to where Maj was sitting with her folks. On second thought,
maybe the strange expression on his dad's face wasn't so
odd. Maj and her family all looked up as he slowly approached her, not sure what to say. He sat down beside her.
Maj looked at her parents and nodded. Her family got up
and went to the main desk.

For a few minutes neither of them said anything. Finally
Maj ran her hands through her hair. "I don't know about

you, but being interrogated twice in three days is two times too many for me."

Daniel looked at her. "I know. I'm sorry you had to go through this again."

"I just feel like we're sinking deeper and deeper into this whole mess," she said.

Daniel nodded. "Yeah. I feel terrible about bringing you guys into this now. I had no idea the hacker was this ruthless."

Maj looked at him. "Don't forget, the hacker brought me into this by targeting me, too. And we were lucky. I'll bet that janitor guy had no idea what was going on, and now he never will. It's funny, a few days ago we were only worried about ourselves and our reputations, and now we find out peoples' lives may rest in our hands."

A door opened down the hall, and Maj and Daniel both looked up to see the detective and Captain Winters come out of the questioning room and head for the main desk, to be met there by Daniel's parents, who stood beside Maj's folks in a human wall around the detective.

Daniel looked back at Maj. "Are you going to be all right?" he asked.

"I guess so. How about you?" she said.

Daniel shrugged. "Depends on how the talk with the 'rents goes, I guess. My dad can't possibly believe I'm guilty of hacking and murder, though. Part of me hopes this is the event that makes my dad listen to me, and another part of me doesn't. I suppose I'll find out soon enough, one way or the other." He got up to leave, then turned to look back to her.

"Maj?" Daniel said.

"Yeah?" she looked up at him.

"Thanks for everything," Daniel said. "Tonight, the whole thing. I really appreciate it."

"I'll appreciate it, too, when this jerk is behind bars where he belongs," Maj said. "But you're welcome."

"They'll get him," Daniel said. "I know they will. Now at least they know where to look."

"They'd better," Maj said. "That reminds me—I think we need to talk to Winters about our suspects."

"You're right," Daniel replied.

Daniel and Maj went over to Captain Winters, standing to one side as their parents questioned the detective about what their children had seen, and what the detective was going to do about it.

"Sir, do you have a moment? There's something we need to tell you."

Winters nodded, and motioned them to one side of the hall where they wouldn't be overheard.

"We think you need to know that we set the hacker up to act tonight," Daniel said, explaining about their suspicions that the culprit was someone inside Net Force, and about their plan, with Mark's help, to figure out who was responsible. "We only told three people that Mark's program would be on site tonight—Ryan Valas, Carter Donley, and Sheila Devane. We cleared Sheila to our satisfaction the night Maj's identity was used. We're pretty sure, because of the timing of the hack, that one of those two men we targeted is behind this."

"That's a pretty big accusation, Daniel, one based on pretty thin reasoning," Winters pointed out. "The hacks have all been late at night, so the timing tonight could have been coincidence. Both of those men are highly placed agents with superb records."

"But they have the motives, opportunity, and training to do it, and they are all fairly new to Net Force. And Valas, especially, knew the Net Force Explorers well enough to target us. We think they're pretty good suspects, and tonight proved to me, anyway, that one of them is our guy—"

"I'm going to talk to Mark about this, but if what you're telling me is true, all your evidence is circumstantial, and none of it is even admissible in a court of law, given the way you got it—"

"Maybe, but it's at least a place to start," Maj pointed out. "What if we're right? Can't you open up an investigation? We may have brought matters to a head in a way that got a man killed tonight. This guy has to be stopped before he kills again!"

"Look, I find it hard to believe either Valas or Donley is a killer. But you are right about one thing—Net Force has

to get to the bottom of this before it happens again. I'll talk
to Mark first thing in the morning. I'll take everything he has
and everything we've learned tonight to Internal Affairs. In
the meantime, I want you to promise me that you won't say
a word about this to anyone other than Mark and Megan, if
I promise to get the investigation rolling from our end.
You've already risked far too much chasing this guy. It's
time for Net Force to take over."

"But, Captain, we were being blamed for the hacking!"
Daniel said. "Did you want us to stand there and let a criminal get away with treason, as well as ruining our lives?"

"You have a point," Winters replied. "This was personal.
I can understand that. But when we debrief this case, I promise you that we're going to talk about where your responsibility ends, and Net Force's begins. Now I think it's time to
get you home before you can get into any more trouble." He
herded them over to their parents and the detective in time
to hear him saying—

"—The kids are clearly not suspects in this murder, but
they are material witnesses. Until we catch this guy, I want
to know exactly where I can find them. Do you understand?"

Winters nodded. "That goes double for me. There will be
no official reprimand or disciplinary action brought by Net
Force against either Daniel or Maj for the hacking attempts
or this murder. The events of this evening have cleared them
completely. The fact that the victim they found was a member of Net Force means they'll need to cooperate with the
Net Force and police investigations, that's standard procedure. I'll schedule a meeting with both Maj and Daniel as
soon as possible to learn all that I can from what they've
stumbled into here. But it's very late, and I think we've got
the basics covered for now. I'll be in touch with all of you
tomorrow to set up an official briefing."

Maj's parents and Daniel's parents thanked Captain Winters and then each took their own child out of the police
station for what promised to be *very* long drives home.

When Daniel and his parents got outside, Ramos said to his
wife, "Why don't you take the zoomer and follow behind

Daniel and myself? Do you mind doing that alone? I'd like some time to talk to Daniel."

Great, Daniel thought.

"All right," his mother replied, going to the small electric car and getting in. In seconds the little vehicle was fired up and ready to go, its headlights cutting through the darkness.

"Come on," Ramos said to Daniel, motioning him toward the family's other car. Daniel walked around to the passenger side and got in. *He just doesn't want to blow up in front of Mom again.* He buckled up and waited for the eruption to begin. *Why won't anybody but my friends listen to my side of the story?*

Strangely, Ramos also got into the car without saying a word, started it up, and pulled onto the street that led to the freeway. He checked to make sure that his wife was following them in the zoomer, then headed for the freeway. Neither Daniel nor Ramos said a word until they were heading north toward Georgetown, when Ramos broke the silence.

"It seems I owe you an apology."

Daniel, who up until this point had been staring out the window, savoring his last view of the world outside his room, turned to look at his father so fast his neck popped. Ramos was still looking straight ahead, his concentration on the road. If what he'd just heard hadn't been so shocking, Daniel would have assumed he had imagined his father saying anything at all.

"Excuse me?" Daniel asked.

His father continued as if Daniel hadn't spoken. "But before I say anything else, I want you to swear on your word of honor that you are not involved with anything illegal." Ramos's gaze remained fixed on the road ahead. Despite that, Daniel felt like a deer caught in headlights.

A man's word is his bond, Daniel thought, remembering how many times his father had drilled that saying into him, *And once it's broken, that bond can never be repaired.* He didn't know why his father was asking for his word now, instead of earlier, but he knew the answer to the question.

"I swear, Father, on my word as a Sanchez, that I am not involved with anything illegal," he said. "I'm only trying to find out who's behind this and bring them to justice so I can clear my name."

His father didn't answer right away, and Daniel knew his words were being searched for evidence that he was lying. *I know I haven't done anything wrong,* he thought, *except when I've tried to clear my name. Maybe some of that was a little wrong. But I was desperate. If he wants to hold me accountable for that, so be it.*

His father looked at him, nodded once, then turned his attention back to the road. "I suppose that's why all of this happened?"

"Because I needed to prove I was innocent? That's pretty much it. Nobody except my friends believed in me. I tried to tell everybody I wasn't the hacker, but despite the fact that Maj was targeted, too, everybody thought I had done it. So I figured it was up to me to catch the real culprit, because it was the only way to prove I was right. I didn't expect it to turn out like this. Even when I called the police after Maj and I found the body, I still didn't believe it. I'm sorry you had to come down here in the middle of the night," Daniel said. *We're actually having a conversation for the first time in I don't know how long. No matter what he says, I need to keep my temper. There's no reason to go off half-cocked.* He looked away from his father, worried that the ever-present anger he felt toward his dad would show on his face.

Again Ramos surprised him. "I'm proud of you, son," he said.

Daniel looked at his father, unsure of what to make of this complete turnaround from a few days ago. *Who is this?* was the only thought that kept running through his mind. *By now he should have locked me in the trunk, with plans to keep me there for a decade.* Daniel kept silent, not sure how to respond, and afraid of saying something wrong if he did.

"Granted, this is not how I would have wanted to discover you could take responsibility for yourself, but what's done is done."

Easy for you to say, Daniel thought. *You aren't the one who almost had his life taken away.* And may still no matter what you do—there's a dead body back there, and the killer's still loose.

"I'm sorry I didn't believe you the first time when you told me that you hadn't done anything," Ramos said, his words coming slowly. "No matter what our differences have been in the past, when the situation is as serious as this, I ought to take my son's word over that of his accuser."

"Thank you," Daniel said.

"Of course, that doesn't excuse a lot of what you've done tonight, including sneaking out of the house the minute my back was turned, and stealing my equipment," Ramos said. Daniel looked at him, frowning, only to relax slightly when he saw his father's face light up in a rare smile, which faded just as quickly as it came. "You showed courage and initiative, but you placed your friend Maj in serious danger. And, worse, you had no backup and no secondary plan in case your first one didn't work."

"True," Daniel said. "But I was scared, nobody believed me, and I was working with the resources I had at hand."

"Yes, but you shouldn't have been doing anything of the sort. I would rather have had you come to me with your suspicions so we could have tackled this together. I realize that you wanted to clear your name yourself, but sometimes you have to know when to admit you need help," his father said. "Now that Net Force is going to step up their investigation, you can relax and let them handle it. Then, once this whole thing has blown over, we can discuss the upcoming quarter. Agreed?"

And be right back where we started from? Not if I can help it, Daniel thought. "Sure, as long as you are willing to listen to me, and take into consideration what I'd like to do with my life."

"I have always said that when you start acting like a man, you will be treated like a man. Although the steps you took tonight were in the wrong direction, your heart was in the right place. I'm afraid your mother is probably still going to ground you for this, and I agree she has the right. However, I will try to reduce your sentence so you will see the sun before next June."

"Thanks, Dad," Daniel said. "No offense, but if I had thought you would believe me, I would have come to you. But I didn't think there was any hope of that. Our last few conversations didn't hold a lot of promise for parental support of my innocence."

"Your mom told me about the conversation you two had the other night. Daniel, I want you to come to me when you've done something wrong, or when you know you are in trouble. It's when you try to sneak around me and avoid responsibility for your actions that I lose my temper. I know I seem harsh sometimes, but I only want to help you," Ramos said.

"But I tried to come to you. You didn't believe me," Daniel said. "My friends did. What else could I have done?"

"It was because of your past behavior that I didn't give you the benefit of the doubt," Ramos said. "Unfortunately, I needed the proof I saw tonight to make up my mind that you were innocent, that you were capable of taking responsibility for your own actions. I'd like to think things will be different between us from now on. I'm willing to compromise on some things, to be less strict, as long as you are willing to come to me with your problems."

"All right," Daniel said. "I'll try." *We'll see how it goes.*

"Fair enough," Ramos said. "I will try, too."

By now they were turning down the street their house was on, and for the first time in a long while Daniel was able to approach his home with feelings other than dread and anger bubbling inside him. He kept stealing looks at his father as they pulled into the driveway. *I've never seen him like this before. Maybe things will be different. But that doesn't change the fact that I've still got to find this hacker before he kills someone else. He's my responsibility—I made the plan that tempted him to murder.*

Daniel's mom pulled in the zoomer beside their sedan and got out. She looked like she wanted to say something to them, but Ramos interrupted her.

"I think we've all had enough excitement for one evening. It's almost daylight. Let's sleep on this a little and discuss it in the morning, all right?" His tone, although lighthearted, left no room for disagreement.

Daniel and his mother both nodded. There was a small smile on his face, a puzzled look on hers, as Ramos herded them both into the house. As soon as Daniel got up to his room, he pulled out his foilpack and dialed a number. "Jimmy? Yeah, it's me. I know, it's been a *really* long night. What you got? Really? That's great. You did what? Man, I told you . . . Where? Listen, this is very important. What was he driving? Yeah, and he was dressed how? Oh, that is beautiful, man! Thanks, I really owe you one. No, I can't get over there right now. I've been up all night as it is. Just sit tight and I'll get ahold of you later. Great." Daniel flipped the phone closed as a satisfied grin spread over his face. "Oh, baby, we got you now."

Daniel slept in the next morning, waking up around noon. Yawning, he stumbled to his computer and found several requests from Mark, Megan, and Maj to contact them. Daniel jumped online and found the three of them at a virtual sidewalk café in Paris.

" 'Fare you well/Do we but find the tyrant's power tonight/ Let us be beaten, if we cannot fight,' " Daniel said as he strolled over to them.

Three blank looks met him as he sat down.

"You're awfully chipper after what happened last night," Maj said.

Mark and Megan nodded.

"I thought you weren't even supposed to be on the Net," Megan said.

"I wasn't, but the situation has changed. I assume you filled them in," Daniel said to Maj, who nodded.

"I told them what happened. And that I've pretty much been cleared. I thought I'd let you tell them your own good news."

"I'm not only cleared. I know who the chameleon is."

The other three leaned forward, the expressions on their faces revealing their shock.

"What? How?" Mark asked. "I went over that recording for two hours last night, and I couldn't get anything other than bare physical measurements out of it. Caucasian male, height approximately 185 centimeters, weight about 95 kilos, stuff like that."

"That's because my intel doesn't come from online or from our surveillance of Net Force HQ. Last night, just in case, I asked some friends to stake out the addresses where each of our suspects lives. When I called them back, guess who went out for the evening? Ryan Valas. And—get this— he drove to an address in Wheaton, where he went to a home in the burbs, let himself in, stayed for about fifteen minutes, and finally drove out of the garage in a late-model maroon sedan, license number HFY-645, leaving his own car behind."

Maj jerked as if she had been stung. "That's the license plate of the car we followed last night!"

Daniel nodded. "That's right. My snoop even got close enough to see that the driver was dressed in a janitor's uniform as he was leaving the Wheaton house. And guess who lived at that address until yesterday? Harry Jameson."

"But why would Valas kill him?" Maj asked. "He has a perfect cover already in place as a member of the CIA assigned to Net Force. His hacking program has left him free and clear every time he's used it. Why would he risk the whole thing by killing a janitor and going to Net Force in the guy's car?"

"Maybe the janitor knew something about Valas that incriminated him," Megan suggested. "And Valas knew it and had to stop him."

"Or maybe the janitor saw something odd and confronted him," Daniel said.

"You mean like blackmail?" Maj asked.

"Not necessarily. The janitor could have just seen Valas at Net Force at a time when he was supposedly not there, and asked him about it. We'll probably never know what set the killing off," Daniel said. "But I'll bet it was something more than just needing an identity—otherwise Maj and I would be dead."

"You don't think Valas suspects we're after him, do you?" Mark asked. "Or Net Force? It's pretty clear Net Force never even considered him as a suspect, until last night. And even then, Winters sounded awfully dubious about our accusations."

"No, I don't think he knows we're after him, because if he thought somebody was watching, he would have scrapped the hack last night," Daniel said.

"If he doesn't suspect that he was being watched, then how did he shake us last night?" Maj asked. "That tracker of yours was working fine, you and I both saw it. He had to do something to it to stop it from working. Unless it broke."

"I know, I thought about that. The only logical conclusion I can come up with is that he had a scrambler in the car, a portable device that neutralizes electronic bugs," Daniel said. "My dad used to use them all the time, and I'm sure the CIA has them as well. Valas activated it when he left the freeway, just in case somebody was following him. He *is* a trained spy. And, if we're right, and I think we are, he'd just committed a murder and was driving around with the evidence handy. Valas has probably been playing both sides against the middle for a while. I imagine he didn't get where he is without being very careful."

"Okay, but that doesn't answer the first question. Why would he go to all this trouble, including commit a murder, when he's already securely inside Net Force as a high-ranking official?" Megan asked. "He has access to all but the most confidential files. Why bother killing a man when incriminating one of us has been working for him to get even those few files he can't get legally?"

"I told you. The only things I can think of are blackmail and disposing of evidence. Or maybe he's trying to reinforce his position by having another intrusion happen when he's supposedly not even at the base, thereby incriminating someone else again," Maj said. "Maybe he's already framed somebody else for the murder. . . ."

The four teens looked at each other. "Don't even make me think about that," Megan said. "But why do it the way he did? He's just made things hotter for himself at Net Force by murdering that janitor. Why didn't he just go after one of us and borrow one of our identities? That's been working for him. Mark and I were online last night, and near Net Force," Megan pointed out, frowning.

"I'm sure he didn't spot us," Mark said.

"Oh, yeah, how sure? Last night you were surprised that he sent the program through a data pipeline. How do you know he didn't see us?" Megan asked.

"Because if there had been anyone trying to corrupt or

take over our data streams, my security programs would have discovered it," Mark replied.

"Yeah, but, Squirt, we already know that it doesn't have to happen that way. If it *is* Valas, he can set up a whole system of fake logon and intrusion, remember? I was nowhere near Net Force when I got nailed for hacking," Daniel said. "And he's a wizard with security—it's his specialty."

"Daniel, you were online, you just weren't near Net Force Headquarters. Maybe Valas, if that's who's doing this, is copying your logon signal at the source, your computer, and creating his 'copy' from there," Mark said.

"Maybe so, but if that's true, how did he co-opt Jameson's signal when the guy was already dead?" Daniel asked. "I don't know that—and I bet you don't, either. But if Valas was driving that car, and he was, we've got our traitor. We can figure out how he did it later. Right now we need to decide what to do with this info."

"Look, we need to go to Captain Winters immediately and tell him about it. With your buddy as a witness to back up our claims," Maj said.

"Actually, there's a little problem with that," Daniel said. "This particular group of kids doesn't exactly have squeaky-clean records. My friend won't make a statement, and nobody will ever get close enough to him to catch him and force him to talk. All we've got to give Winters is hearsay evidence."

"What? Did you tell your friend how important this is to you?" Mark asked.

"Yes, and that's how I got him and the others to scope out the places in the first place. But think about it, even if he did come in, would it do any good? The word of a juvenile delinquent against that of a respected CIA agent? Who would you believe? My friend or Ryan Valas? No, we need more evidence before we go to Winters again," Daniel said. "He's already got enough to start looking at Valas. We need something to clinch the case."

"What more? Do you want to find Valas with a smoking hard drive in his hand? Not only is this guy a spy, but he's also a killer, in case you may have forgotten what we saw last night. If your 'friend'—and I use that term loosely, given that he's not willing to go to bat for you—doesn't come forward to testify on your behalf, then it's time we let the pros handle it. Face it, Daniel, we've done all we can," Megan said. "We leave it alone and let Net Force take it from here."

"I say we put it to a vote, either continue on our own, carefully, while Net Force pursues its own investigation, or leave it alone and let the professionals get this guy without any more help from us," Maj said, looking around at the other three. Seeing no disagreement, she continued. "Those in favor of leaving it to Net Force, raise your hand," she said, raising her own. Mark and Megan raised their hands as well. "Opposed." Daniel's hand half-rose, then fell back to the table. "Okay, then," she said. "It's three to one. We leave it to Net Force."

"All right, all right, you win. But let me talk to my boy again, see if I can't change his mind about coming in and talking to the Captain. That's one thing we can do that will really help Winters—agreed?" His friends all nodded. "If my friend testifies, we really do have something to add to the case for Net Force, something that will clinch it for them. I'd feel much better about going to the higher-ups with real evidence, not hearsay," Daniel said.

"Okay, why don't you get in touch with us as soon as you talk with this guy, and let us know what's going on," Mark said.

"No problem." Daniel stood up and disappeared from the table, leaving the other three staring after him.

"Well, that didn't go exactly as we planned," Mark said.

"I don't think he completely trusts Captain Winters after being suspended," Maj said. "And think about it—if we'd left it to Net Force in the first place, Daniel and I would still be prime suspects for hacking, and maybe worse."

"Yeah, but it's not just you two in trouble, now; it's all of us. When you guys found that body, the rules definitely changed. I was ready to wash my hands of this whole thing last night, until you talked me out of it," Megan said.

"I wanted to wait to talk to Winters because I was hoping that I could find something in that online surveillance that would give us a real clue to the identity of the hacker. But I got nothing but dead ends," Mark said. "If Daniel can pull his friend in to testify, Valas is toast. You know, I just had a terrible thought—you don't think this is a delaying tactic on Daniel's part, something to put off talking to Winters while he tries to get to Valas himself? He's been a little crazy lately with all the stuff that's been happening."

"Don't forget, Daniel was the one to call Net Force in when we found the . . . body," Maj said. "He handled it pretty well. I just hope his parents didn't come down on him too hard for what he did."

"I say we give Daniel a couple of hours, then go to Captain Winters with everything we know, including the fact that there is a witness out there to tie Valas to the body. I'm sure Net Force can track down Daniel's mysterious friend," Megan said.

"Maybe Megan's right," Maj said. "We've given Daniel the benefit of the doubt before; let's give it to him again," Maj replied. "Besides, going to Captain Winters a few hours later shouldn't make any difference, right?"

When Daniel logged off, he sat there for a moment, knowing what he had to do, and how his father would react. *I'm sorry, Dad, but I've got to disobey you one more time. I need proof to clear my name, and right now Jimmy's the only one who's got it.*

He reached for his foilpack again and speed-dialed a familiar number. "Jimmy? Yeah, it's me. You all right? No, no, you just sound kind of strange, that's all. Yeah, I know the feeling. Look, we've got to talk. Really? You mean that? Can you come over here? What? It's okay, I'll be right there. We can go in together. Thanks, man, you're really gonna pull me out of the fire. I'll be there in about a half hour. Later."

He then left a message for his father on his virtmail account. "Dad, I know you're going to be angry when you get this message, but I've got one final loose end to tie up before we go to Net Force. I'd like to meet you there in about two hours. I haven't forgotten about our conversation last night. I'm just trying to live up to it. I love you. Bye."

After sending the message, Daniel activated Mark's trap-door program for the last time. He grabbed his jacket, popped his window open and climbed out onto the roof. Walking quietly over the side of the garage, he eased himself over the edge and grabbed the iron ivy trellis that was attached to the wall. Using it as a ladder, he let himself down and started walking down the street. A few minutes later he was in a bus heading for the south side of Washington.

The bus let Daniel off near a natural wood-sided duplex, with an attached garage for each house. There were no cars in either driveway. *Jimmy's parents must not be home*, Daniel thought as he walked up the driveway to the front door.

Ringing the doorbell brought no response at all. Daniel tried peeking in through the windows but saw no one in any of the rooms. He knocked on the door, and was surprised when the door swung open at his touch.

"Jimmy?" Daniel called as he stepped inside the house. The interior of the duplex was a split-level, with stairs leading up and down. Looking down, Daniel saw an empty hallway leading to the bedrooms below, while the upstairs contained a kitchen, dining area, and living room with the ever-present veeyar console, all deserted. The house was silent, seemingly empty. Daniel's steps sounded unnaturally loud on the linoleum floor.

Where the heck is Jimmy? Daniel wondered. *He's a flake, but he made it sound so important that I come over as soon as possible.*

"Jimmy?" he called again, hearing the slight echo of his voice carry through the house.

"I'm down here," a faint reply came from the lower hallway. "In my bedroom."

Daniel started down the stairs, peering down the dark hallway for his friend. He knew Jimmy's room was the last door on the right, and he headed for it, not even stopping to knock before stepping inside.

"Man, am I glad you want to talk to Captain Winters—" Daniel said as he walked into the room, right into a spray of fine mist.

Immediately Daniel's face and eyes burned as if he had been stung by bees. Caught completely by surprise, he still knew better than to breathe in. It felt as if he was choking to death. Some of the chemical got into his mouth before he could shut it, and he felt his tongue and throat go raw as the droplets burned their way into him. Gasping in pain, he rubbed at his eyes and skin, which only worsened the burning.

Daniel stumbled out of the bedroom, coughing and gasping. He collided with the wall in the hallway and fell to the floor, coughing and choking and crying helplessly. All he could think about was the fire inside his nose, mouth, and eyes. Daniel heard water running and felt a cool rag tossed on his face.

A familiar voice said, "Here. Clean yourself off with this."

Daniel grabbed the wet rag and held it to his face, sucking in the cool water from the cloth. The gas was diluted somewhat by the water, but his eyes and skin still itched where they had been sprayed.

"All right, that's enough," the voice said, yanking the cloth away. "You'll be all right, though you won't feel very good for a couple hours. Trust me, it won't be your worst problem." Daniel opened his eyes to see a blurry figure standing above him. This was immediately replaced by a close-up view of the floor as Daniel's captor rolled him over onto his stomach and wrenched his hands behind his back. Daniel felt a sudden pain as something flexible and tough bit into his wrists. He felt himself being grabbed by the collar of his jacket and hauled to his feet. The room spun as he tried to regain his equilibrium.

"Perfect, you came right when Jimbo here called. You two boys are now my aces in the hole," Daniel heard Ryan Valas say.

Daniel's mouth was still burning, and he swallowed to try and ease his swollen throat. Valas yanked him over to the downstairs bathroom and pushed his head toward the sink. "Spit. Right there. It'll help."

Daniel obediently did so, coughing and gagging to try and clear the acrid taste out of his mouth. "Water?" he asked, still hacking.

"You've got three seconds," Valas said as he filled a glass, keeping his other hand secure on Daniel's collar. "I want you to know that I'm not being kind out of charity. I don't care if you live or die. That'll be up to you—and whether you cooperate with me or not. But I need you to be able to talk later," he said, holding a glass to Daniel's lips. Daniel gulped down as much liquid as he could before Valas took the glass away and washed it thoroughly. "Can't leave any evidence, now, can we?" He put the glass back and looked at his watch. "Time to go."

Valas kept a tight hold on Daniel's arm as he steered him back toward Jimmy's room. Through his tearing eyes, Daniel saw Jimmy, bound and gagged, lying on the bed. The one thing Daniel could see clearly was the fear in Jimmy's eyes. Daniel knew his own eyes held that same fear.

Valas cut the tie that held Jimmy's legs together and hauled him to his feet. Shoving Jimmy next to Daniel and keeping them both in front of him, Valas escorted the two boys out of the house.

"How?" Daniel croaked as Valas pulled him toward the garage.

"That trap with the fake program Gridley's boy tried on me was what tipped me off that someone was looking. When I saw your buddy here casing my house, I knew something was up," Valas said.

"I told my friends. They know where I am," Daniel said, trying to keep his balance as Valas pushed him out the door to the garage.

"Too bad you won't be here by the time they figure out you're in trouble. You can't beat a guy who's already two steps ahead of you," Valas replied. "Three steps, actually. Now I just need to round up your interfering little friend Mark, and I'll have all the cards I need to win this game. And you're going to help me get him."

"You leave my friends out of this and I'll do whatever you say," Daniel gasped.

"You'll do that anyway," Valas said, shoving them roughly across the garage.

By now they were at the car, and Valas had opened the trunk. "The accommodations aren't the best, but then, you both got yourselves into this, didn't you?"

"No, *you* got me into this," Daniel managed to croak before Valas shoved Jimmy and him into the trunk. Daniel twisted himself so he didn't crack his head, although he did land painfully on one shoulder. With Jimmy crammed right next to him, Daniel already felt claustrophobic. And the trunk wasn't even closed yet.

"Now we're going for a little drive. Keep quiet, and you keep living," Valas said, opening his hand to reveal a familiar small aerosol sprayer. "Make any kind of noise, and I spray this into the trunk. It would be really bad if you couldn't wipe it out of your eyes, eh?"

Daniel tried to look cowering and terrified. It wasn't much of a stretch. "Don't worry," he rasped. "We're not going to try anything," he said. *Yet*, he thought.

"Good, that's very smart," Valas said as he closed the trunk. Daniel heard the garage door open, then the car started, and he felt the sensation of movement.

As soon as they started moving forward, Daniel whispered, "Jimmy? Shh! I've got my foilpack wallet. See if you can reach my back pocket."

He felt Jimmy wriggling around, then felt a hand scrabble down his back, dig into his jeans pocket, and pull out the foilpack.

"All right! Now see if you can get it over by my head," Daniel said in a thread of a voice.

He heard panting and more movement as Jimmy tried to get into position. A second later a flat piece of plastic smacked Daniel on the side of the head.

"Pray this works," Daniel said, nosing the foilpack open. He hit the speed-dial button with his nose and the code for Captain Winter's number. He heard the familiar buzz as the phone made the connection. "Captain Winters? I need your help. Ryan Valas has just kidnapped me and a friend—we're in the trunk of his car! And he's going after Mark Gridley next!" Silence. "Hello? Captain Winters, are you there?" Looking down at the phone, Daniel realized that the light that usually came on wasn't glowing, which meant the connection hadn't been made. Daniel pressed several buttons with his nose, but nothing happened. The foilpack wasn't working. One of the blows he'd sustained in the last few minutes had clearly killed it.

Damn, Daniel thought, *I just hope Winters believed us last night when we told him Valas was his man.* The car swung through a turn, slamming him against the wall of the car. He grunted as Jimmy's elbow caught him solidly in the ribs. Awkwardly Daniel tried to arrange himself so that he was lying on his side. The past few minutes had drained him both physically and mentally. *The most important thing I can do is try to stay calm and look for a way out,* he thought. *Valas said I had to talk later, so he needs me for something. He won't kill me as long as he needs me. As long as that's true, I've still got a chance to escape. Worthless phone, can't even be in my pocket without breaking—*

My pocket! Daniel thought, squirming around until he could reach his right jacket pocket. Even with all of the tumbling around he had done, the small stun gun he carried all the time was still there. Daniel's half-numb fingers closed around it and gripped it tightly. Deliverance. *All I have to do now is get close enough to use it on him*, he thought. *Like that'll happen soon.* He palmed the tiny weapon. *I hope it's tougher than that stupid foilpack,* he thought.

Daniel now concentrated on listening for unusual sounds that the car might drive by, cattle lowing if they headed out of town, perhaps, or the sound and smell of the river as they drove over it. He had heard and smelled nothing out of the ordinary so far, but he kept his senses alert, listening and waiting as the car kept traveling.

15

"I don't think we should give Daniel any time to work things out himself. This is too important," Mark said to Maj and Megan.

"Why?" Megan asked.

"Don't forget, it's not just the hacks anymore. Valas has already killed somebody. A Net Force employee. We have to tell Net Force what Mark's friend saw." Mark took out a small icon and activated it. "It's time to call in the big guns," he said, dialing a number, "Luckily, my dad is actually home today."

A few seconds later Jay Gridley appeared in Mark's site. "Hey, son. Hi, Maj, Megan. You know, you could have actually come downstairs and knocked on my door," he said, smiling at the three kids.

Mark's expression was serious. "Maybe, but I wanted you to talk to Maj and Megan, and this was the quickest way to make it work. Daniel Sanchez has figured out who is responsible for the hacks at Net Force." Mark went on to explain about what Daniel's friend had seen last night. "I'm worried. I don't trust Daniel not to go after Valas himself. If he does, it could get Daniel killed. I know that what we're telling you is hearsay evidence, but Valas is our hacker. He's already killed one Net Force employee. Net Force needs to act now! Could you get Captain Winters for us please? He'll verify everything about last night."

"Hold on a minute," Jay said, looking to his left. "I'm calling him now." Now his expression grew serious. "While we're waiting, son, why don't you explain your role in all of this?"

"He'll be explaining *our* role in all of this, Mr. Gridley," Maj said.

"All right," Jay said, just before all of them heard a soft chime. "That must be Captain Winters."

Sure enough, Captain Winters appeared. "Hello, Jay, what's up?" Then he looked around. "It appears I'm the last one to know about whatever's going on here. Why doesn't someone fill me in? Mark?"

"Okay, but before I start, could you please send a police car over to Ryan Valas's's house and see if he's there?" Mark asked. "It could be a matter of life or death."

Jay nodded. "I can do better than that, I promise you. I'll take care of it. Mark, why don't you start talking?" Jay popped out for a second to organize the manhunt.

Why does it always seem to be me giving bad news to the Captain? Taking a deep breath, Mark began, "You're not going to like this, Captain, but . . ."

"So, let me get this straight," Captain Winters said. "I ask you to keep an eye on Daniel to make sure he doesn't do anything foolish, and you three let him go?"

Mark tried to interject but was stopped by Winters's upraised hand.

"Now," Winters continued, "you are sure Ryan Valas, a trusted CIA agent, is our hacker and killer, and you think that Daniel might have gone after him himself? Is that it, more or less?"

"Yeah," Mark said. "We'd have come to you sooner, but you guys weren't taking us seriously. I once asked my mom about the possibility of it being an inside job, and she dismissed the idea. Even last night you sounded like we were out of our heads when we suggested Valas was the mole.

Then Daniel's friend got the goods on Valas. Now I'm worried about what Daniel's going to do."

"If you're right, you let a Net Force Explorer head off into extreme personal danger," Captain Winters said. "What were you thinking? I told you to keep an eye on Sanchez, not throw in with him on some crazy mission. I don't understand why you didn't come to me first."

"James, I understand where you're coming from, and I agree that some kind of disciplinary action will have to be taken, but for now, I think the kids are right. We have to put together a plan to find Valas and bring him in. We also need to find Daniel and his friend, and make sure they are safe," Jay said. An urgent beeping filled the site. "That must be the police dispatch," he said. "Just a minute."

Jay popped out again. Mark quickly turned to Captain Winters. "Captain, we came to you almost as quickly as we could. Maybe I should have kept Daniel here, but he had a point. You guys didn't pay us too much attention when we told you the mole was inside Net Force. Daniel's friend was the first real clincher we had on Valas, and Daniel wanted to bring him in to report to you. So I let him go after the guy. Then I had second thoughts, and I called my dad."

Captain Winters looked at Megan and Maj, who both nodded. "Mark's right, Captain. We felt that we had taken the investigation as far as it could go. The only thing we were waiting for was real proof. But Valas is really dangerous. We decided you needed to know what was going on now," Maj said.

"That's noble, but that doesn't make it smart," Captain Winters said. "Somebody should have called me the minute Daniel found out from his friend that Valas was the killer. You shouldn't have let Daniel go out there alone. But Jay's right. At this point we have to pool our resources and go after Valas. We'll deal with you kids later."

Jay rejoined the conversation. "That was the Washington police. Valas isn't at home. Daniel's not at home, either, and his parents have no idea where he is. They're on their way here now. James, pull together everything we have on Valas, personnel file, the works. I'm heading to the office, I'll meet

up with you there. Mark, Maj, Megan, you three stay put.
We'll contact you if anything happens."

"But, Dad, you may need me. I'm your only link to what's
going on right now," Mark protested.

"No, son, it's past time for us to step in. Don't worry,
we'll get Valas," Jay said. "You need to be here for Daniel.
I want that boy, and his friend the witness, in our hands and
safe until Valas is put away. That goes for all of you! Nobody
leaves until you hear from me. Got it?"

"But what do we do if Daniel calls here?" Mark asked.

"If that should happen, then call me immediately," Jay
said. "I'll dispatch an agent to get him right away. Above
all, don't go anywhere."

With that both Winters and Gridley disappeared from
Mark's site. Mark tuned in to the real world around him for
a second and heard the front door close, then the garage door
opening. Activating his own home's security camera, Mark
watched his father's car pull out of the driveway.

"Nuts," he said.

"Well, now what?" Maj asked.

"I don't know," Mark said. "I can't believe we're shut out
of this one, after all the work we did."

"What else is new?" Megan asked. "You knew that if we
actually did find anything, it would be taken over by Captain
Winters immediately."

"Yeah, but it's still annoying." Mark sat down and rested
his chin in his hands. "What if Daniel's in trouble? It's our
fault for letting him go. He should have called by now."

"It'll be all right," Megan said. "You know Daniel. He's
probably just shooting the breeze with his friend, figuring out
how to make the coolest entrance into Net Force, eyewitness
in tow."

"Maybe. But what if he's not?" Mark said.

"I don't know. Anybody got any ideas?" Maj asked.

Silence descended on the group.

Mark's foilpack phone chirped.

"Hello," he said. "Daniel?"

Then they all watched as Mark's eyes widened. He hit the
button to patch the phone signal into their online environment
as an audio feed.

16

Daniel braced himself for action when he felt the car come to a stop. The trunk had grown stuffy during the long ride, and Daniel would have given Valas whatever he wanted if he'd just left the lid open a little for some air to circulate. His tongue felt swollen, though the worst effects of the tear gas had worn off, and there was a bitter taste in his mouth. His eyes had stopped watering some time ago, but they still felt raw and itchy, as if someone had poured sand in them.

A door slammed, and a few seconds later Daniel got his wish. The trunk opened. He squinted against the sunlight and saw Valas reaching for him. The CIA agent dragged him roughly out of the trunk.

Through a fresh veil of tears, Daniel saw that they were in the middle of an abandoned industrial area. Empty factories, their windows broken, squatted amidst rusting and broken manufacturing equipment. Weeds grew rampant through the cracked concrete and asphalt. Daniel shivered at the thought of being left out here, dead or alive, where no one would find him for days, weeks even.

Valas sat him down on the uneven pavement beside the car, closed the trunk with Jimmy still inside it, and pulled a laptop from inside the car. He set it up on the closed trunk.

He took a satellite phone out of his pocket and hooked it up to the small computer, then turned the computer on.

"Just got to set up a few little surprises for your buddy Mark, then you'll get to talk to him," Valas said in between muttering commands to the portable. Daniel watched him work for a few minutes, trying to recognize any similarity between the man he had watched lecture a week ago with the cold-eyed criminal he was looking at now. He gave up on that after a while, finding it impossible to think about, and concentrated on trying to figure out a way to escape. His fingers searched the surrounding area for a shard of glass or sharp rock to cut his restraints with, but found nothing. He tried straining against the binding, but only succeeded in cutting off the blood flow to his hands.

"Ah, the phone line is clear. How convenient." Valas picked up the cell phone, then squatted down by Daniel. "All right, you are going to say hello to him and tell him you're all right. Don't try to give him any clues as to where we are, because we'll be long gone by the time anyone gets here. Instead, use the few seconds you'll have to convince Mark to do exactly what I tell him," Valas said, letting Daniel see the pistol holstered under his suit jacket. "*Comprende*?"

Daniel nodded, his mouth suddenly very dry. Valas dialed the number and held it up to Daniel's ear. He listened to the dial tone ring and ring, all the while thinking, *Please pick up, Mark. Please answer.*

"Hi . . . Mark? It's me, Daniel," the hoarse voice came over Mark's phone link. Maj and Megan both looked up at the same time. "I'm all right, I'm not hurt, but I'm with someone who wants to speak to you."

"Daniel, where are you?" Mark asked, motioning to the two girls to be silent.

"He's with me," Ryan Valas's calm voice answered. "Just listen. If you try to contact anybody before I tell you to, Daniel will disappear. If you try calling anyone other than who I say, Daniel will disappear. Don't bother tracing the call, as I'll be gone before you can get a lock. I want your search program, on datacube. If you want Daniel to live, you will deliver it, in person and alone. Do you understand that,

Mark? Make sure you bring the real thing this time—your friend's life depends on it. Of course, I don't need to mention again that you will come alone and tell no one about this call."

"Where are you? How will I get there?" Mark asked. "I'm a kid. I don't drive."

"Call this number," Valas said, giving Mark a string of digits. "Ask for Vinnie. He'll send a cab for you. The cab-driver will have directions. I'll be checking with them in a few minutes to make sure you did make that one call. I'm monitoring all phone signals from your house. Remember, you have thirty minutes." With that, the connection was broken.

"Mark, you're not actually going through with this, are you?" Maj asked.

"What else can I do? Valas has me cold. I don't have time to wait for Net Force to try and find him. I don't dare take the chance that he's bluffing about me contacting someone. Daniel's only chance is for me to give Valas what he wants, and hope that he's smart enough to realize that he'd better not do anything to me if he doesn't want the head of Net Force and all the rest of the agency on his tail for the rest of his life. I don't have a choice. The one thing in our favor is that he doesn't know you girls were here online with me. Give me a minute, then find my dad and let him know what's going on."

He called the number Valas had given him, which was for a downtown cab company. Vinnie answered—Ryan had done his legwork. Mark gave the dispatcher his home address and told them to send the arranged cab there as soon as possible. He downloaded his snooper program into a data-cube, then signed off before either of the girls could think of a way to stop him.

Mark took the datacube from its receptacle and headed downstairs to wait for the cab. He grabbed his jacket and put it on, checking for the universal credit card in his pocket. He figured there was enough credit on it for whatever he needed—whether it was cab fare or funeral expenses.

Mark locked the front door and sat on the step, waiting in

the fading light of the setting sun. Squaring his shoulders, he looked down the street for the cab. He checked his watch, then set the timer function, guessing he had about twenty-five minutes left until Valas's deadline passed. He had no idea where he was going. He checked his watch again, then scanned the street. *Come on, where are you? My friend's life is on the line here!*

After what seemed like forever, a green-and-white four-door sedan with a white sign on top and "Carroll Cab Co." on the side pulled onto the street and over to the curb in front of Mark's house. Mark met it there and got into the back-seat. The man nodded and punched up some prearranged location on his GPS system. The address showed up as an abandoned industrial dock on the north side of Washington, D.C. *Is Valas planning to skip town by boat? Once I get Daniel back, can we just call the Coast Guard and have them deal with this?*

Mark looked out the window at the distant Washington skyline speeding by. Most of all, he couldn't believe how fooled he had been by Valas. *I liked him. He just seemed like he wanted to help,* Mark thought. *He's the last person I would have figured to do something like this.* Indeed, a part of him was still hoping somehow that it wasn't true, that it hadn't been Valas speaking to him on the phone. Mark knew he wouldn't completely believe this whole thing until he saw Valas with his own eyes.

And then what? This is still the guy who's holding my friend hostage. It's happened, and I've got to deal with it. Now I have to get Daniel back, by whatever means necessary. Which, of course, is why I'm on this fool's errand. My dad's gonna kill me for this. Assuming Valas doesn't beat him to it.

Almost before he knew it, the taxi had pulled up to the abandoned dock. Mark looked up and down the long grassy strip of land that led down to the docks. No one coming, no one going. He sighed and handed his card over to the cabbie.

"Hey, kid," said the cabbie, who, perhaps sensing Mark's preoccupation, had been silent until now. Or maybe he was in on it? The cabbie's next words dispelled that thought. "They told me not to wait for you, but I don't like leaving you here. Why are you coming way out here? No one's around."

Boy, don't I know it, Mark thought. "I know," he said.

"You want me to wait?" the cabbie asked.

Yes, yes, oh God, how I want to say yes, Mark thought. Instead he kept his voice casual as he replied, "No, but why don't you swing back here in fifteen minutes or so? If you see me, you've got a fare back to the city."

"Sounds good. You sure you're gonna be all right out here?" the cabbie asked.

I certainly hope so, Mark thought again. "Like you said, there's no one out here. I'll be fine, thanks."

"Okay, here's your card," the cabbie said, pushing it through the slot cut in the bulletproof glass. As Mark reached out to take the card, he glanced at the cabbie, and what he saw caused him to do a double take.

The cabdriver had dusty blond hair and a narrow face with extremely light blue eyes. *Where have I seen this guy before?* Mark thought to himself, his brows furrowing. *Valas said he had set up the cab ride already. Maybe this guy is an accomplice?* Just as quickly Mark dismissed the thought. *After all, if he was working with Valas, he could have just taken the cube from me right away. Frack, Mark, get a grip!*

"You all right, kid?" the cabbie said.

"Yeah, you just reminded me of someone, that's all. It's nothing. Thanks for the ride," Mark said.

"No problem. I'll get something to eat, swing back around in about fifteen, twenty, minutes. If you're here, great, if not, no big loss, all right?"

"Sure, thanks," Mark said, getting out of the cab. As he walked across the empty lot to the docks, he resisted the urge to look back. After a few seconds he heard the engine of the cab as it drove away.

A cold autumn wind was blowing in off the river, and Mark shivered and zipped up his jacket. He looked around, unsure as to where to go. Just when he was about to pick whether to go up or down the dock, his foilpack rang.

"Hello?" Mark said.

"Good evening. Do you have what I want?" Valas's voice

said. Mark swore he could hear the man grinning over the phone.

"Yeah, I got it. Where are you?"

"Look south, along the docks. See the light?" Valas asked.

Mark did as he was directed. Sure enough, there was a small blue light flashing from what looked like a few dozen yards out on the river.

"Come join us, won't you?" Valas said, then hung up.

Mark looked around, making sure he was alone, then started walking toward the flashing light. A helicopter flew by high overhead, and Mark looked up at the sound, following the sound as it headed for parts unknown. Strangely, the chopper didn't have its operating lights on, and Mark couldn't spot it against the twilight sky.

Still, I wish I were aboard it, or anyplace else, rather than out here, Mark thought. By now he had reached the landing, and he saw a concrete jetty, surrounded by large rocks, extending out about fifty meters into the river. The jetty was surrounded with a waist-high concrete wall that ran the length of the walkway on both sides and met in the middle to form a horseshoe shape. He stuck his hands into his pockets and, keeping an eye on where he had last seen the blinking light, stepped onto the concrete path.

"Well, here comes your little friend now." Valas was holding his pistol at the back of Daniel's head, and he had a small pair of binoculars in his other hand with which he scanned the surrounding area. "And it looks like he followed my instructions to the letter. There's hope for all of you yet."

Daniel glared up at his captor, not able to say anything because of the thick strip of duct tape covering his mouth. He had thought more than once about trying to get away from Valas, but the right opportunity hadn't presented itself yet. Besides, where could he go for help way out here? He turned his gaze back toward Mark, who was only about a dozen yards away.

"Just relax, stand there, and this will all be over soon," Valas said, the pistol muzzle digging into Daniel's skin. "If you don't follow instructions, well, you'll find out how well you can swim with your hands tied behind your back and a bullet in your lungs."

Daniel looked at the dark water, occasionally whipped into a whitecap by the rising wind. His bound hands were slowly moving toward the place he'd stashed his little stun gun, his only chance of getting out of here alive. Bit by bit he reached into the denim, careful to move only when Valas was distracted, feeling for the weapon resting there.

The wind was blowing stronger now, whipping Mark's hair into his eyes. He shook his head to clear his vision and kept walking forward. Now that he was closer, he could make out two black forms in the darkness. When he was about three meters away, he stopped and waited.

"Mark? Come closer." Valas's voice was faint against the loud lapping of the water against the rocks. "Do you have your foilpack with you?"

Mark nodded and took a couple steps forward.

"Take it out and throw it into the river," Valas said.

Mark did so, losing sight of it in the darkness. He heard a distant splash as the foilpack hit the Potomac. He turned back to Valas. "Let's just get this over with," he said, trying to keep his voice steady.

"Ah, always the businessman. Very well. Show me the cube." Valas's voice was totally emotionless.

"Let me hear Daniel say he's all right," Mark said.

"Negotiating already? Good, very good. You boys continue to surprise me," Valas said. "I'm sure Daniel wants to say hello. Just a moment,"

Mark heard a sound like cloth ripping, and another noise which almost made him cry out with relief.

"Ow!" Daniel said. "Hey, Mark. I'm all right—" Valas clapped something over Daniel's mouth, cutting off his friend's voice.

"All right, he's fine. Now show me the cube," Valas commanded.

Mark took the cube out of his pocket and held it up.

"Come over here, to the left side of the jetty," Valas told him.

Slowly Mark walked toward Daniel and Valas. As he did

so, he glanced at Daniel's face and was surprised to see him wink and nod at him. Mark started to frown, but realized that Valas could still see him, and kept moving. He reached the left side of the walkway and found a thin black case he recognized.

A light came on, illuminating the sleek plastic lines of a portable computer. "Insert the cube and step away, back to where you were," Valas said.

As Mark bent to insert the datacube into the port, his attention was distracted by the roar of a high-powered motor out on the river. Surprised, he looked up to see what looked like a large cabin cruiser heading downriver. He heard the flat slaps as its hull cut through the small waves on the Potomac. The noise, even at this distance, was deafening. The boat swerved to come within about fifty meters from shore, then powered out again in a large plume of water.

What kind of idiot pilots a boat like that? Mark thought. He didn't look at Valas or Daniel but inserted the datacube in the side of the laptop and walked back to his original position.

"We're going to walk over to the computer," Valas said to Daniel, who slowly complied. Mark could only see one of Valas's hands on Daniel's arm. The other was behind the boy, probably holding a weapon. He watched as the two walked over to the computer. Valas took his hand off Daniel's arm, reached for a small headset, and attached it to his ear. He muttered several commands, keeping an eye on Daniel and Mark all the while. The screen began listing the datacube's contents, and Valas took a quick look.

Mark looked at Daniel, who met his gaze with his own eyes and looked sharply downward. Mark followed his gaze and saw Daniel wiggling his fingers from behind his back.

He's up to something, but what? Mark thought. Daniel moved his head almost imperceptibly toward Valas, who was shutting the computer down and packing it up. The CIA agent straightened and slung the computer over his shoulder, then grabbed Daniel again.

"This is all of it, I trust. You certainly wouldn't lie to me, would you, Mark? Not with Danny here"—Valas tapped

Daniel's head with the barrel of a deadly-looking pistol—"in the line of fire."

"You've got everything," Mark said.

Valas opened his jacket pocket and looked at a small device clipped to his inside jacket pocket. "Very good, you are telling the truth. You've done well, Mark. I'd say you have a long and very successful career ahead of you. This"—Valas held up the metal case of the computer—"will just hit the market a few years early in a special private auction I'll hold shortly. You were right—it's good. The best I've ever seen. I've got nice bids from all sorts of covert organizations for it."

"Okay, you got what you wanted. Now let Daniel go and we'll leave you alone," Mark said.

He saw a flash of white as Valas grinned. "Sorry, sport, I'm afraid I can't do that just yet." He held up his hand as Mark started to protest. "You see, I need Daniel, Jimmy, and you to take a little trip with me for a few hours, just long enough to ensure that I get far away from Washington. I like having hostages—gives me somebody to talk to." Valas motioned behind him, where Mark saw a small powerboat moored to the jetty. "Not to mention somebody to stand behind if people start shooting."

"Why? You'll get away clean," Mark said. "There's no one around to stop you. Just leave us tied up. It'll be at least half an hour before we can get loose to call anybody or get help. Besides, I'm sure you probably disabled every phone anywhere near here."

"Perhaps, but I'll need your cooperation a little bit longer. I like having Jay Gridley's son handy as a bargaining chip. Makes me feel secure somehow. When I'm through with you, I'll let you all go and be on my way, and everybody will be happy."

"You don't need us for that. You've got a clean escape route right up that river. We'll just be in the way," Mark said, almost crying with frustration. *If I get on that boat, we're all dead*, he thought.

"I just can't take that chance, Mark," Valas said. "You're coming with me."

Mark started to retort angrily when his eyes went wide as

he looked behind Daniel and Valas. Four black-clad man-sized shapes had risen from the rocks that formed the base of the jetty and were noiselessly climbing over the wall. Mark saw the winking red dots of the laser sights on their submachine guns as they took a bead on Valas's back.

At that moment a powerful gust of wind blew across the jetty, causing Valas's laptop case to blow away from his side. Valas took his hand off Daniel's shoulder to steady the case.

It was just long enough.

"Get down!" Mark cried to Daniel as he hit the concrete.

17

From his vantage point, Mark saw the whole thing. It was as if time had frozen for a few seconds, and everyone was fighting their way through it, moving in slow motion.

Instead of falling to the ground, Daniel actually leaned *backward*, onto Valas, who had looked up at Mark when he had yelled. Mark saw the pistol behind Daniel's head waver and almost point toward him. There was a loud crackle, a gunshot, and then both Valas and Daniel were falling to the ground, Daniel trying to roll away, and Valas just lying there, limp and boneless. Two seconds later two members of the Net Force squad had Valas covered and disarmed.

Mark was bent over Daniel when the other team members came to check on them. "Are you hurt? Are you injured?"

"I think I skinned my elbow when I fell down, but other than that, I feel great!" Daniel rasped.

"TacCom, this is Team One, the area is secure. Target is neutralized, repeat, target is neutralized. The kids are okay, repeat, the kids are okay, over," one of the squad members reported.

"What happened to this guy?" one of them said, rolling Valas over to bind his hands after patting him down. "He's out cold, and he doesn't look too good."

"Stun gun," Daniel said. The Net Force agent had cut Daniel's bindings, and he was sitting up, massaging life back into his arms. "For a CIA agent, he did a terrible frisk. Nonexistent, in fact. Speaking of which, could somebody go get my friend Jimmy? He's out there on Valas's boat, tied up in the cabin."

There was a flurry of motion as a couple of agents headed to take care of it.

Mark sat down next to Daniel, feeling the rough concrete beneath him. One of the agents looked at him. "That was a gutsy move, kid, trying to distract him with a shout. Pretty brave, too, coming out here by yourself."

"Yeah, well, I'm just glad you guys showed up when you did," Mark said.

"So am I," the agent said. "Here comes the chopper, with your dad and Captain Winters in it." He signaled to another agent, and the two grabbed Valas by his arms and dragged him off the jetty toward a waiting van.

The other two agents waited until the helicopter landed. Mark's parents, Captain Winters, and Daniel's parents ran out to the jetty. The two mothers each ran to their respective sons, while the fathers joined the reunion a few seconds later. Captain Winters dismissed some of the agents, then gently put Valas's laptop in a large plastic bag and picked it up. He leaned on the wall of the jetty and waited.

Finally, when all the hugging and crying was done, Mark said, "I was beginning to think you guys would never show up."

"Megan and Maj called me right after you logged off," his dad said. "They replayed the conversation you had with Valas for me, and all we had to do was wait for you to call the cab company. We intercepted the vehicle they sent for you, and substituted one of our operatives. The guy who drove you here is named Hans Feldon, and he works at headquarters. As soon as he got the final destination from the cabdriver, we scrambled our team. We've been here the entire time. We were just waiting for the right opportunity to step in."

"That's were I've seen that guy before," Mark said, snapping his fingers. "Net Force."

"Once we had the address, it was a simple matter of getting the strike team in place to take out Valas when he met with you for the exchange," his father said. "The unit came in off that boat that went by a few minutes ago, and swam up to shore. When we heard he wanted all of you to go with him, we decided to move. Obviously it worked, because we're all here. But you and I are going to have a long talk about following orders. I told you to stay put."

"Umm," Mark said, stalling for time while he thought up a worthy excuse.

"I'm sure you all want to get your children home as soon as possible," Captain Winters said. "We're going to need to debrief these boys before that'll happen. We've got all of this on tape, plus Valas and his laptop. It shouldn't take us long to get what we need. The helicopter can take some of us back to headquarters, and there are a couple of vans waiting for the rest of us. After a few questions to sort all of this out, we can discuss how to handle the charges—"

"Actually, Captain, I'd prefer it if we could get that out of the way right now. After everything that has happened, I'm sure Net Force will see fit to drop all charges against my son, right?" Ramos said.

"Based on the evidence, I have no doubt that Daniel will be exonerated of any charges that may have been made against him," Captain Winters said, "though I believe none were ever actually filed."

"And," Jay said, "I would like to commend Daniel for his determination to catch Net Force's hacker and bring him to justice. Although he did act impetuously, and ended up putting his own life in danger, as well as my son's, he took the initiative in trying to prove his innocence, and in doing so, brought to light a potentially dangerous leak in Net Force."

Mark cleared his throat loudly. Everyone looked at him. "Well, he didn't do it *all* by himself, you know."

For a moment, there was complete silence. Jay was the first to smile, then he chuckled a bit. Soon everyone was laughing, as much to release the tension that had built up over the evening as over the humor of Mark's injured pride. Captain Winters was the first to speak.

"I'm not sure I'd point that out, if I were in your shoes,"

Winters said. "While I agree that catching Valas was difficult and commendable, there were several breeches of protocol that both Daniel and Mark will have to answer for before this whole matter can be cleared up. I *will* discuss these with you, I promise. However"—as he spoke a slight grin crossed his face—"I think that what happened here today will cause these two to think twice before they run off with a half-baked plan and without informing anyone."

Daniel and Mark both looked at each other and nodded.

"Mr. Sanchez, I don't believe there will be a problem reinstating your son as a Net Force Explorer. We'll just have to teach him a few things about reporting to his superiors when it's warranted, that's all."

Daniel and his father exchanged glances. "Thank you. I have a few issues to discuss with him as well. After all, he did leave the house when he was grounded, more than once, he borrowed the car after I specifically told him he couldn't, and he borrowed several rather expensive pieces of equipment without asking. By the time he's through serving his punishment for all this, he'll probably have studied enough to graduate from college, not just high school."

Daniel rolled his eyes at his father's exaggeration.

Ramos paused for a moment, then smiled and continued. "All that aside, I'm proud of you, son."

Daniel was standing there looking at his father with a slightly dazed expression on his face. Without saying a word, he reached out and hugged his dad.

Ramos put one arm around his son and the other around his wife, drawing them close to him. "I think it's time for us to get moving."

"Yes, Dad," Daniel said. "I just have two things to do first."

He went first to where Jimmy stood between two Net Force agents, looking a little the worse for wear and a lot apprehensive.

"You're a hero, man," Daniel said. "You just brought down an international spy. How's it feel?"

"Kinda weird," Jimmy said. "You sure these guys aren't gonna arrest me?"

Daniel laughed. "Nah. They're probably gonna pin a medal on you, instead."

"Jeez, that'll ruin me in the crowd I hang with."

"Then it's time to negotiate with the guys on either side of you. Thanks. I can't ever repay you for what you did." He shook his friend's hand.

Then he walked over to where Mark and his family were standing, and went up to Mark. "I owe you . . . well, everything, I guess."

Mark smiled. "It's just what any Net Force Explorer would do for another, that's all."

"I don't know about that, but . . ." Daniel extended his hand. "Thank you, for everything."

"Don't forget Maj and Megan," Mark said, then clapped a hand to his cheek. "Oh, no! I left them at my site! For all they know, we're still Valas's hostages!"

Daniel laughed loud and long, a refreshing sound after the past few weeks. "Don't worry, Squirt, I'm sure they'll deal with it. Just give them a call when you get in the chopper."

"Yeah, I guess so. Anyway, you're welcome," Mark said. "Besides, I know you'd do the same for me if it ever came down to it."

"You got that right," Daniel said.

He turned and walked back to his family, and they headed over to the helicopter.

Mark turned back to his parents and smiled. "Boy, am I glad that's over with. Well, all's well that ends well. I'm beat. I can't wait to go home and sleep for about a week." He noticed the amused look on his father's face contrasting with the grim, not-quite-a-scowl expression on his mother's. "What?"

"If you think you're going to get away with disobeying your father and putting your own life in danger—no matter what the reason—you've got another think coming," his mom said.

"But, Mom—" Mark started to protest.

"Don't even try to explain yourself, young man. Just march right over to that helicopter and get in. We will discuss this tomorrow," his mom said.

Mark glanced at his father, a pleading look in his eyes.

Jay Gridley shook his head. "Sorry, son, but you got your-self into this one, and you're going to have to get yourself out. Good luck. You're going to need it."

"Great, just great. Daniel gets himself taken hostage and everything's just fine for him. I practically save his life and I get grounded for a year. That's justice for you," Mark mut-tered as he headed to the helicopter. Behind him, his parents followed, trying not to smile.

"You're not really going to come down that hard on him, are you?" Jay asked his wife quietly.

"Probably not, but I think I'll let him sweat for a while," she said. "Short of assigning him his own Net Force agent to watch him, I don't know how we can keep him out of trouble."

"I know. I don't think Net Force is going to authorize any more of these baby-sitting missions in the future," Jay re-plied.

He gave his hand to his wife and helped her into the he-licopter. Once he was safely inside, it lifted off into the night, leaving the harbor and everything that had happened there behind.

Virtual Crime. Real Punishment.

Tom Clancy's Net Force®

Created by Tom Clancy and Steve Pieczenik
written by Bill McCay

*The Net Force fights all criminal activity online. But a group of teen experts
knows just as much about computers as their adult superiors.*

They are the Net Force Explorers...

From the #1 *New York Times*
Bestselling Phenomenon

Tom Clancy's
NET FORCE

Created by Tom Clancy and Steve Pieczenik
written by Steve Perry

Virtual crime.
Real punishment.

**AVAILABLE WHEREVER BOOKS
ARE SOLD OR
TO ORDER CALL: 1-800-788-6262**